THE HANGMAN STRIKES

Laura ran toward the spot where the masked men were hoisting her husband onto a horse and slipping a noose around his neck. In the rainy darkness, powerful hands seized her, dragging her back toward the house. Desperately, she lunged for the iron washtub hanging near the door, lifted it, and let it crash down on her assailant's head. Before he could free himself, she ripped his gun from its holster. He just had time to see her pull the trigger before the shot hit his belly.

Suddenly, Laura heard leather slap a horse's rump. Lightning flashed as she turned to see her husband rudely lifted from the saddle. The sound of his neck popping told her she was too late to help him now . . .

The Midnight Hangman

Morgan Hill

A DELL BOOK

Published by
Dell Publishing Co., Inc.
1 Dag Hammarskjold Plaza
New York, New York 10017

Dell ® TM 681510, Dell Publishing Co., Inc.

ISBN: 0-440-16375-7

Printed in the United States of America

First printing—April 1982

The Midnight
Hangman

Chapter One

~~~~~~

They came out of the night, eight of them, indistinct shapes leaning in their saddles against the slanting rain. With their hats pulled low and slickers wrapped tight, seven of the horsemen formed a semicircle in front of the house. The eighth halted his mount under a tall cottonwood twenty yards away. With slitted eyes, he peered malevolently toward the soft yellow of the two windows.

"Lane!" bellowed one from the semicircle. His powerful voice cut through the darkness and penetrated the log walls of the farmhouse.

Inside, Vance Lane laid down the book he was reading and made his way to a window. The lanterns burning behind him made the outside a black void.

From a rear bedroom his wife called, "Vance, did you say something?"

Lane was trying to see through the rain-drenched window when lightning flashed blue-white and silent overhead, illuminating the yard briefly. Laura Lane, twenty-four and beautiful, entered the room carrying a hairbrush. She was clad in a long woolen robe and slippers. Her long, dark hair hung loosely about her graceful shoulders.

As her husband peered through the window, she said, "Vance, what is it?"

Vance was about to answer when the same harsh

voice again pierced the rainy night. "Lane! Come on out!"

Ice formed in Laura's veins. Hastening to the window, she said, "Vance, is it—?"

"It's them, honey," he said, turning toward her. "I think there's seven of them."

Laura's large brown eyes widened. Her hand went to her mouth. "What are we going to do?" she asked with trembling voice.

Brushing past her, the muscular farmer went to a corner of the room, grasped a Winchester .44, jacked a cartridge in the chamber, and headed for the door.

"You can't fight that many!" gasped his wife. "They'll gun you down!"

Lane hesitated.

The voice outside rasped, "Lane! We're runnin' out of patience!"

Vance shook his head. "I thought this nightmare was over."

"Don't try to shoot it out with them," pleaded his wife of less than two years. "They're too many."

"You know what they'll do," he said with clipped words. "They'll hang me like they did Russ Morton and Ed Cleaver."

Laura bit her quivering lower lip, fighting tears.

"Lane!" came the wicked voice again. "If you're not out here in ten seconds, we're comin' in!"

Vance flashed his terrified wife a helpless look. Putting the rifle in her hands, he said, "Bolt the door when I go out. Don't open it for anyone but me. If they try to come in, shoot through the door." Before Laura could argue, he was outside and the door was shut.

Laura slid the bolt in place and dashed to a window, pressing her nose to the glass.

The rain struck Vance Lane in the face as he moved off the porch. The seven riders in the semicircle dismounted. As they approached Lane, lightning flashed, exposing the black hood masks over their faces. Round holes were cut for the eyes and small slits for the mouths.

"Your grace period is up, Lane," said a large man. It was the same heavy voice that had called out earlier.

"We're on this land legal," retorted Lane, "and you cattle kings know it. You can't keep hanging people and getting away with it. There's plenty of land for everybody. Why do you have to be so greedy?"

Ignoring the question, the big man snapped, "You had a note stuck on your door same as the others. We gave you time to pack up and clear out. You dare defy us?"

With that, they closed in and seized Vance Lane. The farmer was a strong man, but no match for seven men. The eighth man tossed a rope over a protruding limb of the cottonwood tree.

A frenzied wildness, born of desperation, bolted through Vance Lane. He lunged against his assailants, dumping two of them in the mud as they dragged him through the rain toward the tree. Suddenly Laura flung open the door. Lightning split the sky, revealing the rifle in her hands. Her face was deathly pale; her eyes were bulging with a mixture of fear and anger. "Let him go!" she screamed.

The two masked men who had gone down in the mud now moved toward Laura as the others dragged the struggling farmer to the tree. With her heart pounding against her ribs, Laura stepped off the porch, finger curled on the trigger. "I said let him go!"

The first man to reach the enraged woman lunged for the rifle. As his fingers closed on the barrel, it dis-

11

charged. One of the horses whinnied and dropped to the ground. The slug had struck it in the neck. The man wrenched the Winchester from Laura's grasp and flung it into the darkness. She started to run toward the spot where the masked men were hoisting her husband onto a horse.

The second man seized Laura's arm and spun her around. "You get back in the house, lady," he growled, "or we'll hang you, too."

Laura clawed at his face with her free hand, digging her fingernails into his eyes. He let out a painful cry and swung at her blindly with his fist, and Laura went down. Vance Lane twisted and kicked as the others fought to slip the noose over his neck. "Leave her alone!" he kept shouting.

The gallant woman rolled in the mud, shaking her head. Lightning illuminated the scene as she gained her feet and darted toward the cottonwood. Powerful hands grasped her and spun her again. This time it was both men. They dragged her toward the house as she kicked and screamed. As they reached the porch, one of the men stumbled, losing his grip on her arm.

A hatchet, used for chopping kindling, hung from the outside wall beside the door, unnoticed by the man who still held Laura. Quickly she closed her fingers on the handle, lifted it off the nails that supported it, and hacked savagely into the man's masked face. Releasing his grip on Laura, he staggered and fell off the porch, the hatchet still buried in his face.

The other man lunged for her. Laura jerked a galvanized washtub off the wall and smashed it over his head. Quickly she ripped the revolver from his holster and dogged back the hammer. Holding the gun in both hands, she slipped away from the stumbling, groping man and she fired point-blank into his belly. The man jackknifed as if struck by a battering ram.

Immediately following the roar of the gun came the sound of leather slapping a horse's rump. Laura swung her gaze toward the cottonwood tree. Lightning flashed again. Through the driving rain she saw Lance leave the saddle, hands tied behind him. The sound of his neck popping as he reached the end of the rope told her it was too late. She could not help her husband now.

The gun's roar turned the attention of the hangmen toward the house. As Vance Lane swung by his neck in the darkness, the masked men ran toward the soft yellow lights which were the windows and the open door. The first man to reach the porch yelled toward the eighth man who still sat his black horse near the cottonwood. "Boss! She's killed Dobie and Jim!"

Five men charged into the house, dashing from room to room. They overturned furniture and flung open closet doors, searching for the small female who had just killed two of their men.

"Grab the lanterns!" said the big man with the heavy voice. Two men took the lanterns from the Lane house and plunged through the door into the darkness. The others followed. As they rounded the house toward the outbuildings the rain sizzled as it struck the lanterns.

The big man barked orders, sending the masked men into every structure, including the privy. There was no sign of Laura Lane.

At the barn they found the door open and swaying with the wind. Inside, there were two halters, two bridles, two saddle blankets, two saddles . . . and one horse. Fresh droppings in an empty stall clinched it. The woman had ridden away bareback in the darkness.

"No sense tryin' to follow her in this rain," said the

large man huskily. "Her husband's dead. She ain't gonna be no problem now."

"Yeah," agreed another. "Let's load up Jim and Dobie. We need to get to the Jack place."

The masked murderers hunched against the rain as they loaded the two corpses on one horse. "It was Dobie's horse she shot, boss," said one, squinting toward the quiet man who had never left his saddle.

In an even tone, the quiet man said, "Make sure there's nothin' identifiable in the saddlebags. Let's go. We've got two more stops."

The lifeless body of Vance Lane swung heavily in the wind as six riders rode away from the circle of light cast by the two lanterns on the ground.

Lightning slashed the ebony sky with jagged fire as the six dark figures rode into John Jack's yard. The middle-aged farmer and his family had retired for the night. The boss of the outfit glared through the holes in his mask and spoke to the big man. "Maze, I don't want any slip-ups this time. That Lane woman cut a hole in our ranks. Now let's get this farmer outside and in the noose fast. Make sure the old lady and the kids stay in the house."

"Will do," agreed Maze McLeod.

The big man quickly gave orders as the boss found an old oak tree and waited. The masked men dismounted and plodded through puddles to the front door of the house. The rain set up a dull roar against the tin roof of the porch. McLeod drew his gun and banged on the door with the ball of his fist. The others pulled their revolvers from under their slickers.

The huge man waited, then hammered on the door again.

Presently a yellow light appeared through the windows and the latch on the door rattled. A short, stocky man with a shiny bald head opened the door and

14

peered into the rainy darkness. Holding the lantern level with his face, he said, "Who is it?" Suddenly his eye caught sight of the grim masks. He tried to slam the door.

McLeod stuck his foot in the way. As the door rebounded, the thick-shouldered man forced his way in and grasped the shorter man. A second masked man twisted the lantern from Jack's fingers. Two others aided McLeod and wrestled the farmer through the door.

"Who are you?" demanded John Jack. "What are you doing?"

As they dragged him toward the aged and gnarled oak tree, Maze McLeod said, "You were given time to load your wagons and pull out, Jack. Now, are you defyin' us?"

"We've got as much right to this land as you cattlemen," snapped the bald-headed farmer. "We homesteaded it legally."

"We ain't arguin' with you sodbusters," retorted McLeod. "You don't leave, we send you."

Jack's bare feet dug into the mud when he saw the masked figure astride the dark horse next to the oak tree. A hangman's noose swayed in the wind. "No!" cried the farmer. "Not like Morton and Cleaver!"

"Your neighbor Vance Lane is dancin' on air, too, John," came a wicked voice from behind.

Suddenly there was a commotion at the door of the house. "Pa!" screamed nineteen-year-old Jonah Jack.

Quickly the youth was shoved back into the house by the two masked men who stood on the porch. While the elder Jack's hands were being bound behind his back out in the rain, Jonah fought against the two who had forced him back into the house. One of them clipped Jonah on the jaw just as Mrs. Jack appeared holding a double-barreled shotgun.

"Get away from that boy!" she bellowed.

Jonah had gone down from the blow. He scrambled to his feet dizzily. For a brief moment he staggered between one of the killers and his mother. The man seized the youth, pulling him toward his own body. Instantly he whipped the gun from under his wet slicker and put the muzzle to the base of Jonah's skull.

"Now woman," said the baneful masked man, "you put down the scattergun, or I'll splatter the kid's brains all over this house."

Two girls in their mid-teens appeared wide-eyed behind Emily Jack as she slowly lowered the twin muzzles. Quickly the other man relieved her of the shotgun. Her eyes were wide, unbelieving.

"Mama, what are these men doing?" asked one of the girls. "Where's Papa?"

Emily looked through the open door and darted outside, shouting, "John! John!"

From the drizzling darkness John Jack cried, "Stay in the house, Emily!"

The storm lit the night just in time for the terrified woman to see a huge man slap the horse's rump with a leather strap. The startled animal leaped forward and the farmer left the saddle.

Emily screamed as her husband's body fell from the tree limb with a sickening snap. For a moment the hanged man kicked and spasmed. Then life left his body forever.

Emily Jack swore vehemently at the dark forms that stood around the tree.

Maze McLeod looked past the screaming woman at the two men who stood on the porch. One held Jonah while the other blocked the door, keeping the wailing girls inside the house. Like his mother, the youth was violently cursing the hangmen.

Within moments, Emily and her son were also forced back in the house by the masked men. All but the boss gathered inside with them. He remained in the saddle, back turned toward the driving rain. Peering through the holes in his hooded mask, he watched the scene just inside the door.

Mrs. Jack was now sobbing incoherently. "If you sodbusters would've obeyed orders, this wouldn't have happened," came the heavy voice of the big man.

"Who are you to give us orders?" demanded young Jonah, his face livid with rage. "We've got as much right—"

One of the hooded men backhanded him across the mouth savagely. Blood burst from his split upper lip. Jonah dashed to a nearby cupboard and yanked open a drawer. Just as he palmed a revolver, a heavy fist chopped him down.

While the angry youth struggled to his feet, the man who hit him retrieved the gun. "Kid," he said with gritted teeth, "you're gonna force us to get tough with you."

Wiping blood with his sleeve, Jonah Jack hissed maliciously, "We ain't leavin' this valley! We're stayin'. Do you hear me? I'll take over where my pa left off. And I'll hunt every one of you dirty killers down. *I'll kill every last one of you!*"

A cold voice spoke from outside. "Bring the brat out here."

Powerful hands seized Jonah and ushered him through the door. As the rain touched Jonah's bleeding face, the dark figure on the black horse spoke again.

"*Hang 'im.*"

Jonah's eyes bulged. Emily Jack ran for the door, crying, "No! No! No!" A heavy fist caught the woman

17

on the jaw. She went down in a heap. The frightened girls rushed to her as the hangmen forced Jonah toward the swaying form of his dead father.

The boy's lips parted, but no sound came forth. He was numb with terror. One of the hangmen went after the horse which had borne the elder Jack. Jonah's eyes were riveted to the lifeless form of his father as his own hands were being tied behind his back. A gusty wind, raw with autumn's early coldness, swept slanting sheets of rain against his shivering body.

Through the holes in his mask the eyes of the man who sat on the black horse were white and wild. He spoke in a level, flat voice. "You not only can take over where your old man left off, kid. You can swing with him."

Jonah Jack's tongue cleaved to the roof of his mouth.

A rope sailed upward, then dangled from the oak limb. The youth felt himself rise and thump into the same saddle where his father had been moments before. As the nervous horse was forced into position, John Jack's legs brushed against Jonah's shoulder. The boy gasped and whimpered, blinking against the rain in his eyes. The rope, wet and stiff, was cinched roughly around his neck.

"You were right, kid," said the man on the black horse. "You ain't leavin' this valley. Tomorrow they'll plant you in the sod and you can stay here forever." With that he nodded to the big man who stood behind Jonah. The leather strap hissed and popped on the horse's rump.

Jonah's body collided against his father's with a heavy sodden sound, then swung free. As the shadowy figures trotted away, father and son swung side by side in the wind. Their inert forms hung, whipped and dripping with rain.

18

Chapter Two

~~~~~~

Stark terror gripped Laura Lane as she bounded off the porch and plunged through the darkness toward the barn.

Her ears echoed with the sound of the gun she had held. She could still see one man buckling and falling next to his comrade, who lay with the hatchet buried deep in his masked face.

Stumbling through the darkness, Laura wondered what she had done with the gun. When both hands reached her face to wipe rain from her eyes, she realized it was gone, then she heard the loud voices of the hangmen above the roar of the rain. Suddenly her hand was on the latch of the barn door. Groping her way through the absolute darkness, she was aware of a whimpering moan coming from her own lips.

The image of Vance hanging by his neck, illuminated by the eerie flashes of lightning, kept returning unwanted into Laura's mind.

With trembling fingers she found the first stall. Sliding the bolt, she spoke softly to the bay mare. "Come on, Dolly. We have to go fast." The horse nickered softly as the gate swung open and the frightened young woman sank her fingers into the heavy mane. Desperate for her own life, Laura found the strength to mount the horse without the help of a stirrup.

Dolly seemed to sense the urgency of the moment.

Without guidance she bolted for the open barn door and plunged into the rainy darkness.

Laura had never ridden bareback, but she clung to the mare like a cockleburr. Lightning swept across the hills and brightened the path for a brief moment. Laura eyed the trees looming overhead, thinking of her husband. She was unable to tell what direction Dolly was running in. At the moment it made no difference. Any direction was all right as long as it carried her away from the cold-blooded hangmen.

As wind and rain lashed her face, Laura Lane thought again of Vance. How horrible it must have been for him those last few moments . . . staring death in the face . . . knowing the last sound he would hear was the leather strap on the horse's rump. The sound of his neck snapping reverberated in her mind. There was one consolation. Death for Vance was quick. He didn't have to dangle and choke till life ebbed away. A severed spinal cord had ended his life instantly. But this reflection did little to ease the ache in her throat, or thaw the icy knot of grief inside her.

Suddenly Laura heard a heavy rumbling that seemed to come from the dark forest behind. She turned to look. It was hard to tell what she heard with the wind whistling in her ears, the rain beating down, and Dolly's own hoofs pounding the earth.

If the hangmen caught her, she would die, too. Trees and bushes were a blur in the repeated flashes of lightning. The charging animal crashed through a heavy thicket, the rough branches ripping at Laura's sleeves as she ducked her head.

The merciless lashing of the branches stopped and Laura raised her head. A wet branch whipped her face, stinging her violently. She could feel welts rising on her skin as she lay her head once again next to Dolly's muscular neck.

Between lightning flashes, the quilted blackness around her shut out the shapes of trees and bushes. Laura gripped the thick mane, struggling to stay on her sliding, wildly plunging horse.

One thing Laura knew now for sure. Dolly had not taken a southern course. Open fields lay in that direction, and they had been traveling through trees and brush since leaving the house. Had the bay chosen to go north, they would be on a steep climb by now. So they were galloping either west or east.

The mare slowed down at a dark object that lay across the path, then bolted hard and leaped it, almost throwing Laura. She righted herself, then looked back. Apparently Dolly had jumped a large fallen tree.

Again it seemed that there were horsemen on her heels, though she could see nothing in the darkness behind. Fear and cold throbbed through her body.

The gallant mare fought the storm and the darkness as if she knew the life of her frightened rider lay in the balance. Laura loved her for it. Time edged ahead. Dolly's thundering hoofs continued to eat up distance. Her sides were now heaving. Laura could feel the fevered heat of the mare's laboring body beneath her own.

Suddenly in the thick darkness, Dolly stumbled. Laura felt herself sailing through the air. Ragged branches tore at her face. A sharp splinter of fiery pain spiraled across her back. Then her body went numb and darkness closed in.

Lightning still split the sky as the six slicker-draped riders drew rein under the wind-swept cottonwoods that fringed the yard on the Braxton farm. One rider dismounted and led the horse bearing the two corpses deeper into the trees. Returning, he heard the boss saying, "If you can get another clap of thunder like that one a few minutes ago, you can kick in the door and they'll never know it. Then you can be into the bedroom and take 'em by surprise before they can get up any resistance."

"We'll give it a whirl, boss," said Maze McLeod.

"Don't wait too long," said the figure on the dark horse. "If you don't get the thunder—" At that instant, a bolt of lightning slashed the sky. The boss waited for the booming thunder to subside. "If you don't get another one like that within a couple minutes, bust it down anyway and go on in."

Five dark forms plodded across the muddy yard, heads ducked against the rain. The man on the black horse lifted a final rope from his pommel and looped it over a cottonwood limb.

Inside the house, Anne Braxton came awake when the thunder rattled the bedroom window. Her husband stirred next to her, rolled over in the bed and began snoring again. Anne was just going back to sleep when lightning cracked above the house and brightened the room. Slipping from the bed, she crossed the room to the window. For a brief instant, the wind ceased lashing the glass with rain and lightning lit up the yard.

Anne blinked as she saw the five obscure figures moving out of the trees toward the house. Her heart skipped a beat. A prickling at the base of her neck ran quickly down along her spine.

The frightened woman whirled and ran to her sleeping husband. "Roy!" she said, shaking him. "Roy, wake up!"

The farmer stirred.

"Roy! There are men out in the yard! They're coming toward the house!"

Roy Braxton opened his eyes. Groggily he looked up at the silhouette of his wife. "What is it, honey?"

"There are men out in the yard. They're com—"

As thunder shook the house, Anne's words were cut short by the crashing, splintering sound of the outside door being broken open.

Braxton sprang from the bed. "My gun is out there in the kitchen!" he exclaimed in a heavy whisper. "Get in the closet, Anne! Don't come out till they're gone."

Yellow light flared from the kitchen area as one of the hangmen touched flame to a lantern. Anne was trembling. Her breathing was spasmodic. Braxton ushered her to the closet and pushed her gently inside. "Stay there," he whispered. As he closed the closet door, she was near panic.

Lightning brightened the room again. Braxton looked about for something to use as a weapon, but there was nothing.

The husky farmer was thirty-three and vigorous. He would take them on with his fists.

They were coming down the hallway now. The lantern light threw their grotesque shadows on the wall. Braxton had no idea how many there were. He flattened his back against the wall just inside the bedroom door. Standing there in his long underwear, he wished he had boots on his bare feet.

Doubling his fists, Roy Braxton braced himself and waited. Abruptly the first man entered. The husky farmer's right fist caught him flush on the jaw and he went down like a pole-axed steer. The second man swung his revolver at Braxton and missed. Braxton's meaty fist slammed his mouth and he fell backward into the third man, who held the lantern.

As the lantern hit the floor and the room burst into flames, Roy Braxton saw that the men were masked.

23

He put his head down and charged into the close-knit group huddled in the narrow hallway.

Flame climbed the walls, sending billows of smoke to the high ceiling. Fists flailed as the masked men struggled with the muscular farmer.

Inside the closet, Anne Braxton smelled the smoke. Under the door she could see the light from the flames. The noise of the fight had moved to the kitchen area. Anne opened the door and stepped out. The bedroom was bright from the flame in the hallway. A huge man was on the floor, shaking his head. His hat had come off and the frightened woman saw the hood.

One look at the flames and Anne knew she must go out the window. Running to it, she released the lockpins on the sides and raised it. Just before plunging through, she looked back to see the big man on the floor rip off his hood. The blazing fire in the hallway illuminated his face. He looked up to see the woman staring at him.

Anne whirled through the window as Maze McLeod rolled to his knees. The solid punch had left a haze clouding his brain. Anne was outside before Maze could stagger to the rain-soaked sill.

Outside, Anne ran through mud toward the front of the house. At the instant she reached the corner, four men came piling through the door onto the porch. Her only hope was to get into the kitchen and find Roy's gun.

A fifth man emerged through the door, staggering. Lightning flared and Anne could see that three men had her husband down in the mud, tying his hands behind his back. She saw the big man working his huge frame out the bedroom window.

The terrified woman darted through the door into the burning kitchen. Furniture lay scattered and bro-

24

ken. Smoke burned her eyes as she moved through the room, trying to spot the gun. Roy usually kept it in a corner by the cupboard. It was not there.

The heavy kitchen table lay next to the end of the hallway. It was about to catch fire. One end of the tablecloth was aflame. Terrified, Anne pawed through the broken chairs, shattered dishes, and scattered articles. No rifle.

Suddenly a massive form filled the door. It was the big man she had seen in the bedroom. Anne backed toward the fire. The huge monster had murder in his eyes. Rainwater beaded on the hood, which he had replaced on his head. He attacked like an enraged bull.

Quickly Anne bent down and seized the half-consumed tablecloth. As McLeod closed in, she flung the large flaming cloth at his face. It swirled and covered his head. The big man roared, blindly trying to pull away the cloth.

Anne plunged out into the storm. Her gaze swung to the clump of cottonwood trees. The fire from the house gave her enough light to see her husband dangling limply by the neck, his feet six feet from the ground. Her legs went rubbery. "Roy . . ." she gasped.

A vague figure astride a dark horse looked past the men who stood on the ground and shouted loudly, "Get the woman!"

Four masked forms wheeled about. Suddenly Maze McLeod bolted through the door of the house, the blazing cloth wrapped around his neck and shoulders. He reached the edge of the porch, lurched up on his toes. For a wild moment he seemed to hang there, hands clawing at the sky. Then he pitched head first into the mud.

The dark foursome dashed to their burning companion. The boss's attention was drawn momentarily to the hooded man rolling in the mud. Anne Braxton turned and darted toward the rear of the house. The rock-strewn ground jabbed her bare feet. She must hide quickly *Where?* The barn. No. That's the first place they would look.

The tool shed. No. The feed shack. No. They would find her there.

Fifty yards behind the house, through a heavy thicket, was an irrigation ditch. The hard rain beat her face as she fled across the clearing and plunged into the thicket. Pain stabbed her feet as she weaved her way toward the ditch.

The hangmen were coming now, shouting at each other. It would take them a little time to search the outbuildings. Anne's lungs felt like they were on fire, her mouth was dry. Lightning cut the sky overhead. The irrigation ditch was swirling with white foam.

Halting at the edge of the swollen stream, Anne looked back toward the house. Flames were leaping skyward from the roof. The killers were shouting as they moved from building to building.

The weary woman stumbled toward a tree and braced herself against it. Her breath was coming in short gasps. In spite of the cold rain, her face was hot. "Roy," she sobbed. "Oh, God, why? Oh, Roy . . ."

For several moments Anne Braxton wept for her murdered husband. Lightning lashed the sky. Thunder answered angrily.

Then she heard them. They were coming through the thicket. Anne ran down the bank of the ditch to a spot where a clump of bushes grew, stretching their branches over the water. Recklessly, she jumped into the dark swirling waters, clutched the overhanging branches, and pulled in close. She held her nose out of the cold water. Her body quivered with the cold.

* * *

Laura Lane felt cold rain pelt her face as the dark haze in her brain began to dissipate. At first she thought she was only waking from a bad dream. Then the awful truth slammed home. *Vance was dead.* Murdered by a vile gang of hangmen, cattlemen who were set on driving the homesteaders from the valley.

Slowly Laura rolled over and pulled her knees up. Once on all fours, she tried to stand. Lightning lit the murky sky, followed by the voice of thunder. For a moment the whole rain-drenched world seemed to spin. She braced herself against a tree. Abruptly Laura became aware of the sharp, burning pain in her back. She vaguely remembered a spiraling pain before passing out. *Must have raked it on a rock or some sharp object,* she told herself.

Suddenly she thought of the valiant mare that had carried her to safety. Peering through the rainy gloom she looked for Dolly. The animal was nowhere in sight.

Slowly Laura became aware that she was freezing cold and soaked. Her teeth were chattering, and her whole body shook. She must get out of the rain . . . someplace where she could dry out and get warm.

Barefoot, she began walking through the rain-filled night. Her weakened legs gave out and she found herself kneeling in the mud. Her head felt light and dizzy.

Laura lifted her whirling head to the rain. Stinging pellets came down, cold and impersonal. Stumbling, groping, she pressed her shivering body through the swaying trees. Several moments passed.

All of a sudden Laura stepped over a ledge and tumbled head-over-heels down a steep embankment. She was stopped abruptly by a barbed-wire fence. Sharp barbs tore into her side, ripping the robe she wore. Crying out in pain, she pulled her robe loose and began moving along the fence. She reasoned that a fence meant a farm or ranch. There would be a house somewhere near.

Stumbling, lurching, Laura followed the fence. Her bare feet were cut and giving much pain. After a while the fence became a combination of wire mesh and barbed wire.

At last she came to a gate. It was also made of barbed wire and was closed The wooden bar was drawn tight next to a heavy fencepost, held there with a thick wire loop. Her stiff fingers worked at the loop, but the bar would not release. Lightning flared, exposing the dark outline of a house positioned about thirty yards from the gate. Swaying as she clung to the bulky fencepost, Laura shouted at the top of her lungs, "Help! Help me! Please, there in the house. Help!" But the wind whipped the words away, carrying them vainly into the night.

The bruised and battered young woman dropped to her knees. She would crawl underneath the gate. Moving slowly, she slid on her belly. A barbed prong snagged her robe. Weeping with a low moaning sound, Laura worked at loosening the barb.

Suddenly out of the darkness a large dog came on the run, growling. Twisting around with every ounce of her waning strength, Laura headed back where she came from. The big hound snapped and bit at her ankles. A piteous scream escaped her lips. She seemed frozen to the spot. Kicking wildly, she felt the burning fangs tear into the calf of her left leg. Then the robe gave way with a ripping sound and she rolled under the wire out of the dog's reach.

The vicious beast poked his head between the taut strands and snapped savagely. Laura lay in an inch-deep puddle and sobbed. Her bleeding leg burned like fire. Above the wind and rain, she heard a heavy masculine voice come from the direction of the house. The dog retreated from the fence, stopped growling and looked toward the house. The man spoke again. It sounded to Laura Lane like he said, "Sic 'im, Brutus! Sic 'im!"

Again the barking, snapping hound rammed his head through the wires. The worn and wounded woman rolled further away, mud clinging to her bruised and battered body. "Please!" she sobbed. "Help me! Help me!" Her words trailed off into weakening sobs. Little by little she inched away from the dog. Laura was glad the bottom wire was so close to the ground and that the dog was so big. Several times he backed up and tried to squeeze underneath. Only his great size stopped him.

After crawling for what seemed like an hour, Laura collapsed with her face in a wet bed of pine needles. Once again she was beneath tall, swaying trees. She could feel her heart thumping under her, next to the ground. The earth seemed to rock and swing under her body.

Then she passed out.

Chapter Three

~~~~~~

It was high noon when Dan Colt rode the big black gelding into LaJara. He had camped on the New Mexico–Colorado border and headed north into Colorado at dawn.

Colt had followed the irregular trail of his outlaw brother Dave for several weeks since catching a glimpse of him north of Albuquerque. There seemed to be no pattern to Dave's path of travel. Sometimes he went in complete circles. At one point he had gone as far east as Clovis, then had ridden north toward the Canadian River.

Dave was now on a northwesterly course. The prospect was grim. If Dave got high into the Rockies, Dan could easily lose his trail.

As the tall, blond Colt guided the shiny black horse down LaJara's dusty street, his ice-blue eyes studied the weather-worn buildings. The wind was picking up. Dust devils skipped up the street. The noonday sun ducked behind a cluster of dark clouds.

Knowing Dave's weakness for poker, Dan had found the best places to check were the saloons. If his identical twin had been in the town, he would have played at least a game or two.

Shifting his muscular frame in the saddle, Dan ran his gaze up the street. The faded fronts, warped boards, and splintered timbers betrayed the age of the town. The tall man noted that some of the people along the street eyed him warily. This could mean that Dave had been here and caused trouble . . . or that this was one of those towns where all strangers were objects of distrust. Dan had lost Dave's trail a mile or so out of town. It seemed likely that he would pay LaJara a visit.

Colt was just swinging from his saddle in front of the Lucky Nugget Saloon when a band of riders rode into town from the north. The wind whipped their dust upwards, scattering it behind them. As they drew near, one of the riders shouted, "Hey, boys! There he is!" Goading their horses, they skidded to a halt where Dan stood. Five revolvers were instantly lined on him.

"Git them hands up!" shouted one.

Dan gave them a cold, annoyed look. Without lifting his hands, he said, "You talkin' to me?"

"What are you, some kind of lunatic?" rasped another.

"I'm not—"

"We been shaggin' after you for nearly two days," cut in a third man. "You must be plumb loco, circlin' 'round and comin' back."

Colt opened his mouth to speak again when the first rider who had spoken said heatedly, "We was gonna gun you down and drag your cheatin' carcass back to J. D. Now you've saved us the trouble. J. D.'ll be happy to know that he can have you all for hisself."

"I sure am!" came a voice from the batwing doors of the Lucky Nugget.

Dan Colt turned toward the voice. A tall, lanky man in his early thirties swaggered across the boardwalk. He wore a Colt .44 slung low on his hip. He fastened narrow-set eyes on Dan. A hardness slipped into his rawboned features. "I don't know what you hoped to

32

gain by comin' back," he said through his teeth, "but you just signed your own death warrant."

Dan had been through this before. Since he had begun to trail his brother he had lost count of the times that he had been mistaken for Dave. It seemed that Dave had a knack for stirring up trouble and getting out of town before it reached the boiling point. Wearily, he said, "You're makin' a mistake, friend. I'm not Dave Sundeen. My name's Dan Colt."

The slender gunslinger ejected a humorless laugh. "What do you take me for? Some kind of idiot?"

"It's a long story," rasped Colt.

"*Story* is a good word for it, Sundeen," said the gunman. "Now before I blow your guts to the highest tree, I want you to reach in them saddlebags and get what's left of the money you cheated me out of. I can see you spent part of it on new duds and the black horse."

"You're makin' a mistake, mister," said Dan feverishly. "I'm not Dave Sundeen and I don't have your money."

"There are five guns pointin' at you!" hissed J. D., eyes bulging. "One word from me and these boys will blow you to kingdom come."

"I thought you wanted to save that privilege for yourself," snapped Colt.

"You're tryin' my patience," retorted the gunslinger. "Now I want you to put that money in my hand and tell me you're sorry you cheated me. Then I'm gonna give you a sportin' chance to go for your guns."

"Why didn't you challenge my brother when you caught him cheating?"

J. D. spat. "I didn't find out you'd cheated until you left town and you know it!"

"It's best that way," said Dan coldly. "My brother is wicked with his guns. He's faster'n a rattler's tongue." Cocking his head, Dan said, "I don't even know your name, mister."

"I told it to you when we shook hands before the game. It's J. D. Clements and you know it."

Somewhere along the line that name had drifted into Dan's ears. Clements was better than the average gunhawk. He had to be. He had lived to see his thirties. "Why don't you just chalk it off to bad experience, Clements," he said firmly. "You'll never see your money again."

"I'll see it when it comes out of those saddlebags," retorted Clements. "Now dig it out."

"I'm tellin' you for the last time," Dan said, face flushed. "I am Dan Colt, not Dave Sundeen. And your money is not in my saddlebags."

"You could've picked another alias, Sundeen," chided Clements. "Somebody who doesn't know that the famous Dan Colt is dead is liable to believe you. Might challenge you."

"I thought that was what *you* were doin'."

"I am. You're gonna square off with me. Right after I get the apology and my money."

Temper flared inside Colt. "Since you're not getting either, we just as well square it off."

J. D. Clements's face went rigid. Shifting his beady eyes to one of the five riders, he said, "Wes, search his saddlebags."

Colt's icy voice matched his eyes. "You touch those saddlebags, cowboy . . . the next thing you touch is a coffin."

Wes had dismounted and taken two steps toward the big black. He stopped and looked Clements in the eye, then Colt, then Clements again.

"Go on, Wes," lashed the gunhawk. "There's four guns on him."

"I promise you, Clements," said Dan Colt evenly. "I'll get this cowboy and at least two more before I'm dead."

Wes's face went sick. Fear leaped into his eyes. "I ain't gittin' myself killed for no gamblin' money, J. D.," he said shakily.

Clements's eyes widened. "Wes," he snapped. "You do what I tell you."

The cowboy swore. "How do I know he *ain't* Dan Colt? If he is, he *will* take out three or four of us on his way out. I don't aim to be one of 'em." With that, Wes wheeled and started down the street.

J. D.'s face was livid with rage. "Hawker!" he bellowed. "You come back here and search those saddlebags!"

"Do it yourself," said Wes Hawker, walking away.

"I'll shoot you down like a mangy dog!" yelled Clements.

"You'll have to shoot me in the back," Hawker called over his shoulder. "You got a lotta witnesses!"

Clements had not noticed until that moment that a sizable audience had gathered.

Dan Colt's voice cut the air. "You other stumble-bums put your guns away and get your tails out of here."

The four men who held guns on him eyed each other. A man spoke from the crowd. "You boys better do what he says! I seen Dan Colt once in Abilene. He took out five gunslicks at one time. This feller sure does look like I remember Colt lookin'!"

Four horses were reined in a circle. As the men rode away, J. D. Clements shouted, his teeth bared, "You yella cowards! This dude's lyin'! He's nothin' but a cheatin' card shark. Dan Colt's dead. This liar's name is Sundeen!" Whipping around, he looked Colt in the eye. "You're a dead man, Sundeen!"

"The name's Colt," Dan said calmly, "and I'm still breathin'."

With his narrow, beady eyes glued on Colt's face, Clements moved sideways toward the center of the street. "You ain't gonna be breathin' in less than a minute, you cheatin' skunk."

Dan stayed parallel with the angry gunhawk. The crowd of onlookers moved back toward the faded buildings. Soon the two men stood thirty feet apart in the center of the street. Eager to get it done, Clements went for his gun. He had just cleared leather when Dan's twin Colts spit fire in a double roar. Clements's body jerked as both slugs tore into his chest, spinning him half around. He staggered, then drew himself up stiffly. The .44 slipped from his limp fingers and clattered at his feet. He swayed rigidly upright, then went down, his face hitting the street hard.

The wind carried away the blue gunsmoke as Dan holstered the .45s.

The man in the crowd who had spoken out earlier approached the tall man. "You really are Dan Colt, ain'tcha?" he asked excitedly.

"Have been for about thirty-three years," replied Dan in an even tone.

"You hear that?" the man said to the dispersing crowd. "It really is Dan Colt! I told you!"

Certain now that his brother was not in the saloon, Colt decided to eat lunch in a cafe he had passed earlier, then continue following Dave's trail. Leading the black down the street, he tied him in front of the La-Jara Cafe.

Entering the cafe, Dan threaded his way among the

tables and took a corner table. He pulled out a chair and slacked into it, his back to the wall.

A couple of cowboys turned and looked at him from a nearby table. One of them spoke. "You see what the shootin' was about, mister?"

"Mmm-hmm," replied Dan. "Fella named J. D. Clements just shot it out with a drifter."

The one who had spoken laughed. "Well, another drifter just bit the dust, huh?"

Colt's face was expressionless. "It was Clements that ate the dust," he said coldly.

The eyes of both men widened. The other cowboy said, "Ain't possible, mister. Nobody in these parts can outdraw J. D. Clements."

"Yeah," put in the first one, "are you sure you know which one was Clements and which one was the drifter?"

"I believe I can tell the difference," said Dan levelly. "I'm the drifter."

The cowboys eyed each other, gulped the last of their coffee and bumped into the waitress on the way out. The girl straightened her dress and approached Dan's table. "Chicken and dumplings is our special for today, sir," she said with a warm smile.

"Then chicken and dumplings is what it'll be," said the ruggedly handsome man, returning the smile. "And I'll have coffee. Start with a cup right away, please."

The waitress nodded and turned away. In less than a minute she returned with an empty cup and a steaming coffeepot. She filled the cup and set the pot on a pad. "I'll just leave it with you," she said pleasantly.

"Now you're talkin' my language, little lady," Dan said, tilting his hat to the back of his blond head.

As the waitress disappeared into the kitchen, the

outside door opened. Three townsmen entered. They set their eyes on Colt and approached his table. The first one spoke. "Mr. Colt, I'm Hank Bowman and this is Craig Lyles and George Yates."

Dan stood to his feet and shook hands with each man.

"We'd like to talk to you," said Bowman.

"Sit down, gentlemen," said Dan, gesturing toward empty chairs. "Hope it won't take too long. I've got to eat and hit the trail."

George Yates cleared his throat as they all sat down. Looking at Dan he said, "Mr. Colt, it was my understanding that you had been killed six or seven years ago over in Kansas. Supposed to have been some bird whose brother you had gunned down."

"Can't put a lot of stock in hearsay, Yates," said Colt. "Truth is, I got married and hung up my guns. Went to ranchin' up in Wyoming."

Craig Lyles swung his gaze to the big iron on Dan's left hip. "Looks to me like you unhung 'em," he said, eyebrows arched.

"Had to."

"Oh?"

"Three cold-blooded polecats murdered my wife. Had to get 'em."

Lyles's eyes dropped to the floor. "I . . . I'm sorry. I—"

"How could you know?" said Dan quickly.

"Well, I—"

"It's all right," said Colt assuringly.

"Mr. Colt," said Hank Bowman, "we'd like to make you a proposition. We represent—"

The waitress interrupted. "Would you gentlemen like coffee?" she asked, setting three empty cups on the table. A general consent was given and she poured. "Would you like lunch?" she asked, shifting

38

her eyes from face to face. "Special is chicken and dumplings."

"Sounds great," nodded Bowman.

The others grunted assent. The waitress set her eyes on Dan. "Would you like me to hold yours, and bring it with the others?"

"No, ma'am. Bring mine right away, please. I really am in a hurry."

The girl nodded and left.

"As I was saying," put in Bowman, "we represent the town of LaJara, Mr. Colt. We're the town council. We'd like to offer you a job."

"You see," spoke up George Yates, "we need a town marshal. Ours was killed in a gunfight about a month ago. Ever since, scum like J. D. Clements has been drifting into LaJara."

"We need a man who can handle himself like you do," added Lyles.

Dan's head was already moving back and forth. "Can't do it, gentlemen," he said softly. "I'm trailing my twin brother and I've got to catch up to him."

Bowman opened his mouth. "But, Mr. Colt, we're prepared to offer you a substantial salary and —"

"I couldn't do it if the job paid a million dollars a week," said Dan. "I *must* find my brother."

In desperation, Yates said, "After you find him, would you come back and take the job?"

Colt smiled and shook his head as the waitress laid a steaming plateful of chicken and dumplings before him. "I can't make any promises about after I find my brother."

"That's final?" asked Yates, a note of despair in his voice.

"Yes, sir," nodded Dan. "I can understand your need for a marshal, but it just can't be me."

Dan tore into his meal, finishing while the others

were still eating. Leveling his hat on his head, he stood up and said, "If you gentlemen will excuse me, I must be on my way."

Bowman, Lyles, and Yates stood to their feet. Around a mouthful of dumplings, Hank Bowman said, "Thanks for riddin' us of Clements, Mr. Colt."

"My pleasure," said Dan. He walked to the counter and flipped a double-eagle to the waitress. "This'll buy their meals and mine, ma'am," he said smiling. "The rest is your tip."

"Thank you, sir," smiled the girl.

The stiff wind whipped his hat as Dan stepped outside. Dark clouds hovered over the town. The smell of rain was in the air. Stepping off the boardwalk, the tall, muscular man stroked the face of his black gelding and said, "We'll get you a good drink and be on our way, big boy." Leading the magnificent animal across the street to a watering trough, he let him drink. The wind gusted heavily just as a buckboard passed.

Dan saw a hat sail into the air just as a feminine voice cried, "Wait! My hat!"

The man on the buckboard swore and jerked savagely on the reins. By instinct, Dan Colt bounded down the street, following the rolling, bouncing wide-brimmed hat. He ran a block before he caught it. Returning at a brisk walk, he set his eyes on the pair in the wagon. *Father and daughter,* he told himself.

The man was a muscular forty. Silver tinged his temples. The girl was no more than twenty-one or twenty-two. She was pretty, with large hazel eyes. She smiled and alighted from the vehicle as Dan drew near.

Dan saw fire in the man's eyes. "Vicky, get back in the wagon!" he snapped.

The girl threw him a scornful look and moved toward Dan. As the tall man extended the hat, she smiled again and said warmly, "Thank you, sir. That was very kind of you."

"Couldn't let a pretty lady lose her hat," he said, showing his white, even teeth.

By this time, the thick-shouldered man was out of the buckboard and coming around it, his face crimson.

"I'm Vicky Nelson," said the girl, extending her hand.

Accepting her tiny hand in his own, Dan said, "Glad to meet you, ma'am. My name's Dan Colt."

Chester Nelson bolted in, swung his meaty hand downward, striking Vicky's wrist. The blow broke the handclasp. The girl sucked air through her teeth in pain.

"You cheap hussy!" said Nelson with rage. "Gotta latch on to anything that wears pants. You get in the buckboard!"

Dan felt a prickling of heat run up his neck and over his scalp. "Your daughter was only introducing herself, Mr. Nelson," Dan said with conviction. "She was merely showing appreciation for my retrieving her hat."

Raw fury was instantly evident on Nelson's face. "She's not my daughter, saddletramp," he fumed. "She's my *wife*! And you keep your hands off of her!"

Dan Colt was stunned, but he did not show it. He set his blue gaze on the girl, who stood just behind her husband. "I'm sorry, Mrs. Nelson," he said quietly. "I didn't mean to cause any trouble."

"You didn't cause anything, Mr. Colt," said Vicky. "You were only being a gentleman. My husband doesn't know a gentleman when he sees one."

Chester Nelson whirled and slapped Vicky across the face with a stinging blow. "You shut up and get up in that seat!" The girl staggered and caught herself on the buckboard.

Dan felt his skin crawl. His face flushed. Instinctive in his very being was a tenderness and deep respect for women. Especially graceful, feminine, delicate ones. His spirited manhood was easily outraged at the violation of a lady's ennobled status. In his book there was nothing lower on earth than a male who mishandled a woman. His breath was hot to his own lips as he said fervidly, "Don't you do that again, mister." His pale blue eyes were livid.

Saliva spewed from Nelson's lips as he pointed a stiff finger and said, "You mind your own business, saddlebum!"

"You hit the lady again while I'm lookin' . . . and I'll make it my personal business to give you some of your own medicine," clipped the tall man with passion.

Nelson's eyes bulged. "Are you threatening me?"

"No. I'm *promisin'* you."

The thick-chested man burned Dan's face with his hot glare. Slowly he turned back to Vicky, who leaned against the buckboard, silently weeping. "Why ain't you in that seat yet?" he roared.

Nelson's right hand popped the girl's face again. Her knees buckled.

Fire burned in Dan Colt's veins. He took two steps, sank his fingers into the man's shirt, and jerked him around. A wicked, savage fist slammed Nelson to the ground. The wind caught his hat and whipped it away.

The crowd, which once again had pieced itself together unnoticed, cheered.

Chester Nelson rolled in the dust, fighting to gain his equilibrium. Dan waited, fire in his eyes. "Better just stay down, Nelson," he warned. "Because I'm mad! I'll just knock you down again."

The big man raised up on one knee, making sure of his balance, then stood up. He shook his head and blinked. Focusing on the tall man, he said belligerently, "It'll be you down the next time, saddlebum." Then he charged. He was like an animal, wild-eyed, savage, insane.

The lithe Colt side-stepped and let him run by. The crowd laughed and applauded. Nelson whirled and came again, fists pumping. Dan timed it perfectly and landed an uppercut. Bone cracked as the enraged man was straightened by the blow. Blood poured from his mouth. Instantly Dan closed in with a left hook and a right cross.

Nelson grunted and swung hard at the elusive face of Dan Colt. Dan caught him with a stiff punch on the nose. The big man staggered and a rawboned fist came out of nowhere, shattering his senses. Earth and cloudy sky changed places. Nelson was down again, attempting to rise.

"Better stay there, mister," said Colt heatedly. "I'm still mad."

Nelson called on his reserves and worked his way upward again. Vicky could be heard whimpering. One of the women in the crowd, a portly matron, moved next to her. "Come on, honey," she said soothingly, "let's get you off the street." They edged into the crowd, then turned around to watch the inevitable finish.

Chester, his thick chest heaving, closed in. Adeptly, Dan dodged the huge fists and planted a vicious one-two combination on Nelson's nose. The bloodied man swung again. Colt braced himself and put his shoulder into a hard right. It met Nelson's jaw with a loud, harsh sound. The big man's eyes turned to glass. He hung there for a moment on the balls of his feet. Dan slammed him violently one more time.

Chester Nelson hit the dust flat on his back. He was out cold.

Rubbing his fist, Dan walked to Vicky Nelson and eyed the stark, ugly slash of red on her face. "Are you all right, ma'am?" he asked amid the cheers of the crowd.

Tears were spilling from Vicky's eyes. "Yes, Mr. Colt. I'm fine, thank you."

"Ma'am, I'm not tryin' to butt in where I don't belong, but has he manhandled you before?"

Vicky's hand went to her mouth. The matronly woman beside her looked at Dan and said, "He has, mister. He's a mean beast. I don't know how the poor child takes it."

Dan wanted to ask Vicky why she married the old brute in the first place, but it really was not his business and the answer would not change anything. "I hope he treats you better in the future, ma'am," said Dan. He touched his hatbrim and returned to his horse. Mounting up, he rode north out of town.

Chapter Four

~~~~~~

Dan Colt rode until nearly dark. Dark thunderheads were gathering overhead, and lightning bolts were chasing each other in zigzag patterns across the murky sky. Thunder boomed and the rain came. The tall man found an old abandoned farmhouse and moved in. The gelding spent the night under a lean-to beside the house.

Dan was awakened several times during the night by the loud pop of lightning and the crash of thunder. He was sleeping soundly at dawn when the sound of his black gelding's nicker outside the window awakened him. Climbing out of his bedroll, he pulled on his boots and went to the window. Through the dirty glass he saw a bay mare rubbing noses with the black. The air was cold. He shouldered into his mackinaw.

Colt dropped his hat on his blond head and stepped outside. There he saw a mare, whose eyes widened as she saw him. She whinnied shrilly and trotted away. Making a wide circle, she returned and whinnied again, pawing the rain-soaked earth.

"Looks like she wants to play, old boy," Dan said to the gelding.

His pale blue eyes scanned the eastern horizon, then flitted across the sky to the jagged peaks on the west. There was not a cloud in the sky. He took a deep breath through his nose and let it out through

45

his mouth. "You ever breathe such clean air?" he asked the black.

The mare whinnied again and ran the same circle. *Strange*, Dan thought as he studied the saddle marks on the bay. *She belongs to somebody. Must've found a hole in the fence and got out.*

When she made the circle a third time, whinnying and pawing the ground, Dan said, "Old boy, I think she's trying to tell us something." Quickly he saddled the gelding, put the bedroll in its place, and mounted. The mare was running the circle again. "She sure enough has somethin' on her mind, partner," said Dan, touching spurs to the black's sides.

When the bay saw that Dan was ready to follow, she lifted her majestic head high and trotted into the woods. The morning breeze shook tree limbs, showering horse and rider with raindrops that had clung to leaves and pine needles after the storm passed.

As the mare led Dan due west, the sun climbed over the earth's eastern rim and cast its orange rays on the western peaks. Within moments Dan could see aspen trees on the higher elevations. Their moistened leaves sparkled like diamonds in the sunlight as they fluttered in the wind.

The mare had passed from sight, but Dan could hear her whinnying through the trees. As she came into view, she was standing stationary, bobbing her head. Drawing near, Dan's gaze lined on the limp form lying on a bed of wet pine needles. His jaw slacked. It was a young woman.

Colt's feet hit the ground beside the unconscious girl before the black had halted. Kneeling beside her, he saw the tattered robe, the bloodstains where the barbed wire had nicked her skin, and the large splotch of blood on her back. There were dried crimson spots on her face and a deep gash in the calf of her left leg. Her bare feet were cut and stained with blood.

Dan took her carefully into his arms. As he stood up, she moaned and rolled her head. Her body was mud-caked and cold. He must get her out of the frigid air as quickly as possible. The old farmhouse where he had spent the night was the closest place he knew.

The girl moaned again and opened her eyes. At first Dan's craggy face was a foggy blur. She could only tell that some man was holding her. A cold hollow feeling of terror possessed her. Recognizing the fear registered in her bruised and battered face, Dan spoke softly, "Don't be afraid, young lady. I'm a friend. No one will harm you."

She blinked slowly, attempting to clear the haze that covered her eyes.

"I'm going to take you where you can get warm. Do you think you can sit in the saddle?"

"I . . . I can try. Just a little dizzy," said the girl, her fears subsiding.

"I'll be right behind you," said Dan. "You can lean on me."

The battered young woman nodded painfully. Colt hoisted her into the saddle. "Take hold of the pommel," he said softly. "I'm going to get out of this coat and put it around you." Doing so, Dan boarded the black and sat behind the saddle. The girl swayed, eyes closed.

The bay mare nickered. The girl recognized the sound and opened her eyes. Blinking, she said, "Dolly!"

"I thought she was your horse, ma'am," said Dan. "She's the reason I found you. I slept in an abandoned farmhouse last night and she showed up at dawn. She raised a fuss until I was willing to follow her. She led me right to you."

"Dolly, I love you!" said the girl warmly.

The mare followed as Dan rode through the woods in the dappled sunlight. Reaching the old house, the tall man slipped to the wet earth and raised his hands. "Just lean toward me, ma'am, and I'll carry you into the house."

There was no bed in the abandoned house, but Dan quickly had the quivering girl wrapped in his bedroll on the same spot where he had spent the night before.

A dusty old stove stood nearby. The stovepipe was buckled in one spot, but the stove appeared usable. Straightening the buckled place, Dan found wood enough to make a fire. Soon the stove was giving off welcome heat.

There was water in the well behind the house. From his saddlebags, Dan produced coffee, beef jerky, and hardtack. As the girl took nourishment, her eyes brightened. She stopped shivering and managed a smile for the tall, rugged man who sat on an old rickety chair looking down at her.

"Feeling better?" he asked.

"Yes, thank you."

"My name is Dan Colt, ma'am."

"I'm Laura Lane, Mr. Colt," said the battered girl.

"You've been beat up pretty bad, ma'am. What in the world happened?"

Laura's face pinched. Reaching out from under the blanket, she thumbed a tear from an eye. "They . . . they hanged my husband." Her lower lip quivered. "They were going to harm me, too. I jumped on Dolly and ran away."

"*They?*"

"The ranchers. We have a farm in the valley just west of Alamosa about six miles. The ranchers want all of us farmers out of the valley."

48

"I guess they do," agreed Dan. "But they'll hang now, for murdering your husband."

"There's no way to convict them," said Laura with a note of despair.

"Why's that?" asked Colt, arching his heavy blond eyebrows.

"They wore masks."

Dan nodded and pursed his lips. "How many were there?"

"Seven, I think. But there is one less, now. Maybe two."

"Oh?"

"I shot one in the stomach. I'm sure he'll die if he hasn't already."

"The other?"

"I buried a hatchet in his face. Don't know exactly where the blade went in. Couldn't tell for the hood over his face."

"You have any idea who they were?"

"Yes, but there is no way to prove it. They'll bury them in some obscure place. They'll just say that those particular hired men had moved on."

"You don't think either of the men you wounded or killed were the ranchers themselves?"

"Not a chance. Fargo Wayne wouldn't get his own hands bloody. Neither would Jake Long . . . or any of the lesser ranchers, for that matter. Wayne runs the Box W ranch. Long runs the Circle L. They are the hotshots in the valley."

"We need to get you to a doctor, Mrs. Lane," said Dan, changing the subject. "You've got a bad cut on your back and the gash on your leg is going to need some attention."

"The one in my leg is a dog bite," said Laura advisedly. "I tried to get up to a house for help. A big dog just about ate me up."

"How far is home from here?" asked Dan.

"I have no idea," responded the girl. "I don't know where I am. By the looks of the land and the nearness of the high peaks, I would say Dolly took me due west of the farm. If we head east, I think I can get my bearings."

"Think you can ride?"

"Uh-huh."

"I have a clean cloth in my saddlebags. It'd be best if I bind up the gash on your leg. It was bleeding some when I found you. How's it doing now?"

Laying the blanket aside, Laura exposed the wounded leg. "Still bleeding a little," she said. "I'm afraid I got blood on your blanket."

"It'll wash," said Dan. "I'll pack up and we'll get ridin'. It will be warmer outside now."

As Dan and Laura rode eastward, she told him of the struggle between the ranchers and the farmers in the Del Norte valley. For years ranchers had enjoyed open, unlimited range. Now farmers were coming in to claim land that up until now had been part of the domain of the cattleman. The farmers' claims were fair and legal under the recently passed Homestead Act, but the cattle kings would not give up without a fight.

Dan was aware of the cattleman–farmer war ranging all over the west. Much blood had been shed and there was more to come. Cattlemen were vehement in clutching land they claimed under squatter's rights. Farmers, seeking to carve out a new life on the western frontier, fought to stay on rich and fertile land legally theirs by an act of Congress.

The ride was interrupted periodically as Laura needed water from Dan's canteen. The bay mare followed obediently.

It was late morning when Laura pointed to her

home in the valley and Dan aimed the black's nose toward the place.

Dan felt the young woman tense up in the saddle in front of him as they drew near. He jerked the reins when she gasped and began to cry. Over her head he saw the inert form of Vance Lane hanging limply against the noose. The body swayed slightly in the breeze.

Quickly Colt nudged the black and circled around, approaching the house from another angle where the body could not be seen. Easing Laura from the saddle, he carried her inside the house through the back door. He toed the overturned furniture out of his way as he carried the weeping widow into a bedroom and placed her gently on the bed.

"Ma'am, I'm going to ride into Alamosa and get the doctor. Will you be all right while I'm gone?"

Laura fought to control herself. Biting hard on her lip, she looked at Dan through glistening tears and nodded. He made a quick examination of the gash in her left leg. The cloth was moist with blood. "It's still bleeding some. I'll hurry."

"M-Mister Colt," said Laura. "Would . . . would you take Vance down . . . first? I can't just let him hang there . . ."

"Sure, ma'am. Where would you like me to put the body?"

"There's . . . there's another bedroom across the hall. Just—"

"All right. I'll just shut this door so you don't have to see."

The tall man picked up furniture as he passed through the house. On the porch floor was a galvanized wash tub laying on its side. At the edge of the porch was a hatchet. The blade was covered with dried blood.

51

A dead sorrel mare lay in the yard, a bullet in her neck. Two lanterns were set on the ground. One had run out of fuel. The other was still burning. He leaned over and snuffed the flame, then turned his attention to the corpse. *Why can't people live and let live?* Dan asked himself.

Vance Lane's neck was broken. He had died instantly; his face was not bloated as was the case when the hanged victim died of strangulation. Dan walked to a nearby wagon and pushed it underneath the swaying body. Taking his hunting knife from the saddlebag, he climbed the tree and sawed through the rope. The body dropped into the wagon. Carefully he cut away the cord that bound Lane's hands behind his back. Then he lifted the noose from the dead man's head. Dan was about to lift the body from the bed when the sound of a galloping horse met his ears. He turned to see a middle-aged man coming toward him on a sweating horse. The big animal scattered mud as it skidded to a halt, sides heaving.

The rider's eyes bulged as he looked at the lifeless form in the wagon. He flicked his gaze toward Colt. "Oh, no!" he gasped. "Not Vance, too." He swung from the saddle, eying the heap of rope laying under the tree. Dan had removed the rope from the limb and let it drop.

"Who are you?" the man asked Dan.

"I found Mrs. Lane about ten miles west of here, unconscious. All bloody and bruised up. Just brought her home," replied Colt.

The man swore. "Is she all right?"

"I was just going to ride into Alamosa and get the doctor. Dog attacked her somewhere out there in the dark last night. Pretty bad gash in her left leg. Has a deep cut on her back. Some barbwire cuts."

"I didn't catch your name, stranger," said the man.

"Dan Colt," said the tall man, extending his hand.

"I'm Ray Arnold, Colt. My farm parallels Lane's on the south," he said, pointing with his chin. "If you'd like to stay and look after Laura, I'll ride home, change horses, and go after Doc Cummings."

"I'd feel better about not leavin' her here alone, Mr. Arnold," nodded Dan. "When you rode up, you said 'not Vance, *too*.' Was someone else hanged last night?"

Arnold's face reddened. "Yeah," he said stiffly. "They strung up two of our farmers, Russ Morton and Ed Cleaver a few weeks ago—"

"Mrs. Lane told me about them."

"But last night," continued Arnold grimly, "the bloody devils rode onto John Jack's place . . . about three miles west of me, and hung John and his son, Jonah."

Dan Colt breathed an oath under his breath.

"That ain't all," said Ray Arnold shaking his head. "Then they rode to Roy Braxton's farm . . . about a mile further west and strung *him* up."

"What about their families?" quizzed Dan.

"They beat Mrs. Jack, but didn't harm her daughters. Mrs. Braxton got away from them. She had to hide in an irrigation ditch. Almost froze to death, but she'll be all right. They burned the Braxton house down, though. Anne—that's Mrs. Braxton—is staying with some other neighbors. The Healys."

"Does anybody know who did it?"

"Naw. They wore masks."

"Laura said the same thing."

"Everybody knows it's them stinkin' cattlemen," said Arnold crustily. "We just can't prove it. But I'm sure the good Lord knows Fargo Wayne and Jake Long are behind it. They're the two big hogs in the valley." Wheeling, the farmer walked toward his horse, saying, "I'd better be on my way. I'll be back with the doctor by midafternoon."

Dan carried Vance Lane's body into the house and laid it on the bed in the room across the hall from Laura. He covered it with a blanket and pulled the door shut.

He tapped lightly on Laura's door.

"Come in," came her voice from within.

Dan entered. Laura was sitting up on the edge of the bed. Her face was ashen. "What are you doing, ma'am?" he asked.

"I . . . was going to . . . try to get some water . . . and wash off some of this blood . . . and mud," she answered, fingertips to her temples. "But the whole room is spinning."

"Mrs. Lane," said the blond-headed man, "you're in no condition to do that. You'd best lie down until the doctor comes."

Turning her wan face toward him, Laura said, "Doctor Cummings is coming here?"

"Yes'm. While I was removing your husband's—uh . . . while I was outside . . . your neighbor, Ray Arnold, came by. When I told him what happened, he volunteered to go after the doctor so you wouldn't have to be left alone."

Easing back down on the bed, she said, "Bless his heart. He's a good neighbor."

As Dan helped Laura cover up, she asked, "Did Ray say why he rode over here?"

"Ma'am," said Dan evasively, "it'd be best if you just rest right now."

Laura's eyes widened. "They didn't quit here, did they?"

"Hmm?"

"The hangmen. They've hanged someone else."

54

Dan nodded woodenly. "Yes, ma'am."

Laura's face twisted in disbelief. Surely this was a nightmare. "Who else?" she asked, not really wanting to hear it.

"They strung up a man named John Jack and his son. Jonah, I think he said his name was."

"Oh, no. Not the boy, too." Laura's eyes moistened.

"And then they hanged a farmer named Braxton."

The words seemed to cut through right to Laura's heart. Her pale lips parted, but no sound came forth.

Dan leaned over and squeezed her shaking hands.

Laura struggled and found her voice. "Did . . . Ray say anything about . . . Anne?"

"Yes, ma'am. She got away from them. Hid in an irrigation ditch. They burned the Braxton home down. She's staying with neighbors."

Laura broke into sobs. "Oh, poor Anne. She's my best friend, Mr. Colt. I must go to her."

"You can't right now, ma'am," insisted Dan. "You've lost a lot of blood. Your leg needs attention. You must rest now."

Laura knew the tall man was right. She would have to have the doctor's attention and regain her strength before she could go to Anne Braxton.

It was nearly sundown when Ray Arnold returned with Doc Cummings. Arnold and Colt waited in the kitchen until Cummings left Laura's room. They heard the door open and close and met the doctor in the hallway.

"How is she, Doc?" asked Arnold.

"She'll be all right," the middle-aged physician replied. "I had to put sixteen stitches in her leg. The dog really cut her. Also had to put a few in her back. I cleaned all the spots I had to treat, but what she really needs is some woman to sponge bathe her completely . . . and to wash the dirt and blood out of her hair. I gave her some medicine to help ward off a cold. She got chilled pretty bad lying out in the rain last night."

"I'll dash home and get my missus," volunteered Arnold. "She can just stay the night if Laura needs her."

"That would be good," agreed the physician, buckling up his black bag. "She's got some fever. Be best if she had someone watching after her for a day or two."

Ray Arnold looked at Dan Colt. "What about Vance? Laura say what she wanted to do about burial?"

"No," replied Dan. "I'll talk to her about it in the morning. If it's all right with her, I'll sleep in the barn tonight. If she needs me to dig the grave, I'll do that before I leave."

"Guess you *were* headed somewhere when you found Laura," mused Ray Arnold aloud.

"Yessir. Trailin' a man northward."

Cummings eyed the twin Colts thonged to Dan's muscular thighs. "You a bounty hunter?"

"Nope," said Colt bluntly. "Man I'm trailin' is my brother. These guns are for snakes and coyotes I meet along the way."

"Ever met any with two legs?" asked the physician with a sly grin.

"Once in a while." Pointing out the door, Dan said, "There were some like that out there in the yard last night."

Chapter Five

Sunrise brightened the eastern sky as Dan Colt rolled out of the blankets in the hayloft of the barn. He forked hay to Dolly and Vance's gray stallion, plus the two draft horses and his own black gelding.

As he crossed the yard to the house, Dan saw smoke billowing from the chimney. Apparently Mrs. Arnold was up and preparing breakfast. His stomach growled.

Stepping into the kitchen, he caught the aroma of bacon frying and the tempting smell of hot coffee. Edith Arnold, a well-rounded woman in her fifties, looked up from where she stood at the cupboard and smiled. "Good morning, Mr. Colt," she said cheerfully. "Hungry?"

The tall, handsome man ran his tongue around his lips. "Yes'm. I think I could eat a grizzly bear."

"Don't have any of those," she chuckled. "But think there's enough to fill a hungry man here. Maybe even enough for us girls to have a smidgin'."

"How is Mrs. Lane this morning?" asked Dan with a note of concern.

"Much better. Her fever's gone. She seems stronger."

"That's good. How long till breakfast's ready?"

"I'd say ten, fifteen minutes."

"You got some hot water?"

"Mmm-hmm."

"Think I'll borrow a little and scrape off these whiskers."

Dan shaved outside by the well pump and ran a comb through his thick locks. Returning to the kitchen, his mouth watered at the sight of the hot food that adorned the table. Mrs. Arnold was out of the room, apparently with Laura. He dropped into a chair, looked again at the food and waited.

Presently Edith Arnold appeared through the hall door. "Laura's going to eat with us," she said smiling.

Laura Lane stepped through the door and Dan Colt's eyes widened. He hardly recognized her. All he had seen was a bloody, mud-caked girl with hair matted and stringy, clad in a tattered robe. Now she was clean and wearing a fresh dress which accentuated a lovely figure. Her long, dark hair was shiny, curling down about her shoulders.

Dan drew back the chair and snapped to his feet. He had noticed through all the blood and dirt that she had pleasant facial features. Now he realized she was stunningly beautiful.

As Laura limped to the table, she smiled faintly. "Good morning," she said weakly, but with warmth.

Dan helped her into a chair. "Are you the same Laura Lane that I found out in the forest yesterday?"

"I guess I do look a little different," said Laura, smiling faintly.

The blond man helped Edith Arnold into a second chair and sat down in his own. As he settled himself in his seat, Laura set her large brown eyes on his angular face. "I want to thank you for what you've done, Mr. Colt. You have inconvenienced yourself tremendously, I'm sure, to help me."

"I couldn't leave you lying out there in the woods, could I?"

"You must have been going somewhere. I certainly interrupted your travels."

Dan thought of Dave. Where would his outlaw twin be by now? "I was trailing my brother, ma'am." He paused awkwardly. "But it's all right, I'll pick up his tracks again."

They ate in silence. Edith washed and dried the dishes. Some time later, Dan was on his fourth cup of coffee when he edged up to the subject of Vance Lane's burial.

"Ma'am," he said, setting his hazy blue eyes on the pale features of the bereaved and battered woman, "will you be wanting any help with . . . with the burial?"

"Well, I . . . I think my neighbors—"

"Certainly we will take care of it, honey," put in Edith. "We'll—"

Mrs. Arnold's statement was interrupted by the sound of horses approaching the house. Laura tensed, eying the door. Dan shoved back his chair and went to the window. Pulling back the curtain, he said, "Couple men wearing tin stars."

"That'll be Sheriff Palmer and one of his deputies," said Edith confidently. The stout woman went to the door and pulled it open. "Howdy, Sheriff," she said as heavy boots sounded on the porch.

"Mornin', Mrs. Arnold," came a husky voice. "Is Laura able to talk?"

"I believe so," replied Edith, looking over her shoulder at the girl, who was still seated at the table.

Laura nodded.

Edith widened the door. "Come in, gentlemen."

As the two lawmen entered the kitchen, they gave Dan a lingering look, then turned to Laura. Dan guessed the sheriff to be about forty-five . . . the deputy about twenty-two. They removed their hats. "I want you to know I'm mighty sorry about Vance, Laura," said the sheriff tenderly.

"Me too, ma'am," said the deputy. "He was a mighty fine man."

Tears touched Laura's brown eyes. "Thank you," she said softly.

"Sheriff, this is Dan Colt," interjected the older woman.

"Glad to meet you, Colt," said the sheriff, extending his hand. "I'm Sheriff Bradley Palmer." Gesturing to the younger man, he said, "This is Deputy Ron Castin."

As Dan shook hands with Castin, Palmer said, "Is Dan Colt your *real* name?"

"Yes," came the steady reply.

The sheriff's brow furrowed. "There used to be a gunhawk by the same name," he said, eying the irons on Colt's hips. "Wore a pair of twin Colts. But he was shot in the back over in Kansas. Buried by his killers. Nobody ever found the body, at least."

"The reason that they never found the body, Sheriff," said Dan, "is because the ambush story is untrue and I'm still alive."

Ron Castin's eyes widened. "You mean you really *are* Dan Colt, the gunfighter?"

"The same," responded Dan evenly. "I hung up my guns and went to ranchin' up in Wyoming."

Eying the guns again, Palmer said, "Looks like you done strapped 'em on once more. How come?"

"Circumstances," said Dan coolly.

Palmer studied Colt's features for a long moment, then turned to the young widow. "Laura, I need to ask you some questions."

Laura nodded.

"Would you like some coffee?" asked Edith.

Both lawmen accepted a steaming cup and slacked

into straight-backed chairs. Dan thought it best not to appear in a hurry. The sheriff was turning something over in his mind. He returned to his own chair.

Looking at Laura across the table, Palmer said, "What time did they ride in here last night?"

"It was about nine . . . nine thirty," replied the young widow.

"How many were there?"

"I think there were seven. Vance . . ." Laura's face pinched. "Vance saw them coming. He said it looked like seven."

"How did they get in the house? The door looks intact."

"Vance went out to talk to them. He . . . he left the rifle with me. Told me to shoot through the door if they tried to come in. He told them we were on the land legally. They grabbed him. I went out and put the rifle on them. They took it away from me. The gun went off and hit one of their horses."

Palmer spoke to his deputy. "That explains the dead horse out there."

"Ray Arnold says you got away on your mare," said the sheriff.

"Yes," nodded Laura.

"But not before she shot one of the skunks and cut open another one," put in Dan Colt.

Palmer's eyebrows arched. "Really?"

Laura explained the details of the shooting, the hatchet incident and her ride in the night, closing with the subsequent rescue by the tall blond man.

The sheriff eyed Dan with suspicion. "How did you happen to be in the area where Laura fell, Colt?"

"I'm on my way north from New Mexico," replied Dan, trying not to show the annoyance he was feeling.

"Where you headed?" prodded Palmer.

"Don't know exactly."

61

"Just drifting, eh?"

"Nope," said Dan curtly. "I'm trailin' my brother. Wherever he lands, that's where I'm headed."

The sheriff let his gaze linger momentarily on Dan's face. "Have we met somewhere before?"

"Not as far as I know," said Colt blandly.

Returning to Laura Lane, Palmer asked, "I assume they wore masks here also?"

"Yes."

"Was there anything about them you recognized?"

"No, Sheriff," said Laura. "Nothing." She paused and asked, "Have you any ideas?"

"Only that they must be cattlemen. Those notes that were stuck on all the farmers' doors after Morton and Cleaver were hanged made it clear who's behind the hangings. But there are a lot of cattlemen and a lot of hired hands."

Castin spoke up. "Laura, do you have any idea why they chose to pick on you, the Jacks, and the Braxtons?"

"John and Roy and . . . and Vance were the backbone of the Farmers' Association after Russ and Ed were murdered."

"Do you mind if we look around outside, Laura?" asked Palmer.

"Not at all. I wish you could find something to lead you to them," she said bitterly.

"May already have," said the sheriff, fishing in his vest pocket.

"Oh?" said Laura.

Palmer held up a round silver saddle ornament with two narrow strips of black leather attached. "Found this under the hangin' tree on the Braxton place. I would say it came from a fancy black saddle. If I could find the saddle, I'd have one of the hangmen."

"Well, let's hope you find it," said Edith Arnold.

"What we're thinkin'," put in Deputy Castin, "is that maybe the rider won't notice it's missin'. Maybe he'll come ridin' into town on that saddle and we'll spot it."

"Why don't you just make the rounds of the ranches and look for it?" asked the young widow.

"These men are desperate, Laura," responded Palmer. "If I didn't find it on the first ranch I investigated, they would alert each other that I was examining saddles. The owner of this ornament would check his saddle and realize it was missing. The saddle would disappear and there would go my one piece of evidence."

The sheriff stood to his feet. Castin followed suit. "We'll scour the grounds and be out of your way," Palmer said to Laura.

"You're not in the way, Sheriff," said Laura. "I want the men who murdered my husband brought to justice."

"Sounds like you exacted a little justice of your own," observed Palmer. "Few men can live with a hatchet in their face or a bullet in their gut. Remind me to stay on your good side."

The two lawmen moved to the door. Palmer turned and fixed his eyes on Dan Colt. "Why is it when I look at you, I get the name Sunday . . . or Sunshine . . . or Sundance in my brain?"

Dan's blood turned cold. "I must remind you of someone else," he said, disguising his apprehension.

"Guess so," said the sheriff, placing the saddle ornament back in his vest pocket. "Let's go, Ron."

Dan and Edith Arnold stood in the door and watched the two lawmen examine the grounds. The deputy spent several moments rifling the saddlebags on the dead horse. Dan watched Palmer pick up a mud-caked Winchester. He held it up and looked toward the house. "Is this Vance's rifle?" he called.

Dan turned to Laura, who was still seated. "He's found a rifle."

"I'm sure it's the one they took away from me," she said blandly. "They wouldn't leave their own."

Dan called back to the lawman as he passed through the door, "It's Vance's!"

The tall man walked to the sheriff and took the Winchester. "I'll clean it up for her," he said, turning toward the house.

Behind him, Dan heard the double click of a revolver hammer being dogged back. "You just hold it right there, *Sundeen!*" came Palmer's sharp voice.

Dan started to turn.

"Don't turn around!" barked the sheriff. "Just put the rifle down, then unbuckle your gunbelt. One quick move and I'll split your spine."

As Dan eased the muddy Winchester to the ground, Ron Castin left the trees and came on the run. "What are you doin', Sheriff?" he asked, drawing his gun.

"It just came to me who this bird is," clipped Palmer. "He's Dave Sundeen. Lawman killer and escapee from Yuma. I've got a wanted poster on him at the office."

Castin's mouth dropped.

"Get his guns," said the sheriff.

At the kitchen door, Edith Arnold stared at the scene and spoke to Laura Lane. "Somethin's wrong, honey."

"What's the matter?" asked Laura.

"The sheriff's got a gun on Mr. Colt. Deputy's taking his guns."

Laura shoved back her chair and limped to the door. "What is he doing?"

"Guess we're about to find out," observed the stout woman.

Bradley Palmer held his revolver on the tall, blond man while his deputy cuffed Dan's hands together behind him. The three talked for a moment, then Castin headed for the barn. The sheriff ushered Colt toward the house. Laura limped onto the porch. Edith followed.

"Sheriff, what are you doing?" demanded Laura.

"This *hombre* is no more Dan Colt than I am," said Palmer, a glint of triumph in his eye. "He's a wanted criminal. He shot a lawman in Arizona. Escaped from Yuma prison."

The young woman's soft brown eyes swung to Dan's face, held there a moment, then flashed truculently at Palmer. "I don't believe it!" she snapped. "No criminal would have bothered to do what Dan—Mr. Colt did for me."

"Unless he thought there was something in it for him," retaliated Palmer.

"Sheriff, you're wrong," said Laura with conviction.

"I've got a poster on him at the office, ma'am," said the sheriff. "His name is Dave Sundeen."

"Sundeen is my identical twin brother," spoke up Dan defensively. "He's the one I'm trailin'."

Palmer cursed. "That's a damn fairy tale if I ever heard one!"

Colt's eyes flinted. "There are ladies present, Palmer," he rasped. "Watch your mouth."

The sheriff's face reddened. "You'd better watch your own—" His eyes met Laura's. "Uh . . . I'm . . . uh . . . sorry, ma'am."

"Why do you think he's lying?" challenged Laura. "Some people do have twins, you know."

Palmer's face clouded. "Yeah, but—"

"This man is no criminal, Sheriff," Laura said crisply. "I just know he's not."

"Meaning no disrespect, ma'am," said the sheriff,

"but I can't operate on female whims. This *hombre*'s face matches a poster in my file. I've got to take him in. We'll let the law decide his innocence or guilt."

Ron Castin appeared at the barn door, leading Dan's horse.

"Let's go, Sundeen," said Palmer.

Laura stepped off the porch and gripped Dan's arms. Looking into his eyes, she said, "I know you're telling the truth. I'm so sorry. If you hadn't stopped to help me, this wouldn't be happening."

"It isn't your fault, ma'am," said the tall man softly.

The young widow's eyes misted. "Thank you for what you did." She threw a hot glance at Bradley Palmer.

"Mount up, Sundeen," said Palmer, dodging Laura's glare.

The deputy helped Dan aboard the black. A cold, sinking feeling descended over the blond man.

Laura watched through watery eyes until the three riders faded from view.

Chapter Six

At the north end of the Del Norte valley, four men huddled in the early morning in a cabin tucked among the tall trees in a shaded box canyon. Sweat beaded on the finely chiseled forehead of a slender young man who wore long, thin sideburns and a pencil-line mustache. The handsome youth leaped to his feet and began to pace the floor.

"Don't worry, boss," said Maze McLeod, dabbing lightly at the burns on his face and head. Patches of hair were missing. "If the ornament came off when your horse scraped the tree, the boys'll find it."

"It has to be there," said the boss, running his fingers through his thick black hair. "Too many people in this valley have seen my saddle. That little piece of metal could put my neck in a noose." Reaching in his vest pocket, he produced a gold pocket watch. He noted that his two riders had had sufficient time to ride to the Braxton place and return.

"Here they come, boss," said one of the other men.

Thundering hoofs skidded to a stop. Two sweaty riders plunged through the door. The slender young man eyed them expectantly. "Well?"

"Boss, we got trouble," said the first one to enter. "That stupid sheriff got there just ahead of us."

The boss swore. "Heath, can't you ever do anything right?"

"Boss," said Heath Finley defensively, "me and Mel got to the Braxton place not twenty minutes after sunup. Palmer had one of the deputies with him, lookin' the grounds over. We watched him walk straight to the tree where we hung Braxton. He picked up the ornament, looked it over, and stuck it in his vest pocket."

"And, boss," put in the other sweaty rider, "somebody had already cut Braxton down. The body was gone."

"Probably whoever rode and got Palmer," said McLeod.

"Why didn't you two shoot that hick sheriff and get the ornament?" demanded the boss, his features livid with rage.

Finley's face blanched. "Kill a lawman?"

"They bleed and die just like the rest of us," said the boss.

"Yeah, but boss," said Finley's partner, "killin' a lawman can bring all kinds of trouble. And we would've had to kill *two* of 'em!"

"Mel, you're just as spineless as Heath," growled the boss angrily. "I should've handled it myself." Grabbing his hat, he asked, "Did you see which way they headed from Braxton's?"

Mel Trent said, "We took off before they left, but if they were at Braxton's just after sunup, they couldn't have been to Jack's or Lane's yet."

"Maybe they didn't even know we'd hung the others," put in McLeod, still dabbing at his burns.

"Maybe not," agreed the boss. "But wherever they are, we gotta catch 'em and kill 'em. I want that ornament back." Eying Finley and Trent, he said, "Let's go. I want to show you two how to handle a man's job." Turning to Manfred Drake and Lefty Dean, he said, "You two go on into Alamosa and get the groceries."

Dan Colt rode sullenly, his hands cuffed behind him. Sheriff Bradley Palmer rode in the lead, holding the reins of Colt's black gelding. Deputy Ron Castin brought up the rear.

The morning sun was lifting higher in the crystal blue sky, slowly shortening the shadows.

"If this alleged twin of yours exists," said Palmer over his shoulder, "how come he's willing to let you take the blame for his crimes? Some brother, I'd say."

"He doesn't even know I exist," Dan said blandly.

The sheriff ejected a horselaugh. "Now that *is* funny! Mister, you're gonna have to come up with somethin' better than that. They'll slam you into Yuma and bury the key."

The east rim of the valley was ridged with crooked lines of trees and upthrust rocks. The climb to the crest of the rim would weave them on a rugged, rocky trail amid boulders, large and small. Once on top, the ride to Alamosa would be about half an hour. Dan knew his chance of escape would narrow considerably once he was locked up in Bradley Palmer's jail. He remained alert. He must find a way to get out of this situation.

A large black hawk wheeled across the azure sky. Another hawk skimmed low on broad wings and cast a flickering shadow on the green valley floor. Dan Colt eyed the birds with their great pinions flapping free and easy. He thought of his own arms, shackled and useless.

Some time passed without any exchange of words. Deputy Ron Castin broke the silence. "Sheriff, what are we going to do with Sundeen once we lock him up?"

Without looking back the sheriff said, "I'll wire the U.S. marshal's office in Raton. They'll send a man to take him back to Yuma." Silence prevailed for several moments. Palmer twisted in the saddle. "Ever hear of a U.S. marshal name of Logan Tanner, Sundeen?"

The name Logan Tanner clung to the walls of Dan Colt's mind like foul mud. "My name is Daniel Colt, Sheriff," he said, lips drawn tight.

"Whatever your name is . . . I asked you if you ever heard of Logan Tanner."

Colt's mind framed an image of the lawman who had arrested him in Holbrook, Arizona. It was Tanner's refusal to believe Dan's story that ultimately resulted in Dan's imprisonment at the Arizona Territorial prison at Yuma. "Yeah," he replied darkly. "I've heard of him."

"Crackerjack lawman," said Palmer. "Works out of the Raton office."

As if I didn't already know, thought Dan.

Time edged forward slowly. The sun was at its apex in the burnished sky when the lawmen and Colt approached the spot at the valley's eastern boundary where they would begin the ascent up the scabrous path to the rim.

Three sweat-stained riders dismounted unnoticed atop the ridge and tied their panting horses in the shade of some tall pines. Rifles in hand, they ran to a rocky ledge and crouched down.

"They're just starting the climb, boss," said Mel Trent, pointing to the sheriff. "We circled 'em and still beat 'em."

"Let's work our way down to those rocks," said the raven-haired boss, pointing. "We can shoot 'em easy from there."

While the three men picked their way downward to

the designated spot, two hawks swooped out of the valley and circled over their heads.

"Stupid birds are gonna give us away," said Heath Finley.

The boss turned his handsome face upward, fixing his coal-black eyes on the wheeling hawks. "Palmer won't even notice 'em," he said blandly. "He's too dumb."

Mel Trent flattened himself behind a rock and peered over it. "Boss," he said in a husky voice, "I think the one on the black horse is a prisoner."

"What?" said the slender boss, hunkering beside him.

"Looks to me like Palmer's leadin' his horse. His hands are behind his back, sure as shootin'."

Finley joined them, squinting to sharpen focus on the trio. "That answers our question," he said. "They've picked up a prisoner on the way."

The boss studied the winding path ahead of Bradley Palmer, Dan Colt, and Ron Castin. The wind picked up, moaning softly through the tall pines that grew on the crest of the ridge. It sighed down off the flat-topped mesa to the valley floor three hundred feet below.

"We'll let them reach that level area just below those two boulders," said the boss.

"Gotcha," agreed Trent.

"What about the man on the black?" asked Heath Finley. "Shall we kill him, too?"

"Hate to kill a man that has the good taste to ride a black horse," replied the boss. "Tell you what. Let's cut down the two lawmen. If the dude on the black hightails it back down to the valley, we'll let him go. All I want is that saddle ornament. We gotta kill Palmer and the deputy to get it. If he jumps off the horse and stays close, gun him down. We can't have any witnesses."

In less than a minute the three riders would be at the level place where the killers could get a clear shot. They levered cartridges into the chambers of their rifles.

"You two plug the deputy," said the slender man. "I'll take out Palmer. We'll fire on the count of three."

Down below the three horses' hoofs dug into the soft dirt, still wet from last night's rain. The hoofs sent small rocks cascading down the steep grade. Sheriff Palmer eyed the path ahead. "We'll rest the horses at that spot up there where it levels off," he said advisedly.

Looking back at Colt, he said, "What's it like at Yuma, Sundeen?"

"It's a suburb of hell," replied Dan.

"They tell me the guards are meaner'n snakes."

"Most of them."

"How'd you get out?"

"Sprouted wings," said Dan with a note of impudence.

"How high are the walls?" asked Castin, while Palmer glared at Colt with contempt.

"Only about ten feet," said Dan.

"Shucks," chuckled the deputy, "a normal-size man could get a run at a wall that low and hop over it."

"Guards have a Gatling gun in the tower," responded the man on the black. "Prisoners know they're just itchin' to use it."

"Anybody ever make it over the walls?"

"Yep."

"Guards asleep on the job?"

"Nope. When the place gets too crowded, the

72

guards look the other way. Usually two or three will dive over the wall."

Castin was stunned. "You mean they just let them go?" He snapped his fingers. "Just like that?"

"Yep."

"Just because the place is too crowded?"

"Yep." Dan's brain was working at trying to figure how to escape the two lawmen.

"I can't believe that," commented the deputy.

"Well, there is one little hitch to it."

"Oh? What's that?"

"They pay Apaches to kill the escapees. The Indians don't have to return the entire corpse. Just an ankle with the marks where the leg irons had been. Everybody wore leg irons at night and at various other times. Apaches get a pint of whiskey per dead convict."

Castin's face paled.

As they reached the level area, the sheriff looked at Colt with a sneer. "If you're Dan Colt and Dave Sundeen is the outlaw, how come you know so much about Yuma?"

"Because it was me that was sent there," snapped Dan. "Logan Tanner mistook me for Dave. Wouldn't believe there were two of us. Judge and jury were the same way."

"Logan Tanner?" said Palmer, arching his eyebrows. "I guess you *have* heard of him."

"I even saved Tanner's life up in Welcome, Colorado," said Dan in a bitter tone. "He still wouldn't believe me."

The sheriff laughed. "I'm with Tanner. Unless you produce this phantom twin, I won't believe you till the day I die."

Suddenly the sky seemed to explode. Rifle fire

roared overhead, the reports reverberating among the rocks and boulders. It sounded like a dozen guns had cut loose on the three riders. Dan heard Ron Castin grunt behind him as two slugs ripped into his body. Simultaneously, the sheriff jerked and stiffened with the bullet's impact. He peeled out of the saddle and hit the ground hard.

Dan was helpless to guide his horse, but he spurred the animal savagely. As the black leaped, then whirled, deciding to go back down the precipitous path, Dan threw a glance upward, expecting a bullet to strike his body any second. He saw white powder smoke drifting away in the wind.

The frightened gelding paused to keep from running into Castin's horse, then whirled in a complete circle. Dan saw Palmer sprawled awkwardly on a flat rock, just before he felt the black plunge forward again. Castin lay in a muddled heap as Dan and his horse darted past where he lay. The tall man was having trouble staying in the saddle. He wondered why the riflemen were not shooting at him as the gelding thundered down the steep slope, reins trailing.

Once the black almost fell. When he stumbled, Dan nearly left the saddle. He righted himself and clung to the horse's back with all the strength in his legs. Within another minute horse and rider were on the valley floor. Dan hollered, "Whoa! Whoa, boy!"

The gelding slowed, trotted thirty yards and came to a gradual stop. Throwing his right leg over the saddle horn, Colt dropped to the ground. Quickly he looked up the steep slope. Three men were moving down from a higher elevation toward the ledge where the two lawmen lay dead.

Dan sat down on the ground and placed his shackled hands flat. Then he lay on his back and wriggled his rump through, bringing his arms up and pulling his knees up to his chin. He inched the short chain on the handcuffs over the toes of his boots and stood up. Now his hands were in front of his body.

Eying the scene on the ledge again, he saw the three bushwhackers milling about the level place where the bodies lay. Dan hoped they would leave the lawmen's horses behind and not search their gear. His twin Colt .45s were in Palmer's saddlebags.

The bushwhackers wasted little time. They were scrambling toward the lofty rim. Gaining the top in less than five minutes, they stood silhouetted against the sky, studying the valley below. Then they turned and disappeared.

Dan tied the reins together and looped them over the horse's head. Then he gripped the saddlehorn with both hands and climbed into the saddle. He raked the gelding's sides, crossed the flat, and ascended the steep pathway. Reaching the narrow shelf where Palmer and Castin lay dead, he dismounted and walked to Palmer's horse. The saddlebags appeared untouched. He was relieved to reach inside and feel the cool grips of the twin Colts.

A further search produced the key to the cuffs in Palmer's vest pocket. He twisted a wrist to position the cuff for insertion of the key. He slid the key in and the tiny lock clicked and the ratchet bar sprang open. In another moment the second cuff was loose.

Finally free, Dan made his way to where the sheriff still lay sprawled on the flat rock, trying to figure how to handle the situation. Suddenly, he remembered the silver saddle ornament that Palmer had stuffed in there. It was gone. He glanced up the steep slope. Whoever had gunned down the two lawmen was after the ornament.

Dan decided to drape both men over their saddles and take them into Alamosa. No one need know that Palmer had arrested him.

In less than three quarters of an hour, Dan Colt and his dismal train moved down the main street of Alamosa. Residents readily spied the bodies of their sheriff and deputy. Quickly they gathered around the horses as Dan continued moving down the street.

"Who killed 'em, mister?" someone asked.

"What happened?" came another voice.

A considerable number grouped around him as Dan reined in at the sheriff's office. Questions were being fired at him, raising a heavy hubbub. Dan eyed two men who stood near the office door. There was something that Edith Arnold had said that had led him to believe there was a second deputy. Speaking to the two men, he said, "The other deputy around?"

"He's over at the Yellow Rose Saloon," one of them answered.

"Would you mind fetchin' him for me, please?" asked Dan, dismounting.

"Better wait a few minutes, stranger," said the man. "He's got some drifters in there givin' him some trouble."

Dan shot a glance up the street toward the Yellow Rose. Looking back at the man, he said, "Don't let any of these people touch the bodies, okay?"

The man nodded and stepped off the board sidewalk, pushing his way through the crowd.

As Colt approached the saloon he could hear loud voices coming from inside. Threading his way between a hip-shot horse and a wagon loaded with groceries, he ducked under the hitching-rail and elbowed his way through the green-painted batwings.

The bright light outside and the gloom of the saloon made a momentary contrast.

"I told you, sonny," a harsh voice was saying, "we ain't goin' nowhere."

"You'll just bring down federal law on you," came a young voice.

As Dan's eyes adjusted to the comparative darkness, he spied the youthful deputy, standing with his back to the bar. Several customers had lined the walls, making a path for the inevitable gunplay. Four granite-faced roughnecks sat around a table in the middle of the room. Two half-empty whiskey bottles and four empty glasses decorated the table.

The harsh voice came again from a tall, swarthy man with long bushy sideburns and a heavy black mustache. "I got a score to settle with your boss, Deputy. I ain't pullin' outta this stinkin' burg till it's settled."

"What you have in mind is murder," lashed the deputy. "I'm not standing by while you gun down Mr. Palmer."

"You annoy me, kid," rasped the dark-faced gunslinger. Pointing a stiff finger, he said through his teeth, "You go on back to the office and shine your badge. I'm liable to decide to use you for target practice. I ain't vacatin' this town till your sheriff comes back."

The deputy opened his mouth to speak when Dan Colt's voice cut a swath through the room. "The sheriff isn't comin' back!"

Every eye zeroed in on the face of the tall, blond stranger.

"He's dead," said Dan, flicking his gaze to the face of the young lawman, then returning it to the four hardcases. "I just brought in his body."

The deputy's face blanched. Shock registered in his eyes.

Two of the men in the crowd eyed each other furtively, then looked back at Dan Colt.

The tall, swarthy gunhawk eased out of his chair and glared at the deputy. The other three scraped their chairs and stood up.

"No reason to hang around now, is there?" said the deputy. "Can't draw against a dead man."

"Guess that leaves *you*," said the dark man icily.

The deputy's face stiffened.

"I've got this thing in my gut. I've just *gotta* kill me a lawman today." The dark man's eyes were mean.

"Why don't you boys just plant yourselves on your horses and go play tough stuff somewhere else?" came Dan Colt's ragged voice.

The ugly foursome eyed him with disdain. The youthful deputy's protruding Adam's apple dropped, then bobbed into place. These men were professional killers. Dan knew the type. Any one of them could outdraw the inexperienced deputy. It was not in the tall, blond man to stand by and let it happen.

One of the gunmen forced a wicked smile and said, "Who you challengin', whitey?"

"*You*, if you've got the salt to face a *man*," grated Colt.

"Why you—"

"Wait a minute, Lenny," cut in the tall, dark one. "Maybe I'd like to handle mister blue eyes myself."

Another of the four spoke to Dan and said, "Mister, you'd better not tangle with him." He was nodding toward his swarthy champion. "Do you know who he is?"

Dan did not answer.

"Well, he's—"

"I'm Neal Nix!" barked the tall, dark one.

The name had never touched Dan's ears. "Is that supposed to turn my backbone to jelly?" he asked defiantly.

"Don't tell me you've never heard of the man who gunned down Francis Oldham!" bellowed another of the four.

Colt had heard of Oldham. He had been one of the best in his day. Age had caught him and slowed his gun hand. But Dan's temper was up and he taunted Nix. "Frances Oldham?" he asked, emphasizing the feminine ending on the *Frances*. "Who was *she?*"

Nix's eyes caught fire. "You just turned the first shovel in your grave, blue eyes!" he roared. The blood in his angered face made it even darker. "I'll give you your choice. You can die in here, or outside."

Dan Colt's smoky blue eyes bored in on Nix. "No sense bloodyin' up the saloon," he said in a cold monotone. Slowly he backed toward the batwings until they touched his back. He eased through them and let them swing shut. Instantly men began to pour through the door.

Someone shouted, "Gunfight! Gunfight!"

The crowd down the street forsook the saddle-draped corpses and hastened toward the Yellow Rose. The youthful deputy followed Dan into the street. "Mister," he said in a half-whisper, "who killed the sheriff?"

"No time to explain it now, Deputy," Dan said hastily. "I'll tell you about it after I put this fool where he belongs."

"But what if he—?"

"He *won't.*"

The deputy backed away. Dan centered the street. Neal Nix followed suit. His friends detached themselves from the crowd and crossed the street. They leaned against the hitching-rail. Two of them folded arms across their chests as if the outcome of the gunfight was not in question.

Manfred Drake and Lefty Dean stood next to their grocery-laden wagon.

Neal Nix went dramatically into his stance, a wolf-like grin twisting his dark face. Dan stood ready, hands curled like talons just above the grips of his twin Colts. His mouth drew into a grim line. Brittle tension overtook the crowd, which now was breathlessly still.

Then . . . Nix's hand darted downward.

Dan's hands were invisible blurs. The .45s belched fire in a synchronized roar. Both slugs dead-centered in Neal Nix's chest. The impact knocked him flat. He lay motionless, his fingers curled on the gun still in its holster.

As the blue-white smoke sifted skyward, Dan wheeled toward Nix's three cohorts. His ice-blue eyes bolted them hard. "Who's next?" he hissed.

Wide-eyed, they inched along the vacant hitching-rail, shaking their heads. "We ain't drawin' against you," one said weakly.

"Then get out of this town," said Dan, clipping each word.

The three fell down, stumbling over each other. As they unscrambled and headed for their horses, the tall man hollered, "Wait a minute!" They froze in their tracks. Dan pointed to the inert form of Nix. "Pick up that piece of buzzard bait and take it with you!"

As the nervous trio complied, a portly man of sixty stepped out of the crowd and said, "Sir, I want to congratulate you. That's the most adept handling of guns I have ever seen in my life. My name is Fred Carver." He did not offer his hand because Dan was busy reloading the .45s.

"May I ask your name, sir?" asked Carver.

"Colt," Dan said evenly. "Dan Colt."

"I live over in the town of Del Norte, Mr. Colt,

and—" Carver's mouth hung open. "Did you say *Dan Colt?*"

"Mmm-hmm," hummed Dan, punching the spent shell out of his left hand gun.

"I've heard much of you, sir, but I thought—"

"I was dead?"

"Yes!"

"Well, let that be a lesson about listening to gossip," said Colt dryly.

The deputy stepped in. "Did I hear you correctly, mister?" he asked, eyes enlarged. "You are Dan Colt? *The* Dan Colt?"

"Yes. I'm Dan Colt," replied the blond man, slipping a cartridge from his belt and thumbing it into the cylinder.

"My dad used to talk about you, Mr. Colt," said the deputy. "Said he knew you in Wichita."

"Yeah? Who was your dad?"

"Sheriff Bill Caley."

Recognition spread over Dan's suntanned features. "Sure. Your dad and I fought a gang of horse thieves together once. I was one of those distasteful bounty hunters at the time, but I showed up when six of 'em had him cornered. It was at one of Wichita's feed lots. That was one lawman who was happy to see a bounty hunter."

Dan's face clouded. "He was killed over in Hutchinson, wasn't he?"

"Yessir," said young Caley, eyes darting downward. "He was outnumbered in a gunfight again. Only there was no Dan Colt to help him out of that one."

"He was a mighty fine lawman, son," said Dan warmly. "You can be mighty proud."

"I am, Mr. Colt," said the youthful deputy. Sticking out his hand, he said, "I'm Bill, Junior."

Dan met his grip. "I can see the resemblance now."

"Mr. Colt, I thought you'd been shot and killed by a bushwhacker somewhere in west Kansas."

"Guess you can see that's not so."

"Yessir." Bill turned toward the sheriff's office. When his gaze fell on the two bodies draped over the saddles, he said, "Oh, no. Ron's dead, too?"

"'Fraid so," responded Dan.

The bodies of Bradley Palmer and Ron Castin were turned over to the local undertaker. Dan sat in the sheriff's office and related to young Bill the story of the hangings in the valley and the subsequent bushwhacking on the ridge. He avoided the real reason he was riding with Palmer and Castin. Passed it off that he was coming to Alamosa anyway and merely rode along for company. He figured if Bill knew about the arrest, it would only confuse matters. Dan hoped that the deputy would not be looking through the wanted posters any time soon.

"We got word of the hangings from Ray Arnold," young Caley told Dan Colt. "Sheriff Palmer figured it would be the same as when they hanged Russ Morton and Ed Cleaver a few weeks ago. Not a shred of evidence."

"No tracks to follow?" queried Dan.

"No, sir. They chose a rainy night then, too."

"Ray Arnold mentioned a couple of hotshot ranchers as suspects," said the tall man.

"That'd be Fargo Wayne and Jake Long. They've got the biggest spreads and the most cattle. They have the most to lose with the homesteads fencing off the open range."

"Don't they have enough pasture land without using the whole valley?"

"Plenty. The farmers haven't really claimed that much land. But the cattlemen's association has panicked. They're afraid more homesteaders will come. So some of the cattlemen are taking to drastic measures. They're trying to drive out the farmers and frighten any new hopefuls away."

"I guess you'd say murder is pretty drastic," mused Dan aloud.

"I wonder why they killed the sheriff and Ron," said Bill, shaking his head.

"Oh," said Dan. "I forgot to tell you, Palmer did find some evidence."

"What? Where?"

"A silver saddle ornament. Had two pieces of black leather attached. Found it next to the tree where Roy Braxton was hanged. Somehow they found out he had it. Time I reached the place where Palmer and Castin lay dead, the bushwhackers had rifled Palmer's pockets and taken the ornament."

Deputy Bill Caley, Jr. wiped a nervous hand over his brow. "Well," he said with a sigh, "looks like until this county can get a new sheriff, I'm going to be the one that carries out the investigation."

"What do you plan to do?" asked Colt.

"I'm going to talk to the widows and see if they saw anything that would give any leads. Then I think I'll visit the cattlemen one at a time. Maybe I can detect something that will help."

"Do you think the entire cattlemen's association is behind the hangings?"

Caley stared thoughtfully into space for a long moment. Shaking his head, he said, "I doubt it. They're upset and worried, but most of the ranchers are good men. They're not murderers. Could be just one or two behind it."

"And you think the best prospects are Wayne and Long?"

"Only for the reason I already gave you. I can't pic-

ture either of them guilty of murder either. But somebody is."

"At least seven somebodys," said Colt, nodding.
"And one of them rides a black saddle." The tall man
eyed the young lawman carefully. "It could be, Bill, if
you get close to the guilty parties, they might give you
the same treatment they gave Palmer and Castin."

"I was thinkin' the same thing," said Caley. "What I
need is a man sharp with a gun to help me bring those
hangmen to justice."

Dan knew by the look in the deputy's eyes just who
he had in mind. He knew that the inexperienced
youth would probably end up dead if left to handle
the hangmen by himself. His thoughts ran to Laura
Lane. The men who had killed her husband must pay.

Bill Caley studied Dan's angular face, waiting for
his reply.

Dan's thoughts drifted to his outlaw twin. Dave was
probably moving farther and farther away. It was im-
perative that he capture Dave and turn him over to
the Arizona authorities. He would never breathe a
free breath or be rid of the relentless Logan Tanner
until Dave was in custody.

No, Dan told himself. *I can't leave. My own problems will have to wait.* A tinge of a smile touched his
lips. "Okay, pardner," he said. "I'll stick around and
help you clear up this hangin' business. We'll root out
the killers together."

"Great!" exclaimed Caley. "As acting sheriff, I'll deputize you."

Dan flipped palms forward, shaking his head. "No
need for that. If I have to use my guns, they won't
need arresting. If there's any arresting to do, you can
handle it."

"Whatever you say," Bill agreed. "I'm just glad to

have you with me." Cocking his head, he said, "By the way, Mr. Colt. Where were you headed when you found Laura Lane?"

"Uh . . . north toward Del Norte."

"Looking for work?"

"No. Uh . . . trailin' my brother."

"Oh. Family stuff, huh?"

"Yeah," nodded Colt. "Family stuff."

"Is your brother older or younger than you?"

It came out before Dan had time to think. "I don't know."

Bill looked at him blankly. "He's your brother and you don't know which one of you is the oldest?"

Resignedly, the tall man said, "We're twins."

Young Bill smiled. "Twins? What's his name?"

"Dave."

"Dave Colt, hmm?"

Dan did not answer. He wished it *was* Dave Colt. He wished things had been different. Standing up, he said, "Tell you what, kid. You've got the funerals to take care of in the morning. Why don't I head on back to the valley? I can hole up at the Lane place. You come on out after you bury Palmer and Castin. We'll visit the ranches together. In the meantime, I'll talk to the widows. See if there's anything they saw or heard that might give us a lead."

"Okay, Mr. Colt," said Bill, rising to his feet.

"Tell you what, Bill," said the tall man, clapping a rawboned hand on the acting sheriff's shoulder. "I'd appreciate it if you'd just call me Dan."

Caley's ears hitched upward as a broad smile spread across his face. "Sure, Dan," he chuckled. "And you can call me Mr. Caley!"

The two laughed together as Dan headed toward the door.

Bill's face turned suddenly sober. "History sort of repeated itself today, Dan."

"How's that?"

"In Wichita you came to the rescue of lawman Bill Caley, Senior, when he was in a tight spot. Today you did the same thing for lawman Bill Caley, Junior."

"Aw, you'da handled it," said Dan.

"Yeah, right to my grave," said young Caley. Shaking Dan's hand, he said, "Thanks, Dan."

The tall man passed through the door and said, "See you tomorrow."

Chapter Seven

~~~~~~

The sun was a blazing flame as it settled into the clouds over the jagged peaks to the west. As Dan Colt was descending into the Del Norte valley, a grocery-laden wagon rolled to a stop in front of a cabin hidden in a box canyon to the north.

Manfred Drake and Lefty Dean climbed stiffly from the hard seat and loaded their arms with boxes.

"I thought you boys had decided to stay in Alamosa all night," rasped the boss as they entered the cabin.

Drake and Dean eyed the man with the thin mustache, then looked around at the others. Maze McLeod smelled of liniment. His burnt face and head were shiny with it. Heath Finley was draped on a dirty horsehair couch. Mel Trent sat at the table with the dark-haired, handsome boss.

Dean spoke in retaliation. "We stopped at the Yellow Rose to have a drink. Saw a shootout."

"So?" snipped the boss.

"We knew you had kilt the sheriff and deputy," said Drake, "cuz this tall, blond gunslinger brung their carcasses into town on their hosses."

"Yeah?" responded the man with the long, thin sideburns.

"And boss," said Dean, "you remember Neal Nix?"

"The gunnie? We saw him take out another gunnie over in Durango."

"Yeah. He had rode into Alamosa with three mean-lookers like hisself, lookin' to kill Sheriff Palmer."

"And that skinny kid deputy was orderin' 'em outta town," said Manfred Drake. "They wuz gonna gun down that kid when this tall, blond dude come into the saloon. Told the deputy 'bout the sheriff bein' kilt."

"Then this blond gunnie and Nix got to mixin' heated words," put in Lefty Dean. "Challenge come from the blond dude."

"Boss," said Drake, "he's got them real pale blue eyes . . . thet seems like they's looking right smack dab *through* yuh, instead of *at yuh*!"

"Mmm-hmm," said the boss. Looking at Trent, then Finley, he said, "I wonder if this was the fella with the cuffs on."

"Might've been, boss," said Mel Trent. "He probably came back when we left and—"

"Why would a man who had been arrested bother to cart those bodies into town?" cut in Heath. "He'd have found the key and dumped the cuffs . . . and lit a shuck outta there."

"Maybe this blond dude came along and found their bodies, or even seen us shoot 'em," said Mel.

"Did either of you boys get a good gander at the man on the black?" asked the boss, fingering his thin mustache.

"I didn't," answered Trent. "All I ever saw when he got close was the top of his hat."

"Me too," said Finley. "I never saw enough of him to tell what he looked like or what color his hair was."

The boss looked at Drake and Dean. "So how'd the shootout go?"

Manfred Drake took off his hat and sleeved sweat from his forehead. "Boss, you ain't never seen a human with such fast hands! Nix was a pro. A good one.

He went for his gun first . . . and never budged it from the holster. Died grippin' the handle."

"Blue-eyed dude wears two .45s," added Lefty. "Slung two bullets in Nix's chest afore Nix knew whut hit 'im!"

"You didn't hear his name?" asked the outlaw leader.

"Nope," both men said simultaneously.

"If he's that good, boss," said Mel, "we don't need to worry that he was close enough to identify us when we whacked Palmer and the deputy. If he was, he'd have lit into us."

"Right," agreed the boss. "We don't need to be concerned about him." With that, the slender man stood up and placed his low-crowned Stetson on his head. "I better be heading home. You boys take a little tour tomorrow. See if any of those widows are packin' up. Check on the rest of the sodbusters, too. If we don't get some results pretty soon, there'll be another hangin' with the next storm."

Chapter Eight

Laura Lane came out of the room where her husband's body lay.

The sun was setting in a blaze of orange and purple glory as she quietly limped into the kitchen. Edith Arnold was building a fire in the cookstove. Turning to look at the young widow, she said, "You all right, honey?"

"Yes, Edith," replied Laura, sitting down at the kitchen table. Her eyes were red and swollen from crying. "I don't know what I'm going to do," she said with a note of despair. "With Vance gone, there's nothing left for me here. Besides, the rest of the farmers will be pulling out."

"I wouldn't count on that," said Edith, moving from the stove to the cupboard. "We homesteaders didn't come hundreds of miles through rain, hail, sleet, snow, cold, heat, and hostile Indians just to fold up and surrender to a gang of cutthroats. Ray is meeting with the others at Paul Healy's place right now. We're going to do something . . . fight back."

"But there's no way I can run this place alone, Edith."

"Don't give up yet, Laura. There's a way the other farmers can help." The stout woman moved to Laura and pulled her head close to her breast. "We're going to weather this storm somehow, honey. Just you wait and see."

The grieving widow clung tightly to Edith.

As darkness blanketed the land, the two women ate supper. Laura had to force herself to eat. They were just finishing when hoofs sounded outside. Laura's eyes widened in fear.

"Don't worry, honey," said Edith. "I'm sure it's Ray. But just in case . . . " The stout woman picked up Vance's rifle from which she had cleaned the mud during the afternoon.

Heavy boots sounded on the porch. There was a light tap on the door, and a familiar voice said, "Ladies, it's Dan Colt."

Forgetting the pain in her bandaged leg, Laura bounded to the door and pulled it open. "Dan!" she exclaimed. "How—?"

"It's a long story."

Suddenly realizing she was keeping him on the porch, Laura said, "Oh. I'm sorry. Come in!"

Dan removed his hat and stepped through the door. "Hello, Mrs. Arnold," he said smiling.

"Hello," replied Edith, mouth agape.

"Got any coffee?"

"Sure do, son. Sit down." Edith snatched a cup from the cupboard, plunked it on the table, and filled it with hot coffee. As Dan lowered his frame onto a chair, she said, "Got some leftovers, too. You hungry?"

"Yes, thank you."

While Edith scurried about, Laura sat down at the table across from the tall man, eyes wide. "Dan—" Her face flushed. "I . . . I mean, Mr. Colt . . ."

Leaning forward on his elbows, he said, "Ma'am, is it all right if I call you Laura?"

"Why certainly," said the dark-haired beauty. "I want you to."

"Good. Then what's good for the goose is good for the gander. Okay?"

Laura's eyes fluttered. "Okay, Dan."

Edith shoved a plate between his elbows and laid down a knife and fork.

"Dan," said Laura, "what happened? Why did the sheriff let you go?"

"He didn't have any choice," said Colt evenly. "He's dead."

"Dead?"

"Dead?" echoed Edith from the cupboard.

"Both of them," said Dan. "The deputy, too. Ambushers cut them down. We were taking the shortcut to town, climbing the steep grade, when they opened fire."

"Thank God you weren't hit!" gasped Laura Lane.

"They didn't even shoot at me," responded Colt. "I was still wearing cuffs. My horse ran back down to the valley. The killers took that saddle ornament from Palmer's body and left."

Edith piled food on Dan's plate. Between mouthfuls, the broad-shouldered man related the events of the day. He told of the shootout with Neal Nix and of his discussion with Bill Caley.

"Caley's comin' out tomorrow," he concluded. "We're going to visit the cattlemen. One by one."

Hope lit up in Laura's eyes. "You mean you're going to stay and help us?"

"Yes'm. I just decided that I couldn't ride away from here without knowing the hangmen were caught and prosecuted."

"We're glad to have you with us, Dan," said the older woman. "Ray's due here any time now. He'll be glad to know it. The homesteaders had a meeting this afternoon. Gonna fight back."

"Good," smiled Dan, pouring himself more coffee.

"I'm going to make the rounds in the morning and talk to the other widows. See if they saw or heard anything that could help us nail the hangmen."

"Dan," said Laura, "I'd like to go with you. I want to see Anne Braxton."

"I don't think you're up to it, honey," said Edith.

"I could do it if we'd hitch up the team and take the wagon. Could we do that?" she asked Dan, her eyes pleading.

Colt nodded. "Sure. If you think you can take it."

"Thank you," said Laura, a faint smile touching her lovely mouth. "I'll be just fine."

"What about the . . . the burial, Laura?" asked Dan. "Do you want me to—"

"We were waiting for Ray to get here," said the portly woman. "He was going to see if a couple of the men would come over in the morning and dig the grave."

"I'll be glad to do it," offered Dan, looking into Laura's tired eyes.

"Let's see what Ray tells us when he gets here," said Laura. Setting her soft gaze on him, she said, "Now I want to hear about your twin."

Dan was in the middle of a gulp of coffee. He lowered the cup, swallowed, and said, "It's sort of a long story, ma'am. Maybe we ought to wait until—"

The tall man's words were cut short by the nicker of the big black gelding outside. Then hoofbeats were heard. Fear registered in Laura's face.

"That'll be Ray," said Edith.

"You sure?" asked Dan, standing up. "It's more than one horse."

Laura's hand went to her mouth, trembling.

Dan moved toward the door. The hoofbeats stopped and a voice said, "Edith! It's me, hon!"

Mrs. Arnold smiled. "Yep, that's him."

Ray Arnold entered the house with two other men. He hugged his wife, inquired how Laura was feeling, and introduced Dan to Paul Healy and Lloyd Anderson. The two farmers had come to dig Vance Lane's grave by lantern light.

Laura spoke to Healy. "Paul, I understand Anne is staying at your house."

"Yes," replied Healy.

"How is she?"

"She's taking Roy's death pretty hard. But she's planning to stay here in the valley. In fact, at the homesteaders' meeting today she told them no cattlemen were going to run her off. The people cheered her and have volunteered to pitch in and build her a new house."

"Wonderful!" exclaimed Edith. Turning to Laura, she said, "See there, honey? With that kind of spirit, we'll stand our ground. And with Dan's help, we'll round up those dirty hangmen."

Laura touched the scratches on her face and managed a smile.

"If the four of us trade off, we can dig the grave in no time," suggested Dan Colt.

The men agreed. With lanterns, they made their way in the dark to the crest of a small hill west of the house. At the spot described by Laura Lane, they dug the grave. As they dug, Dan gave them the news of the Sheriff and Deputy Castin being killed. He laid before them Bill Caley's plan to question all the ranchers.

The three farmers explained to Dan the precautions that were being taken to guard against any more hangings. The homesteaders were arming themselves to the teeth. Laura Lane, Anne Braxton, and Emily

Jack, along with her two daughters, would stay with neighbors until the hangmen were caught.

"What about the families of those first two men who were hanged?" queried Dan.

"Both widows packed up their kids and went back East," said Paul Healy advisedly.

"Somebody has already cut down their fences," put in Lloyd Anderson. "Ranchers' cattle have free run on their land." He took a deep breath and let it out slowly. "Guess it don't make no difference. Nobody livin' there, anyhow."

The foursome made quick work of making the grave ready for Vance's burial the next morning. When they returned to the house, Laura had already gone to bed. "I told her that if she was ridin' with Dan to see Anne tomorrow," explained Edith, "she should get her rest tonight. Besides, she has the ordeal of burying Vance tomorrow."

Lloyd Anderson and Paul Healy excused themselves and rode away into the darkness.

Ray Arnold said he would stay at the Lanes' for the night. He and Edith would move Laura to their home tomorrow. Dan made his horse comfortable in the barn and crawled into the bedroll in the hayloft.

Morning came with low clouds veiling the eastern horizon. By the time Dan Colt and Ray Arnold had fashioned Vance Lane's coffin with rough pine boards, the sky was a heavy gray.

The two men carried Lane's stiff body outside and placed it in the pine box. They nailed down the lid and hoisted it into the back of the dead man's own wagon. Arnold waved toward the window where his wife stood watching. Presently, the two women appeared. Laura had nothing to use as a veil, so she came with pallid face exposed. In her hand was a large black Bible.

"Would you ladies like to ride in the wagon?" asked Dan.

Laura lifted her large brown eyes to Dan's face. "It's not far," she said quietly. "I would rather walk."

Edith looked toward her husband, who stood beside the wagon. "I'll just walk, too, honey."

Arnold boarded the wagon and clucked to the team. With Laura in the middle, the trio followed. A cold wind gusted across the valley as they climbed the gentle, grassy slope. Ray circled the wagon around to the far side of the grave. Laura's knees buckled when her gaze fell on the yawning dark hole, sided by the somber mound of dirt. Dan supported her by gripping both arms just above the elbows.

Reaching the edge of the grave, Dan left Laura to Edith's strong hands and assisted Ray in lowering the coffin into the hole. Silent tears streamed down the young widow's cheeks.

Dan and the Arnolds stood uneasily, not knowing what to do or say.

Laura stared down at the coffin for a long time. Then, slowly, she set her eyes on Ray Arnold. "You were his friend, Ray," she said softly, extending the Bible toward the homesteader. "Would you read for me? I have the passages marked. John, chapter eleven and First Corinthians, chapter fifteen. The portions about the resurrection."

Ray Arnold's lip quivered and his voice broke several times as he read the chosen passages. He closed with a short prayer, asking God to be near to Laura in her grief and to help the homesteaders to bring the hangmen to justice.

Dreary clouds hovered close and the cruel, unfeeling wind whipped across the bleak crest of the hill. Edith released Laura to Dan's strength and moved to her husband, who had begun to weep.

For a time Dan and Laura stood in reflective silence. Dan thought of his own grief. The picture of Mary's grave on a Wyoming hillside crowded into his mind. A touch of bitter loneliness washed over him.

Leaning hard on the muscular man, Laura struggled with her sadness. Two days before there had been no grief on the top of this hill. She was a happy young woman with a good husband. There had been sunshine, warmth, and joy. Now a dismal grave marred the hill. Vance was gone. There was just empty gloom.

Several minutes passed. Laura took a deep breath and looked up. "I'm ready to go now, Dan."

Ray stepped toward Laura and placed the Bible in her hands. Looking at Dan, he said, "I know you and Laura want to get going to see the other widows. You take the wagon and go on. I'll fill the grave."

The young widow hugged his neck and kissed his whiskered cheek. "Thank you, Ray."

Arnold blinked against the tears threatening to fill his eyes. "You're like my own daughter, honey," he said past the lump in his throat.

Turning to Edith, she said, "You both are like parents to me." The two women embraced.

Dan Colt helped the two women board the wagon, climbed into the seat beside Laura, and gave the reins a light snap. The wagon slowly descended the wind-swept hill. Along with the sounds of the wagon wheels rolling on sod and grating on rough places, Laura was aware of the hollow sound of rocks and clods hitting the pine box.

* * *

The clouds were breaking up and letting some sunshine through as Dan Colt and Laura Lane drove away from the Arnold farm. They had delivered Edith home, where she would prepare a room for Laura to occupy until the hangmen were caught.

As the wagon rattled over the cattleguard and passed through the gate, Laura said, "Dan, tell me about your twin. Why is his last name different than yours? Didn't the sheriff say it was Sundeen?"

"You're sure you want to hear it?"

"Yes. I really do. Besides, hearing about you will take my mind off my own troubles."

"The Jack place is straight ahead?" asked Dan.

"Mmm-hmm. Past that long line of cottonwoods and beyond the creek about a half mile, you'll see four large haystacks. Make a right turn at the haystacks. The next place is Jack's."

"I don't know where to start the story," said the blond man, an icy glare filling his eyes.

"How about the beginning?"

"Well, I really don't know about the beginning," Dan grinned, "except that I'm positive that I was born."

"That's a start." She smiled faintly.

"My parents were traveling in eastern Arizona," began the tall man. "I don't even know which direction they were going. I was two . . . maybe three years old. A man named Ben Mason and his wife, Katie, were traveling from California to Texas. They happened upon the dead bodies of my parents. Robbers had murdered them and stolen what few valuables were in the wagon. They also found little ole *me*. They buried my parents and took me with them to Texas."

"Your twin was not with you?"

"No. I'll get to that in the story."

"Is Texas where you grew up?"

"Yes. When I was nineteen, two gunhawks shot down Ben Mason. I vowed to hunt them down and kill them."

"Did you?"

"Yes'm. That's when I found that I had a natural ability with guns. I became a gunslinger. Was hired many times as a bodyguard. Often helped lawmen bring in outlaws. Took up bounty hunting. Had to make a living some way. It's pretty lucrative."

"Pretty dangerous, isn't it?"

"A little. So I lived by my guns until I married Mary."

Laura showed surprise. "Dan, you never mentioned you were married."

"She's dead, Laura." His blue eyes showed a hint of inward pain.

"Oh," said Laura with furrowed brow. "I'm sorry . . . I . . ."

"You had no way of knowing."

The wagon rocked as it grated over a hard, rough spot in the trail.

"Where did you meet her?" asked the young widow with interest.

"Wichita. Her father was a prominent businessman there. She was as beautiful inside as she was outside."

"She must have been," said the young widow. "I can see you loved her very, very much."

Dan swallowed the lump that bolted into his throat. "Yes'm."

"From what you said, you must have put away your guns when you got married."

"Yes. We moved to southwestern Wyoming Territory. Went to ranching."

100

Laura wanted to ask how Mary had died, but decided against it.

"Things were wonderful for five years," continued Colt. "Then it happened."

Laura's brown eyes swung to Dan's pinched features.

"Three drifters rode onto the place while I was in Fort Laramie." An old familiar flame of hatred seared through Dan's body. "They murdered Mary and left my hired man for dead. Before he died in my arms, he described them." Dan looked down at the small form next to him. "Laura . . . I had met those same three drifters on my way home. Passed the time of day with them. They had just murdered Mary and my hired man."

"So you strapped on your guns and went after them."

"That's right."

"You had seen them, so you knew who you were after?"

"Mmm-hmm."

"I assume you found them."

Dan nodded. "Caught two of them in Holbrook, Arizona. Made them draw against me."

"The third one?"

"Didn't find him till several months later."

The wagon rounded the four large haystacks. Laura pointed to a white barn half-hidden by a stand of elms and cottonwoods, about a mile away. "That's the Jack place." She looked into Dan's eyes. "Why did it take so long to find the third one?"

"This is where Dave comes in."

Laura nodded expectantly.

"As soon as the first two lay dead in the street, I found the town marshal holding a shotgun on me. His name was Logan Tanner. I told him the gunfight was fair and pointed out the crowd of witnesses standing there in the street. He called me Dave Sundeen and said he was arresting me for shooting *him* while resisting arrest some months before."

Laura listened intently as the blond man told her of his trial and how several witnesses pointed him out as the man who shot Marshal Logan Tanner.

"And Laura," Dan said, "before the trial Tanner showed me a wanted poster with an artist's sketch of Sundeen. It was *my* face. I didn't have a chance."

He proceeded to tell Laura Lane of the five-year sentence handed down and the horror of Yuma prison. He explained that not long after arriving at the prison, he met a convict who had been with the gang the day his parents were robbed and killed. The convict told him that they had taken a little blond-headed boy about three years old. One of the outlaws and his wife adopted him.

"Apparently the outlaws had not seen you," said Laura.

"I vaguely remember being frightened and watching my parents die. That's all I remember. I must have watched the whole thing from some obscure place. The convict said he told them his name was Davey. No last name. He eventually ended up with a family named Sundeen."

"And all those years you had no recollection of him?"

"I vaguely remembered a little blond-headed playmate. But that's all."

"How did the Masons know your last name was Colt?"

"Some things they found in the wagon."

Laura thought a moment. "Then Dave doesn't know you exist?"

"Not unless he has a much better memory than I do. I doubt it. We may not have even been three years old yet."

"Dan, how did you ever get out of Yuma? You must have broken out. You said you caught the third killer some months later."

"Water went bad. I was in solitary confinement. They allowed no water to men in solitary for the first few days. Cholera hit everybody but me. Even the superintendent died. A friendly guard who believed my story let me out. He was very sick himself."

"So you've been trailing your twin ever since?"

Dan nodded. "Except for the time I took out to find Carl Fox. The third killer. Once he was dead, I got hot on Dave's trail."

"Have you ever gotten real close?"

"Mmm-hmm. I even saw him down in New Mexico. I was within a few feet of him. But he didn't see me. Got away before I could do anything."

Laura looked at him quizzically. "When you finally catch up to him . . ."

"Yes?"

"If it comes to a shootout . . . well, he *is* your brother. Will you be able to—"

"Draw against him?"

"Yes."

Dan shook his blond head. His pale blue eyes grew hazy. "I don't know, Laura. I just don't know."

Chapter Nine

~~~~~~

Emily Jack and her two daughters were packing bedding and supplies in their wagon when Dan Colt and Laura Lane pulled into the yard. Two fresh mounds lay quietly in the shade near a flower garden. Emily's face was a gray mask of granite. She tried to smile as her eyes met Laura's.

The two women embraced and spoke softly to each other for several moments. Then Laura embraced the girls. Returning to the tall, blond man, she said, "Emily, Rhonda, Janie . . . this is Dan Colt."

Emily Jack's face brightened. "Oh! You're the man who found Laura and brought her home."

"Yes'm," smiled Dan.

"Dan is going to help us track down the men who . . . who killed John and Jonah."

Emily eyed the low-slung irons thonged to Dan Colt's hips. Squinting against the sun, which was now shining brightly, she said, "You a gunfighter, Mr. Colt?"

Dan did not know whether he was in for a scorning or a praising. Bracing himself inwardly, he set his jaw and said, "Yes, ma'am."

"I envy you!" blurted Emily. "If I was a man, I'd oil up my guns and hunt the slimy snakes down. I'd shoot 'em so they'd die slow and painful."

"Yes, ma'am," agreed Dan.

"Emily," said Laura. "Dan wants to ask you some questions. Wants to see if you saw or heard anything that could give him a lead on the hangmen."

"I already talked to Sheriff Palmer," said Emily Jack, "but I'll be glad to answer any question Mister Colt has to ask."

"Sheriff Palmer is dead, Mrs. Jack," said Dan solemnly.

The woman's face stiffened. "What? Dead?"

"Yes, ma'am. Some of the hangmen ambushed him and Deputy Castin yesterday. Castin's dead, too."

Emily swore under her breath.

"Dan and Deputy Bill Caley are going to work together on this, Emily," said Laura. "That's why he wants to ask you some questions."

The middle-aged woman squinted at Dan again. "We were just leavin' for Joe Latham's place. Gonna stay there till them filthy killers are put out of business. But I sure got time to talk if it'll help." Tossing her graying head toward the house, she said, "Come on in and sit."

Dan and Laura followed Emily and the girls into the house.

"Take a chair," said Emily, gesturing toward the big table in the center of the kitchen. "I'll light up a fire and fix you some coffee."

"Don't bother, Emily," said Laura. "We won't be here that long."

"You sure?" asked Emily. "It won't take but a few m—"

"Really, Mrs. Jack," said Dan. "Neither of us care for any."

Emily shrugged and plopped in a chair. Rhonda and Janie joined the adults at the table.

Setting his frank blue eyes on the middle-aged

woman, Dan began. "I know the hangmen were masked, Mrs. Jack, but was there anything at all about any one of them that would help you identify him if you saw him again?"

"There was one I think I would know if I saw him," she answered without hesitation. "It was his size. He was a monster. Would have to stand six six at least. Probably weighs two sixty or seventy."

Dan looked at Vance Lane's widow. "Did you see him, Laura?"

The dark-haired beauty shook her head. "The only two I saw plainly at all were the ones that grabbed me."

"Hey, I heard about that!" exclaimed Emily. "Honey, did you really chop one of 'em's head off?"

Laura's face flushed. "Not quite," she responded softly. "Just swung the hatchet as hard as I could in his face."

"Buried it good, huh?"

"I guess."

"Gut-shotted the other one, huh?" Emily's eyes were wide.

"Guess you'd say that," said Laura, as if the memory of it was distasteful.

Emily wagged her well-rounded head. "I think we oughtta turn *you* loose on them buzzards, honey." Throwing her glance at the blond man, she said, "Don't you think so, Mister Colt?"

Dan smiled and eyed Laura. It was hard to believe such a small, delicate woman could stand her ground against two men and kill them both.

Laura flicked a glance at Emily, then met Dan's gaze. "I guess you just do what you have to do," she said firmly.

"Was there anything else, Mrs. Jack?" asked Dan.

"The rest of them were pretty regular. Except . . ."

"Except what?" queried Dan.

"There was one man who never came in the house. Must've been the leader. Never left his horse."

"What about him?"

"It was the horse." Emily said thoughtfully. "In a flash of lightning I got a good look. The horse was jet black."

Emily Jack was unable to add anything else. Dan and Laura boarded the wagon and headed for the Paul Healy farm.

As the wagon creaked and rattled along, Dan said, "Laura, have you noticed the color of my saddle and bridle?"

"Black," said Laura. "Just like your horse."

"Did you ever notice," asked the tall man, "that brown leather looks out of place on a black horse?"

"Not really."

"Men who care about appearance will always put black leather on a black horse."

"So there is a good chance that the leader would have a black saddle."

"Right," said Dan. That ornament Palmer found had two strips of black leather attached to it. It had to have come from a black saddle. "Unless a professional saddlemaker puts that ornament back on, a close examination would reveal that it had once broken off."

"So if you find ranchers with black horses, an examination of their saddles could lead us to the ringleader."

"It's a possibility." Dan turned and looked at Laura. "Do you know of any saddlemakers in or near the valley?"

"Sure don't."

"Well," sighed Dan. "At least we have a little somethin' to go on."

The sun was midway in the morning sky when they reached Paul Healy's place. The house was built of logs and nestled among cottonwood and willow trees. The barn and outbuildings were to the rear of the house. Across the yard from the house about thirty yards was a wagon shed that rested in the shade of a single cottonwood.

Dan swung the wagon to the shed and pulled it to a halt. He dropped to the ground and circled the wagon. With strong hands he lowered Laura earthward. "You seem to be walking better on the leg," he said.

Laura nodded. "Edith changed the dressing on it last night. Seems to be healing all right."

As the pair crossed the yard, Myrtle Healy appeared on the porch. "Hello, Laura," she said warmly. "I bet this is Mr. Dan Colt."

"Yes, ma'am," smiled Dan.

"I'm Myrtle Healy," she said, offering her hand.

Dan gripped Myrtle's hand. Then the woman of forty-five wrapped her arms around the young widow.

"Anne is going to be mighty glad to see you, Laura," said Myrtle. Turning to Dan, she said, "Come on in the house, Mr. Colt."

As they filed through the doorway, Anne Braxton stood up from where she sat in an overstuffed chair. The room had the odor of medicine. There was a white handkerchief in Anne's hand. The two widows rushed into each other's arms and began to weep.

"Oh, Laura," sobbed Anne, "what is happening to us?"

"At least we're together," sniffed Laura. Drying her tears, she said, "Dan, this is Anne Braxton." Looking back into the tearful eyes of her friend, she added, "Anne, I want you to meet Dan Colt."

Anne smiled. "Hello."

"Mrs. Braxton," said Dan, nodding, touching his hat and smiling.

"Dan found me out in the wilderness and took me home," said Laura. "I rode Dolly away from the hangmen in the dark. Dolly stumbled in the darkness and I fell off. When I hit the ground, I passed out."

"It had to have been an awful experience for you," said Anne.

"When I woke up," continued Laura, "it was still dark and raining. I saw a house and tried to get to it, but a big dog attacked me. I stumbled on in the darkness and passed out again. Next thing I knew it was morning and Mr. Colt was carrying me in his arms."

"Dan is working with Deputy Bill Caley," continued Laura. "They're going to find the hangmen, Anne."

Laura explained to Anne about Sheriff Palmer and Deputy Castin being ambushed.

"I'd like to ask you some questions, Mrs. Braxton," said Dan. "We've talked to Mrs. Jack. I want to see if you can add to what she told us."

"Please sit down," said Myrtle Healy. "I'll put on some coffee." While Myrtle busied herself, Dan and the two widows sat down at the kitchen table.

"Mrs. Braxton," said the handsome man, "I know the men who killed your husband were masked, but did you see or hear anything that would help us identify them? They no doubt are hired hands on one of the ranches."

A wry grin curled Anne Braxton's mouth. "I saw the face of one of them."

"You did?" asked Dan, eyes widening. "How?"

"Roy put me in the bedroom closet when the hangmen broke through the front door. They fired a lantern and came down the hallway toward the bedroom. Apparently Roy punched the first one that came

110

through the door. I heard the man hit the floor. There was a scuffle, then I heard the glass of the lantern shatter. Roy was fighting them toward the kitchen."

Anne stopped and blew her nose softly. "I smelled the smoke and saw the light of the flames under the closet door. I knew I had to get out. I headed for the window. The man on the floor had pulled off his hood. I took one look at his face and dived out the window."

"Did he know you saw his face?" queried Dan.

"Yes. He looked straight at me."

"Would you recognize him if you saw him again?"

"Definitely. The fire lit his face."

Dan shook his head.

"What is it, Dan?" asked Laura.

"It's a wonder they haven't come after Anne," he said, exhaling the words.

Laura's face blanched as she looked at Anne.

"We thought of that," put in Myrtle from her place by the stove. "They may not know where she is."

"They'll find out," said Dan evenly. "We've got to make sure she is well protected."

Still thinking about the man whose face she saw, Anne said, "I think anyone can identify him now."

"What do you mean?" asked Laura.

"There have got to be burns on his head and face," said Anne advisedly. "When I got outside, the others had Roy on the ground, tying his hands. I ran into the kitchen, trying to find Roy's rifle. This man had come out of the bedroom window and followed me." She paused to collect her thoughts. "He came at me," said Anne, swallowing hard. "The rifle was nowhere in sight. The kitchen tablecloth was on fire. I snatched it up and threw it at him, and it settled over his head. He was yelling and clawing at it when I ran out of the house. I know he's got to have some burns."

"Good," smiled Dan. "If we spot him, we'll nail his hide to the wall."

Coffee was poured around by Myrtle Healy.

"Anything else you saw or heard that would help us, Mrs. Braxton?" asked the tall man.

"Not that I can think of."

Dan blew on his steaming cup of coffee. "Now," he said, looking at Anne. "We've got to figure how best to protect you. If you can identify *one*, they are *all* vulnerable. And they know it."

Maze McLeod sat on the porch of the cabin, which was well-hidden in the recesses of the mountains, and watched two chipmunks chase each other through the dappled shade and scamper up a tall pine. The pain in his face and scalp was subsiding and he was feeling better. Only the hooded mask had prevented more severe burns.

He was confined to the cabin for two reasons. One was the weakness he felt from being burned. The other was that by now the Braxton woman had no doubt spread word of her throwing the flaming table-cloth over his head. People would be on the lookout for a man with facial burns.

However, there was a more urgent danger. Anne Braxton had seen his face. By describing him to residents of the valley and surrounding towns, she could be a powerful threat. Like Finley, Trent, Drake, and Dean, Maze McLeod was not employed by one of the ranches. He had come to work for the clandestine young man who promised him great wealth.

McLeod had often been seen by the populace. The Braxton woman's story would bring a full-scale investigation. It would only be a matter of time until the hidden cabin would be discovered and the hangmen caught.

Maze McLeod's stomach was churning. He had not found the courage to tell the boss that Anne Braxton had seen his face. The young man had a quick and vile temper. If he learned that Maze had been so stupid as to pull off the hood in the burning bedroom, Maze's chance toward riches would be gone.

The main idea of the masks was to throw suspicion toward the ranchers for the hangings. If a battle resulted between the cattlemen and the farmers . . . so what? It would only help the rapacious young man in his drive to take full control of the Del Norte valley.

Maze McLeod's boss was cleverly planning and manipulating things to satisfy his own greed. The men who helped him would one day share the wealth when the entire valley was his. They would have unlimited range and could raise great herds of cattle. The railroad would soon be linking up from Durango to Trinidad. It was already operating from Trinidad to Denver. They could load beef on the hoof in Alamosa and ship it up to Denver without running off any fat. The west was growing. There would be no limit to the market for his beef.

McLeod fished in his shirt pocket for the makings and rolled a cigarette with trembling fingers. Blowing the smoke out through his nose, he dabbed around the burns on his forehead with a soiled handkerchief. He wished he could stop sweating. This quandary was going to make him sick to his stomach.

Which should he do? Reveal to his hot-headed boss that Anne Braxton had seen his face? Or take a chance that nothing would come of it?

One thing for sure. The boss would be furious at his removing the mask in front of the woman. He wouldn't understand how Ray Braxton's punch had numbed his brain. He would be fired. None of this valley's wealth would ever be his.

Maze stood up and swore vehemently. He was in a trap. He was going to lose either way, unless . . . He popped a fist into a meaty palm. Maybe the Braxton woman hadn't talked yet. Maybe she was still sick from her ordeal. A lot of things could have prevented her from blabbing off her mouth yet.

If Anne Braxton was dead, she couldn't tell anybody anything.

Chapter Ten

~~~~~~

Fargo Wayne had come up the hard way.

He had been raised on a small Missouri farm near St. Louis. It was a poor farm . . . a rundown place with an old sod shack for a house and dilapidated outbuildings. There was never enough food on the table. In the winter there was not enough clothing to warm their bodies. The shack was drafty and cold.

Bertha Wayne had died of pneumonia when her two sons were very young. Fargo was six, Lincoln four.

Their father scratched out a meager living from what crops he could produce and odd jobs he could pick up in the community. Most of the money he had earned was left on the bar at a local saloon. Sometimes the boys would not see him for days. When he did come home, he was usually drunk. And when George Wayne was drunk, he was mean.

Lincoln had died at twelve years of age as a result of his father's drinking. George Wayne staggered into the sod shanty one day after being gone for nearly a week. It was a freezing winter day. Link had been slow in removing himself from the elder Wayne's favorite chair when his father demanded it. The enraged man picked up the boy and bounced him off the sod wall.

When Link recovered his senses he stumbled out the door, wearing no coat. Fargo started to go after him. Their infuriated father forbad him to go outside, saying Link would come back on his own. Fargo headed for the door, arguing that it was below zero outside and his younger brother would catch pneumonia. George Wayne struck his eldest son, knocking him unconscious.

When Fargo came to, his father was gone. Link had not returned. Fargo bundled himself warmly, packed Link's coat, cap, and gloves under his arm, and set out to find him. It was dark and Link was nowhere to be found.

Fargo returned to the sod shanty. Neither his father nor Link had returned. Afraid for his younger brother's safety, he walked into town and found his father at the saloon. George Wayne refused to join in the search for Link. In desperation, Fargo sought help from the sheriff. The next morning, Lincoln Wayne's frozen body was found in an old abandoned shed three miles from home.

Fourteen-year-old Fargo saw to it that his brother was given a decent burial. His father was too drunk to attend. Fargo left the cemetery and trudged through the bitter cold to the railroad yard. There he caught a freight train headed west. The rails ended at the Kansas border. There he joined a wagon train and made his way to Colorado.

In Denver the transient boy took a job with a local hostler. It was there he learned to love horses.

At sixteen, Fargo Wayne was offered a job by a rancher. Working with horses and cattle, he soon found that ranching was in his blood. When he was twenty-four, young Wayne decided to take advantage of squatter's rights. He journeyed to southern Colorado in search of a place to set up his own ranch.

The young man had saved enough money to buy five cows and a bull. He built a house with his own hands in the broad Del Norte valley and went into the cattle business, naming his ranch the Box W.

At twenty-six, Fargo met beautiful Francesca Martine in Alamosa. His own striking good looks captivated the lovely Spanish maiden and soon they were married.

Fargo went to work and built a larger, more luxurious house for his new bride. His cattle business was doing well. He ran eight hundred head on the average and had six hired hands. He paid them well. Even then he found it difficult to keep them, because of one hard and fast rule. No man could work for Fargo Wayne who drank liquor. The memory of his drunken father had kindled a hatred inside him for liquor and saloons. His mother and brother had both died deaths indirectly caused by drink.

After three years of marriage, Francesca presented him with a baby boy. They named him Scott. Two years later a second son was born. Smith Wayne was a special joy to Fargo. From the day he was born, everyone agreed that the child had a remarkable resemblance to his father. This became more apparent as the child grew.

In their nineteenth year of marriage, Fargo had driven Francesca into Alamosa to buy material for a new dress. Despite their wealth, Francesca enjoyed making her own clothes. It gave her something to do. The two boys were now in their teens. Most of the time they were with their father or out on the range.

As the wealthy rancher and his wife left the dry goods store, they boarded the buggy and headed out of town. Just as they drove past a saloon, a drunken cowboy barged through the batwings, staggering and firing his revolver. One of the bullets hit Francesca in the head.

Fargo Wayne went into a rage and nearly beat the cowboy to death with his fists. He went into a deep depression over Francesca's death. For over a year he spent the greater part of each day at her grave, which was located among a thick stand of willows near the big house.

When Fargo began to come out of the depression, his hatred for strong drink was more vivid than ever. He preached temperance to his sons, warning them of the evils of alcohol. He held a stringent line on the ranch hands. If a Box W man was ever seen in a saloon in town, he was fired without a second chance.

The men liked the high wages they made working for Fargo Wayne. Seldom was one ever seen in a saloon. However, from the time he was eighteen, Smith arranged a secret contact in Alamosa and smuggled whiskey into the bunkhouse. He bought it for a dollar a bottle and sold it to his father's men for three dollars. Smith would keep a bottle stashed for his own use. Sometimes while rounding up strays, he would stay gone for two or three days. He would drink himself drunk and stay gone till he sobered up. Fargo was none the wiser.

Now, at age fifty-five, Fargo Wayne boasted a herd of some six thousand head. But he had troubles.

Homesteaders were muscling in on the open range. They were putting up barbed-wire fences. Not only was it cutting down the size of range for his cattle, but the beasts were forever getting tangled in the fences and damaging their hides.

Not only this problem weighed on Wayne's mind, but it was becoming apparent that someone was stealing Box W cattle. Box W men were riding casually around the valley, trying to see if any of the homesteaders had extra cattle in their pens . . . or were doing any excessive butchering.

Fargo Wayne knew that every ranch the size of the Box W lost a few cattle to rustlers. It was inevitable. When the losses consisted of a single animal now and then, he passed it off as part of the business. But it was almost a certainty that of late the cattle were being driven off in bunches. Rustling had broken the back of larger ranches than the Box W. It could happen here.

Fargo Wayne stood on the wide porch of his large Spanish-style house. His coal-black eyes scanned the slopes and meadows of the valley. The years had turned his thick head of hair from black to silver-gray. Though time had etched some furrows in his finely chiseled face, he was still lean, lantern-jawed, and handsome. His six-foot frame was as muscular now as ever, his back as straight, his shoulders as broad.

It pleased Wayne that he and his son Smith were exactly the same size. The boy was twenty-four now and looked precisely as Fargo did thirty years before. The only real difference was Smith's mustache. Fargo had always worn his full and partially drooped at the ends. Though it was silver now, he had never changed its style. Smith wore that strange pencil-line mustache and had thinned the lines of his sideburns to match it.

The silver-haired rancher was also disturbed with a third problem. Someone in the valley had taken it upon themselves to murder some of the homesteaders. Hooded horsemen had ridden through a stormy night a month ago and dragged Russ Morton and Ed Cleaver out of their homes. When they rode away, both men swung dead by their necks.

And now it had happened again. Night before last, masked killers had hanged Vance Lane, Roy Braxton . . . and John Jack and his boy.

Fargo Wayne ran nervous fingers through his ample gray hair. Who would do such a thing? All evidence pointed to the cattlemen. The warning notes posted on the victims' doors prior to the killings said as much.

But who?

He had known Jake Long for twenty years. Jake was a stern man and was known to be tough. A man had to be tough to make it in this raw country. But Jake was no murderer.

The Circle L and the Box W were the two biggest spreads in the valley. They had the most to lose with the coming of the homesteaders. Town and country people alike were going to point the finger of accusation in their direction.

Sheriff Palmer had convinced the people that it was outsiders when Morton and Cleaver were hanged. Things had quieted down and almost returned to normal. Wayne could walk the streets of Alamosa again without suspicious eyes burning him. Now he would be under suspicion again.

Fargo tried to think of who among the ranchers would take such drastic measures as to ride onto a man's property, drag him out of his house in front of wife and children, and hang him from his own tree. He knew every one of the ranchers well. There was no one who would do such a thing.

Wayne raked the valley again with his eyes. He wished Scott and Smith would get back. He wanted to know about the cattle count.

The sun crawled past its high point in the sky and bent downward.

At first they were two tiny specks on the horizon. Fargo Wayne almost passed them off as a mirage. He squinted, palm-shading his eyes from the glare of the flaming ball in the sky. No. They were real. Couldn't be his sons. They would be coming off the west range. These riders were coming from the south.

Could be Palmer and one of his deputies, Wayne told himself. He was expecting this. The sheriff would have to come out and question him again. He had probably just been at Jim Easterly's place, coming from the south. All the ranchers would be suspects until this thing was cleared up.

The silver-haired rancher squinted again. Maybe it *was* Scott and Smith. They may have swung south for some reason. One of them was definitely on a black horse. Scott was liable to pick any number of horses from the corral. He really laid no claim to any particular one.

But Smith. Fargo had bought the black gelding for him special. It was when the boy turned twenty-one. He was so strikingly his old dad all over again . . . Fargo just couldn't help himself. Well, it isn't every son that's his sire's spit and image. That's why Smith got the black saddle with the fancy silver trimmings and the bridle to match.

Wayne had scolded himself inwardly for being so generous with his second son. He really had not done as much for Scott. He did buy Scott a pair of boots for his twenty-first birthday. Then, of course, Smith had pouted around for a week afterward until his dad broke down and bought him some, too. They cost more than Scott's, but it didn't really hurt anything. Smith's tastes were just richer than his older brother's.

That was why he had upped Smith's pay until he was drawing more than Scott. True, Scott really carried the load around the ranch. But he just didn't seem to need as much money as Smith did. Fargo supposed Scott would be upset if he knew what Smith was drawing. Especially if he knew about all those loans his silver-haired daddy had made to Smith that had never been paid back.

On the other hand, though, Smith had been spending a lot of time lately riding the range alone. Maybe the man who checks waterholes and reads sign for wolves and other predators should be given extra consideration. It was lonely work . . . and Smith had freely volunteered for it.

Smith deserved a little extra now anyway. Fargo had let Francesca talk him into setting up his will Spanish-style. The Spaniards gave preference to the firstborn son. However many children there were, the firstborn son would aways receive a higher percentage of the inheritance.

Even when Francesca died and Fargo had had the will rewritten, he kept it Spanish-style in honor of her original desire. Scott would have a sixty-percent interest in the ranch and Smith forty. The money in the bank would be divided in the same way.

Wayne thought of the day when Smith came to him in private and complained about the will. He felt that it should be reversed. After all, it wasn't Scott who was the image of his father. Fargo didn't like the look in Smith's dark eyes when his request was refused. But the look disappeared when old dad opened the safe in his den and plunked a heavy roll of bills in the boy's hand.

The lantern-jawed cattleman didn't need to squint now. The riders were definitely not his sons. The man on the black was, in fact, just the opposite of Smith. Where Smith was dark with coal-black hair and eyes to match, this man was tanned, but light skinned. The hair showing under his hat and that on his face was medium blond. As the two riders pulled to a halt, Fargo could see that the blond man had sky-blue eyes. He recognized the other rider as Deputy Bill Caley.

"Afternoon, gentlemen," said Wayne, his back held straight.

"Afternoon, Mr. Wayne," replied Caley.

"Slip out of those tailbreakers and come on up on the porch," the rancher said in a friendly tone.

The riders swung to the ground and mounted the red-brick steps.

"Mr. Wayne," said the younger man, "I want you to meet Dan Colt."

The blond man gripped the rancher's hand.

Fargo Wayne released Dan's hand, squinted, and cocked his head. "I recollect there used to be a gun-hawk with that handle." His dark eyes lowered to the twin Colts, then leveled with the sky-blue eyes. "You hankerin' for a pack of challenges wearin' that name, or did you come back from the dead?"

"This is the *real* Dan Colt, Mr. Wayne," put in Bill Caley. "He saved my father's life once. Dad talked a lot about it. When I met this man in town yesterday, he told me things that no imposter could know. Besides that, he saved my life yesterday."

Wayne's gray eyebrows arched. "Oh?"

"You ever heard of Neal Nix?" asked Caley.

"The gunfighter?"

"Uh-huh. He and some friends of his were in town. They had come to kill Sheriff Palmer. The sheriff was out talkin' to the widows of those farmers."

The rancher's eyes flinched.

"Nix was gonna kill me, Mr. Wayne. Dan, here, challenged him."

Fargo's gaze flashed to Dan. "Not hard to tell who won."

Bill's eyes widened. "Mr. Wayne. Nix never even got

his gun out of the holster! He moved first and Dan shot him in the twinkle of an eye!"

"I heard," said the rancher, "that five, six years ago Dan Colt had been dry-gulched and planted six feet in Kansas prairie."

"Truth is," said Colt, "I dropped out of circulation a little over six years ago. Went to ranchin' up in Wyoming. Some lyin' little coward caught on that I had disappeared from the gunsmoke circles and decided to make a name for himself. Spread the word that he had shot me in the back and buried me in an unmarked grave."

Dan ran a finger over his mustache. "If I ever find the little split-tongue, I'm gonna make him eat his words."

Being a man who did not waste words, Fargo Wayne said, "You here about the hangings, Bill?"

Caley nodded soberly. "Yessir."

"I figured Bradley would be here to see me again," said Wayne.

Caley's eyes widened. "Then you haven't heard?"

"Heard what?"

"The hangmen ambushed the sheriff and Ron Castin and killed them yesterday."

The rancher's jaw sagged. Dan studied his eyes.

Fargo gasped. "How do you know it was the hangmen?"

"Can't divulge that information right now," said the acting sheriff. "But we know it was part of the same bunch who hanged Lane, Braxton, and the Jacks."

"Mr. Wayne," said Dan Colt, "you're an intelligent man. You know that every cattleman in this valley is under suspicion."

Wayne nodded gravely.

"I know there's a code of honor among cattlemen," continued Colt. "But we are dealing with cold-blooded murder. Can you think of any rancher or ranchers who would foster or sanction a thing like what happened night before last?"

The silver-haired man shook his head. "I've racked my brain on the matter, Colt, but I can't think of one cattleman in this valley who would do such a thing." Running his fingers through his hair, he said, "I'll admit we are not happy with our range being chopped up with homesteads and fenced off with barbed wire, but if the Congress passes laws that say they can do it, we'll have to learn to live with it. I know all seventeen of the other ranchers in this valley. I'd vouch for every one of them and trust them with my own life."

Dan turned and looked toward the corrals and barns, then swung his gaze in the direction of the bunkhouse. A few hands were working near the barns. "How many men do you employ, Mr. Wayne?"

"I'm never sure exactly," responded Fargo Wayne. "They come and they go. My son Scott would know. He handles the hiring and firing. I'd say . . . oh . . . about a hundred men, give or take ten either way."

"A hundred," nodded Dan.

"That's cowpunchers," added Wayne. "Then there's the cook and my two sons, Scott and Smith."

"When would a fella find all of them here?" asked Dan.

"From midnight to sunup," said Fargo. "Why?"

"We've got a little evidence that needs something to correspond with it," said Dan calmly. "Just need to look around when all the men are in."

"Feel free, Colt," said Wayne. "We've got nothin' to hide."

"Thanks, Mr. Wayne," said Bill Caley. "One of us will be back at sunup."

Fargo Wayne watched Dan Colt and Bill Caley become specks again. A few minutes after they disappeared, he saw Scott Wayne coming from the western edge of the valley.

As the eldest son dismounted, he said, "Dad, there's no question about it. We've lost at least four hundred head in the past month."

Fargo Wayne shook his head. Lifting his eyes to the west, he said, "Where's Smith?"

Scott's face hardened. He struggled to keep his voice soft. "He left me over by Shadow Rock and rode north. Said a waterhole needed checkin'."

Chapter Eleven

Smith Wayne reached the hideout just before sundown. His five men lounged on the porch smoking, as he threaded through the trees and dismounted. His face was a dismal mask.

"What's the matter, boss?" queried Heath Finley. "You look bad."

"We got problems, boys," Smith said dejectedly. "This time the old man sent my brother with me to tally the cattle. I've been doin' it myself. Reportin' only a few missin' now and then. Scott knows now that a few hundred are missin'. We'll have to curtail stealin' Box W cattle for a while."

"How you gonna pay us?" asked Maze McLeod.

"You just don't worry about that, Maze," snapped the boss, eyes flashing. "I'll find another way."

"But those dealers we been sellin' your pa's cattle to are wantin' more," put in Mel Trent. "If we don't sell to them, they might decide to go elsewhere. Then what?"

Smith Wayne's brow furrowed. He ran fingertips along his thin, bristly mustache. "It's just going to take a little more time," he said with a ragged edge to his voice. "I expect to see all those homesteaders packin' up and high-tailin' it anytime now." His dark eyes scanned the faces of Finley, Trent, Drake, and Dean. "You boys see any indications today?"

The four faces were set in grim lines.

Heath Finley spoke. "Yeah, me and Mel seen some indications, boss. Bad ones."

Smith's eyes flashed. "What do you mean?"

"The sodbusters are haulin' lumber to the Braxton place. That can only mean one thing. The widow Braxton ain't plannin' on high-tailin' it. Them fools are gonna build her a new house."

Young Wayne swore.

When Maze McLeod heard Finley speak of Anne Braxton, his blood ran cold. That woman had to die *tonight*. Fixing his hard gaze on Finley's face, he said, "By the way, where's the Braxton widow stayin'?"

"What's it to you?" snapped Smith.

"No reason, boss," said Maze. "Just wonderin' where she was stayin'."

"I can tell if you want to know," piped up Lefty Dean. "Me and Manny seen her today. She's at the Healy place."

"Yeah, boss," said Manfred Drake, "and that ain't all." Smith Wayne swung his flinty gaze toward Drake. "You know that blond-headed gunslick we told you about?"

"Yeah."

"He was there to see widder Braxton today. Him and the Lane woman."

Smith's face darkened. "You don't suppose he's gonna join forces with the sodbusters?" he said through his teeth.

"Could be," replied Drake. "Him and that Lane widder seem friendly."

Smith Wayne swore vehemently. "We've got to act fast, boys," he said, snapping his fingers. "There's gonna be another hangin' tonight."

"But, boss," said Finley, "it ain't stormin'. What about our tracks? A blind Indian could track a rooster through this valley. We better wait till it storms again, so the rain can cover our tracks."

"We don't have time to wait!" rasped the boss. "We've got to get these homesteaders out of this valley. I'll figure out somethin' between now and midnight. You boys just meet me at Shadow Rock at twelve sharp."

"Who you gonna hang, boss?" inquired big Maze.

Smith thought for a long moment. "Let's hang the closest sodbuster to the Box W," he said with a cold grin. "I've got a plan formin' in my head."

"That'd be Tod Moore," put in Heath Finley.

"Right," said Smith.

"The sodbusters will probably be armed to the hilt," said Lefty Dean.

"We'll take them by surprise," said Smith. "Just don't hurt the man's wife any more than you have to. They also got a couple kids. Don't bloody them up if you can keep from it."

Smith strode to his horse and mounted. Looking back, he said, "Maze, you feel like ridin' with us tonight?"

McLeod's head bobbed. "Uh . . . no, boss. I'm still purty weak. I'd better not try it yet."

Smith nodded, lips drawn tight. "You boys bring the rope."

Smith went over the plan in his mind.

As the hooded hangmen, he and his henchmen would ride onto the Tod Moore place a little after midnight. They would lure the farmer to his front door, then a couple of men would break in the back way and put guns on the wife and children. Whatever weapons Moore might try to employ would then be rendered useless.

Young Wayne's warning to his men about going easy on the farmer's wife and children came from a

129

deep regard inside him for women. Part of this was because his mother had been a real lady. His respect for her had spilled over to women in general. Smith had no particular liking for children. On the whole, they annoyed him. But he wouldn't deliberately bring harm to them.

But his most basic nature was one of extreme and powerful greed. He would stop at nothing to satisfy his craving to be rich. *Nothing*. Women, children, friends, or family were not safe if they posed a threat to his plans to one day control the entire Del Norte valley. He would be the richest cattleman west of Texas, no matter who had to be walked on or killed.

Tod Moore would die tonight. Adjacent to Moore's place on the west was Jake Long's spread. After hanging the farmer, Smith and his men would ride in the darkness to Long's place. They would leave tracks that would lead directly to Jake's corral.

Smith was familiar with the gates and buildings on Long's ranch. He and his hangmen would ride through the east gate of the corral, pass through it to the west gate and let all of Jake's horses out. Smith and his men would simply ride among them. Their tracks would be lost in the herd. They could drive some of the Circle L herd into the creek, then walk the creek for a while. Coming out one at a time at lengthy intervals would make tracking them almost impossible.

While the law investigated Jake, it would keep heat off the Box W.

If Moore's death did not drive out the homesteaders, Smith Wayne would take stronger measures. The main thing was to be rid of the sodbusters as soon as possible. If pressure from the law was coming on the Box W, he wanted it to come before he took over the ranch. It was better that old Fargo be under suspicion than himself. After all, since he was going to be the king in these parts, Smith Wayne should have the respect of the people.

He slowed the black's pace as the Box W came into view. Dusk was heavy now, but he would be at the house by dark.

Smith cursed aloud as he thought of the old man's refusal to reverse the will, giving him the high percentage of the estate. It would have removed the obvious motive when Scott was found dead. The law would notice with keen eyes the twenty-percent difference in the inheritance. However, if Fargo altered the will himself, it would put Scott's death in a different light. The man who was already due the larger percentage of the inheritance would be under much less suspicion.

So now Smith would have to take great care to make Scott's death look like an accident.

Darkness blanketed the land as Smith Wayne passed the house. Fargo sat on the porch and peered through the gloom. "That you, Smith?" he called.

"Yes, Dad," answered the man on the black.

"Hurry up, son, Mabel's holding supper. We've been waitin' for you."

"I'll be right in, Dad," responded Smith. "Soon's I put my horse in the barn."

"All right, son," said Fargo. "I'll tell her to dish it up."

Inside the barn, Smith left his gelding saddled. It would save time when he rode out later. If someone happened to go in and find it, he would say that he was hurrying to supper and planned to return later . . . then forgot.

Scott and Fargo were already seated at the table when Smith entered the kitchen. The housekeeper threw him a sour look and finished serving the pasty-thick mashed potatoes, which had been cooking too long.

Smith's eyes met Scott's as he dropped onto a chair. The elder brother's eyes were cold. Smith shifted his gaze to the craggy face of his father. Fargo smiled. Smith returned it weakly, then looked up at Mabel as she placed the bowl of mashed potatoes on the table.

Scott's voice cut the air. "How were things at the waterhole?"

"Huh?" said Smith, meeting his brother's gaze.

"The waterhole," said Scott evenly. "That *is* where you've been, isn't it?"

"Oh . . . uh . . . yeah. Yeah, the waterhole."

"Spring plugged up? Took you quite awhile."

Smith's eyes shifted to his father, then back to Scott. "The uh . . . rain the other night filled it with mud and stuff. I had to dig it all out. Waterhole was gettin' low."

"A six-year-old kid could do it in five minutes," retorted Scott, his mouth pulled tight.

Smith's temper flared. Jaw jutting, he said heatedly, "Get off my tail, Scott! You ain't my boss! I don't have to account to you for every breath I take. You lay off, or we're gonna mix it up! You hear?"

Fargo Wayne fixed his dark eyes on his oldest son. "Scott, you don't need to badger your brother like that. What's gettin' into you? Smith's a good boy. You think he's got a girl friend he's seein' on the sly or somethin'?"

"I don't know what he's doin'," answered Scott, softly. "Just seems to me he spends a lot of time away from home."

Smith's fist banged the table, rattling dishes. He pointed a stiff finger between Scott's eyes. "One more word, big brother, and we're goin' outside."

"Wait a minute, son," said Fargo in an amiable tone. His hand touched Smith's arm. "No need to fight."

Smith Wayne's countenance did a rash change. Instantly, the fire in his eyes disappeared. "I'm sorry, Dad," he said sweetly. "I guess I'm just a little edgy. All this hanging business going on and people lookin' at us cattlemen as if we're the cold-blooded murderers."

Mabel lowered a platter over Smith's plate and scooped off a dark piece of meat. As she moved to the others, Smith flipped the nearly charred steak with his fork. A sour look twisted his face. "Mabel, this meat is charred to ashes," he snapped. "You know I like my steaks rare."

"It *was* rare at suppertime," snapped the portly housekeeper.

"Now look!" bellowed Smith. "You—"

Fargo's hand was on his arm again. Immediately the young man brought himself into control. Looking up at Mabel, he wagged his head and smiled. "Well, one thing for sure, Mabel . . ."

"What's that?" asked the gray-haired woman of sixty.

"I know you *worship* me."

Mabel, who did not have any liking for the egotistical son of Fargo Wayne, grunted, "Worship you?"

"Sure," chuckled Smith. "You just placed a burnt offering before me!"

With that, Smith broke into a bellowing laugh and immediately was joined by his father. Mabel left the room and Scott sat sober-faced, chewing a mouthful of well-done steak.

Moments passed before father and son stopped laughing and settled down to devour their supper.

While the three men ate in silence, Scott was wishing that he *could* mix it up with his spoiled brat brother. The elder brother was two inches shorter, but outweighed Smith by twenty pounds. He had always been stuck with the hard work on the ranch. He was physically stronger than Smith. When they were boys, Smith often taunted Scott to the point of brawling, then ran to his father for shelter. But he knew it would hurt Fargo Wayne to see Smith beat up, so Scott had never manhandled him.

The silver-haired patriarch chewed his food and wished that Scott was more like Smith. Scott was too even-tempered and predictable. Smith might be a bit more fancy-free, but to Fargo Wayne, that made Smith more interesting. He wished Scott was more interesting. Sometimes he seemed to take things too seriously.

Scott would never have thought of that burnt-offering thing. *That Smith is a sharp boy*, thought Fargo.

He finished his meal and touched his mouth with a napkin. "Had a visit from Deputy Bill Caley, today," he said casually.

Scott spoke up. "I was expecting Palmer to pay us another visit. He would have to, after the hangin's the other night."

"Palmer's dead," said Fargo flatly.

Smith's face registered surprise. "The sheriff's dead?" he asked.

"Ambushed yesterday." The elder Wayne nodded. "He and Ron Castin both."

"Caley have any idea who did it?" asked Scott.

"Same gang that's doin' all the hangin's," replied Fargo.

"How does he know that?" queried Smith.

Fargo shook his head. "I don't rightly know. He and

that Colt feller said they had positive proof. One of em's gonna be out here at sunup."

"Colt?" Smith's brow furrowed. "Who's he?"

"You ever hear of a gunhawk named Dan Colt?" asked Fargo.

Smith nodded. "Uh-huh."

"That's who was with Caley today."

"What's Caley doin' ridin' with a gunslinger?" Scott questioned his father.

"All I know is Colt saved Caley's life by takin' out Neal Nix in town yesterday."

"Neal Nix?" Scott gasped. "Colt outdrew Nix?"

"Yep. Caley said Nix went for his gun first. Colt drilled him cold. Nix never even cleared leather."

Scott Wayne whistled. "This Colt must be somethin'."

"Word was goin' around seven or eight years ago that Dan Colt had mopped up two entire gangs all by himself," said Fargo. "One in Wichita. Another in Abilene. They say he can fan a gun and make it sing. Dead accurate, too."

"What's he doin' in these parts?" Smith asked, a queasy sensation rising in his stomach. He was remembering what Manfred Drake had told him earlier. The blond gunslick was friendly with the Lane woman and seemed to be siding with the farmers.

"He didn't really say, son," said Fargo. "But he's actin' like he's wearin' a badge." The elder Wayne paused, then spoke again. "I've got a feelin' with Colt in the picture, these bloody hangmen are gonna be cornered like rats in a corn bin."

"I sure hope so," put in Scott. "The guilty culprits deserve to hang."

"Dad," said Smith, "you say Colt or Caley is comin' back here at sunup?"

"That's what they said."

135

"What for?"

"They wouldn't tell me. Colt said they had some kind of evidence about the hangmen. One of them wanted to check somethin' out when all the hands were here."

Smith Wayne thought of the saddle ornament. His blood ran cold.

Chapter Twelve

~~~~~~

At eleven thirty that night, a lone rider left the Box W ranch under cover of darkness. He walked the black horse until he was out of hearing range of the ranch buildings, then roweled the animal and galloped west toward Shadow Rock.

Finley, Trent, Drake, and Dean were waiting for Smith Wayne when he arrived at the large rock formation. The faint light of the quarter moon did not reveal the worried look on Wayne's face as he drew near and reined in where the four riders were huddled. But the sound of his voice betrayed his uneasiness.

"You bring a rope?" asked Smith, eying the dark figures.

"Got it right here, boss," answered Finley. "Whatsa matter? You gettin' cold feet? You sound upset."

"Cold feet?" Smith swore. "Hangin' Tod Moore doesn't bother me in the least. But we got trouble."

"Whaddya mean?" queried Trent.

"You ever hear of Dan Colt?"

Each of the four nodded.

"He's the blond dude that's taggin' around with Laura Lane."

"How do you know that, boss?" asked Finley.

"Bill Caley had him at the Box W today."

"Seems I heard that the famous Dan Colt was dead," put in Trent.

"Looks like he's very much alive," said Smith.

"Bet this dude's an imposter," said Finley.

"If he is," cut in Lefty Dean, "he's a mighty good one. He took out Neal Nix with no trouble."

"Yeah," agreed Drake.

"We've got to assume he *is* Colt," said Wayne. "Which means he's gotta go."

"You mean we gotta kill him, boss?" Heath Finley's voice was quivering.

"That's exactly what I mean," said Smith coldly. "He's got to die. Just like *anybody's* got to die who stands in my way. Either Colt or Caley is comin' to the Box W at sunup."

"How come?" came Trent's worried voice.

"They wouldn't tell my old man. But they wanted to do some investigatin' when all hands were on the grounds." Smith paused. "I know what they're lookin' for. They want to examine the saddles."

Finley loosed a string of cuss words.

Trying to see Smith's saddle in the dark, Mel Trent said, "Did you put the ornament back on?"

"Yeah," replied Smith. "But it's not fastened on like the others. Anybody who knows saddles will be able to tell that it had come off."

"What we gonna do, boss?" asked Trent.

"I got a feelin'," replied Smith, "that it'll be Colt who shows up with the sun. He's got to die before he reaches the Box W."

Silence prevailed. Smith Wayne's four henchmen knew that their boss would want to be at the ranch to establish his alibi. They waited to hear which ones would be appointed to ambush Dan Colt.

Peering at Drake and Dean through the darkness, Smith said, "Lefty, you and Manny have been a little less than efficient of late. Would you like a chance to bring up your grades?"

Finley and Trent felt an instant wave of relief.

After a few seconds of silence, Dean spoke, "S-sure, boss. We'll do it. Won't we, Manny?"

Drake swallowed hard. "Look, boss. How about all four of us takin' out Colt? After all, we—"

"Now if you're yella, Manny," lashed Smith, "I'll get somebody else to handle it."

"It's not that, boss," said Drake defensively, "I just—"

"Yes or no, Manny!"

"Uh . . . uh, *yes*, boss. Sure, me an' Lefty will handle it."

"What if it *ain't* Colt, boss?" queried Dean.

"Then you'll have to kill Caley," Wayne said coldly.

"Then Colt will be out to the Box W next," said Drake.

"I suppose so," said Smith. "But it'll give me a little time to figure out how to ditch my saddle." Adjusting himself in the saddle, he said, "After we hang Moore, I'll get on home. Finley and Trent will head for the cabin. Drake and Dean, you find a good spot for the ambush. Stay far enough away from the Box W so's they won't hear the gunfire. Whether it's Colt or Caley, they'll still approach the ranch from the same direction the last five miles."

While the five hangmen rode toward Tod Moore's place, Smith explained his plan for leaving tracks to the Circle L ranch. The foursome agreed that letting Long's horses out and mingling their own among them was a smart idea.

As soon as Finley, Trent, Drake, and Dean rode away from the hideout and dissolved into the night, Maze McLeod lifted his huge frame from the overstuffed chair. Strapping on his gun, he donned his hat and picked up a black hood. He blew out the lamp and stepped out into the darkness. Quickly, the big man saddled his horse and rode in the direction of Paul Healy's farm.

The towering cottonwoods around the Healy house loomed against the starlit sky. The quarter moon cast hazy shadows on the ground. The night wind whistled among the thin limbs of the willows.

McLeod spotted the wagon shed standing still in the night beneath a lone cottonwood. Leaving his horse next to the shed, Maze darted across the thirty-yard span to the house. Pausing under the trees that fringed the yard, he pulled the black hood from under his belt and slipped it over his head. The coarse cloth stung his burns.

He stepped on the porch. The boards groaned under his weight. Maze knew that if he knocked, the fearful homesteaders would not open the door. His best bet was to kick open the door and plunge inside. He would hide until Healy came to investigate. After he had overpowered the farmer, he would take care of Mrs. Healy. Then Anne Braxton would die.

Hunching his huge shoulders, McLeod threw his weight against the door. It cracked, but did not open. Backing up a couple of steps, he hit it again. Wood splintered in all directions as the door flew open.

Instantly there were voices, speaking in half-whispers at the rear of the house. McLeod spotted the dark, rectangular shape of the hall doorway. He hastened to the wall beside the hall door and flattened his back against it.

"Who's there?" came a frightened male voice.

McLeod was breathing heavily from his exertion, but remained silent, drawing his revolver.

Muffled footsteps sounded at the far end of the hallway. "Who's out there?" demanded Paul Healy gruffly. "I've got a gun! I'll shoot the first thing that moves!"

Maze could hear Myrtle Healy sobbing with fright in the bedroom. "Paul!" she cried. "Don't go out there! They'll hang you!"

Healy was stealthily creeping toward the door where Maze McLeod waited. The huge man held his place and stifled his breathing. Healy stopped short of the hall doorway, eyes peering toward the front door, which swung loose in the breeze.

As the farmer inched his way forward, Maze caught sight of the tip of a rifle barrel. Just a little bit more . . .

Suddenly, Healy felt the rifle snatched from his hands. It discharged, filling the room with orange flame. A pistol barrel thumped against the farmer's head with a fleshy, sodden sound. Myrtle screamed her husband's name as the unconscious farmer slumped to the floor.

"Mrs. Healy!" bellowed the big man.

Maze could hear only incoherent sobbing.

"Mrs. Healy!" he repeated.

"Y-yes!" sobbed Myrtle.

"We've got your husband out here! He's still alive. Do you want him to stay that way?"

Myrtle choked on her words. "Yes! Yes, I . . . do!"

"We won't hang him if you send Anne Braxton out here!"

Silence.

"Mrs. Healy!"

"Anne . . . isn't . . . isn't here," said Myrtle with quivering voice.

"Don't you lie, Mrs. Healy!" snapped McLeod. "We know she's stayin' here!"

"N-no!" came the reply. "You . . . you can search the house. She's not here!"

141

Paul Healy was showing no signs of coming around. Maze hollered into the hallway, "Mrs. Healy, you got a lantern back there?"

"Y-yes!"

"Light it!"

With trembling fingers, Myrtle Healy fumbled for a match and scraped the head on the side of the table next to the bed. It shot a spark and snapped in two. Fighting hard to control her fingers, she pinched another match. Just as she scratched the match against the table, McLeod's big voice boomed, "Mrs. Healy!"

The second match broke.

"I . . . I'm trying!" she cried.

With the third attempt, a match flared and the quivering woman lifted the glass chimney and touched the flame to the wick. The flame flickered, turned blue, and then came alive. The room was flooded with light.

As the soft glow filled the hallway, McLeod checked the unconscious farmer. Paul Healy still showed no signs of movement.

"Okay, boys!" said Maze loudly. "I'm going back. If anything happens to me, hang him!" Stepping into the dimly lit hallway, he said, "Mrs. Healy. I'm comin' back. You try anything, we'll hang your husband!"

"I . . . I won't," sobbed the terrified woman.

McLeod's huge frame filled the bedroom door. "Now, lady," he said with a foreboding voice, "you produce Mrs. Braxton, or your husband dies."

The grotesque sight of the giant masked man took Myrtle's breath. Struggling to speak, she clung to the bed and stammered, "A-A-Anne is . . . isn't here, mis . . . mister."

"Where's her bedroom?" demanded the huge man.

"J-just to your . . . your r-right there in the hall."

McLeod stepped forward and seized the lantern.

Myrtle whimpered as his heavy boots clomped into the adjoining bedroom.

As Maze pushed open the bedroom door, he held the lantern high. The room was in perfect order. The bed was made up neatly and was untouched. Angrily he crossed the hall and flung open another door. It was a sewing room, with the customary things laying about.

McLeod heard a groan as he stepped back into the hall. By the lantern's light he could see the farmer stirring on the floor. "Mrs. Healy," he called.

"Y-yes," came a timorous voice.

"Come out here."

Quickly the big man strode to where Paul Healy lay on the floor. Kneeling down, he put the muzzle of his revolver to the man's bleeding head. As Myrtle appeared shakily at the hall door, McLeod thumbed back the hammer. The mechanism made a dry, clicking sound that seemed to fill the room. The frightened woman gasped.

Healy's eyes opened. He stared first at the lantern, which set beside him on the floor. Then his glazed eyes lined on the hideous hood that covered McLeod's face. The big man clamped his free hand on Healy's neck, holding his head to the floor. The cold muzzle pressed the top of his skull.

"Now, Mrs. Healy," said McLeod with gritted teeth. "I want to know where the Braxton woman is."

Myrtle ejected a weak whimper.

"Don't tell him anything," groaned Healy.

The big man shoved the muzzle hard against the farmer's head. "Where's Anne Braxton, Mrs. Healy?" The hooded man's eyes were bulging and wild through the holes.

Paul Healy winced and breathed it out again, "Don't tell him anything."

143

Maze flipped the barrel to the side of the farmer's head and fired into the floor. Myrtle screamed and Paul jumped. Maze forced his head to the floor and placed the smoking muzzle against his forehead. The farmer's ears were ringing fiercely. The acrid gunsmoke made his eyes water. "The next one makes you a widow, Mrs. Healy," rasped the huge man. "I'm askin' you for the last time. Where's Anne Braxton?"

Myrtle Healy was in a frenzy. It came from her quivering lips almost without thought, "*She's at Tod Moore's place!*"

Maze could not believe his ears. *Tod Moore's place!* That was exactly where Smith and the boys were headed. Glaring at the terrified woman, he said, "You'd better be tellin' the truth. If I find out you're lyin', you'll both die. *You hear me?*"

Myrtle sobbed, nodding her head. "It's the truth!" Turning her face to the wall, she cried, "Anne! Anne, forgive me! Oh, God, forgive me! Forgive me!"

Big Maze bounded out the door and ran to his horse. Vaulting into the saddle, he could hear Myrtle Healy still sobbing as he kicked the horse into a full gallop. Lifting the hood from his face, he headed north, toward the hideout. There was nothing he could do now. He dared not show up at the Moore place after telling the boss he didn't feel like going tonight.

The scheme was evident. Anne Braxton knew she was in danger. She would be shifted from place to place for her own protection. There was no question in Maze McLeod's mind. Anne had described him to others. This is why they were protecting her. If Smith learned that she saw his face . . . Maze did not like to think about it. Whatever happened at the Moore place tonight, Anne Braxton was going to die by tomorrow night. Maze would see to it.

✿   ✿   ✿

All was quiet at the Moore farm. Milk cows loung-ing quietly in the barnyard paid little heed as five hangmen crept into the yard. Smith Wayne found a giant oak tree with a limb positioned just right. He halted his horse beneath the limb. "Okay," he whis-pered, "Heath, Mel . . . you two go around back. As soon as Lefty and Manny start bangin' on the front door, you get ready."

Eying those two men, he said, "Let out a wild yell when you know Moore is at the front door." Looking back at the other two he said, "That'll be your signal to bust in the back and grab whoever you find first. Doesn't matter whether it's the woman or one of the kids. Just grab one and put a gun to their head."

Addressing Dean and Drake again, the boss said, "The minute Moore shows up, you tell him we have men in the back who've got a gun to the head of one of his family. He's to give up instantly, or you'll give an order for the execution."

"What if they ain't found anybody yet?" asked Drake.

"Then *bluff* him, stupid!" lashed Wayne. "Now get goin'!"

With that, Smith sailed a rope over the limb just above his head. Finley and Trent rounded the house in the thick gloom. Dean and Drake charged onto the porch and began banging on the door and yelling at the top of their lungs.

"Tod Moore," yelled Dean.

"Come out of the house!" hollered Drake.

Suddenly a gun roared inside the house. The front door splintered right between the two hangmen. Both men dived away from the door as the gun barked again.

As Tod Moore blasted the door, the noise of his gun covered the sound of glass shattering at the rear of the house. Finley and Trent were not waiting for a vocal signal.

Inside the house, Tod Moore heard a woman's scream come from a rear bedroom. He had not heard the glass shatter. He wheeled to see two dark forms at a bedroom door, then suddenly two more.

"I got a gun at her head, Moore!" came a sharp voice.

"And I've got another one!" came a second threatening voice. "Drop your gun, farmer, or they both die!"

The clatter of metal against the hard wooden floor echoed through the house. "All right! All right!" said Tod Moore.

"Hey, boys!" shouted one of the dark figures. "Kick the door in. We got 'em!"

Within seconds the front door split and shattered. One hinge gave way and it dangled awkwardly.

"Take him!" barked the same voice.

The hooded man who had just burst through the door seized the sinewy farmer. He offered no resistance. "Please don't hurt my family," he said with plaintive voice.

"Tod!" screamed the farmer's wife.

Two children began to whimper in their beds. "Mommy!" called one. The mother tried to free herself.

"Leave the kid be," snapped the hooded man who held his gun to her head.

"Do what he says, Lila," said Anne Braxton, who was held at gunpoint by the other one. "These beasts wouldn't stop at killing a woman."

Heath Finley squinted through the gloom at the woman. "You're the Braxton woman, ain'tcha?"

Anne did not answer.

146

"Well, honey," said Finley, "in a minute you and your friend, here, will both have somethin' in common." A fiendish laugh escaped his lips through the thin slit in the hood. "You'll both have dead husbands!"

Lila Moore broke into uncontrollable sobs.

Outside, Tod Moore was on the ground, face down. Lefty Dean jerked the knot, cinching the homesteader's hands behind his back. Manfred Drake released his grip on Moore and went after his own horse.

Dean snapped the trembling man to his feet and pushed him toward the giant oak tree.

As Tod Moore neared the tree, he saw the grisly outline of Smith Wayne astride the black beast. Drake led his horse to the tree, stopping the animal beneath the heavy limb. The noose was barely visible in the dark. The lean-bodied farmer was hoisted into the saddle. His breathing was heavy.

Smith Wayne's cold voice grated on Moore's ears. "You could've packed up, sodbuster. Now look what your defiance has got you."

Tod Moore found his voice. Shakily, he said, "I won't be here to see it, but you'll get yours, mister."

Wayne spoke one word. "Lefty."

The leather strap slapped the horse's rump.

Inside the house, Tod Moore's choking and gagging sounds could be heard. Lila collapsed on the floor.

Lefty Dean's voice came from outside. "Let's go!"

Heath Finley said to Anne Braxton, "Better tell the rest of the sodbusters, lady. Get out of this valley while you still can."

As Finley released his hold, Anne Braxton's temper flared. She leaped at the man with the swiftness of a cat. Through the cloth hood she found his left ear with her teeth. She bit down savagely, shaking her

147

head. Finley hollered with pain and tried to shake her loose.

Anne's arms were around his neck with her full strength. Mel Trent was stumbling over Lila Moore's inert form in the dark, trying to help his partner.

Anne held on with the tenacity of a bulldog. She and Finley fell to the floor. The masked man howled, trying to free himself from the angry woman. Warm fluid was in Anne's mouth now. The salty taste of blood met her tongue as she felt the ear rip loose.

Suddenly, a pistol barrel found her head with a solid blow. The darkness deepened as Anne felt herself hit the floor. Then she was swallowed in an inky blackness.

Chapter Thirteen

"You gotta get me a doctor!" whined Heath Finley.

The five hangmen had ridden through the Circle L corral as planned. Smith Wayne was satisfied that their tracks had been obliterated by those of Jake Long's horses. Now they rode the waters of the creek.

"If we bring a doctor out here, our whole scheme goes to pieces," lashed Wayne, who rode just ahead of the injured man.

"My ear's about to fall off, Smith!" snapped Finley.

"Then ride on into town and get it sewed back on!"

"I told you," said Heath defensively, "I'd never make it. This ear is bleedin' somethin' fierce." Heath swore vehemently. "I shoulda killed that Braxton witch!"

"You ain't killin' no woman," rasped Wayne. "You should be man enough to handle a hundred-pound female."

Finley swore again. He had ripped a large section of cloth from his shirt and was pressing it against the bleeding ear. "I gotta git to the cabin and lay my head down, boss," he said pleadingly. "If I don't get this blood stopped, I'm gonna bleed to death."

"Mel will get you to the cabin," said Wayne testily. "But there ain't gonna be no doctor. When he finished sewin' you up, he'd send the law and Dan Colt right to our door."

"We can kill the doc once he sews my ear up," snapped the injured man.

"You don't seem to understand what I'm tellin' you, Heath," hissed Wayne angrily. "You ain't jeopardizin' my plans by bringin' *anybody* out here! Now if you can't ride into town and tell the doc your girl friend saw you with another female and chewed your ear off, then you just lay up there in the cabin till it grows back to your thick head!"

One by one, the hangmen of Del Norte pulled out of the creek. Trent and Finley headed for the cabin. Dean and Drake set out toward the spot chosen for the ambush of Dan Colt or Bill Caley. Smith Wayne aimed for the Box W.

Fargo Wayne's younger son rode with the hope that Tod Moore's execution would be enough to drive the homesteaders from his future domain. With Dan Colt out of the way, they would surely sense their inevitable defeat and get out.

Smith knew that dawn would soon appear as he stealthily led his horse into the barn. In the dark, he unsaddled the animal and slipped off the bridle.

Quietly, he crossed the yard and climbed through his bedroom window, which he had left open earlier. Easing his slender frame over the sill, he felt his way along the bed in the dark. Removing his hat, he hung it on one of the bedposts and lowered himself to a sitting position on the bed.

As Smith pulled off his boots, he felt a strange, unexplainable sensation wash over him. He unbuckled his gunbelt and hung it on a straight-backed chair next to the bed. At the same instant his fingers touched the buckle of his pants belt, his line of sight flicked across the room. There was an overstuffed chair that sat in a dark corner. The same sensation touched Smith Wayne again. Someone was seated in the chair.

Smith squinted, then jumped when Scott's voice cut the thick darkness. *"Where you been, little brother?"*

It took the younger Wayne a moment to catch his breath. Scott stood up, thumbed a match into flame, and touched it to a lantern. The room filled with light. The flickering flame threw awesome shadows on the dark face of Scott Wayne. "I asked you where you've been." The elder brother's voice sounded like hot flint on cold steel.

Smith scowled and slitted his black eyes. "Since when do I have to answer to you?" he blustered.

"You lied to me, Smith." There was frost in Scott's voice.

"What're you talkin' about?"

"I rode out to the waterhole you said you unplugged. There was no sign of mud and debris." Scott's lips pulled tight. "Where did you go this afternoon? And what's this skulkin' around at night stuff?"

"I don't have to tell you nothin'!" blurted Smith. In the same instant, he lunged at the stocky brother and aimed a punch at his face. Scott ducked and grasped Smith's arm and whirled him around, forcing the hand up between his shoulder blades. Smith struggled and Scott shoved the hand upward with a sharp motion. The younger brother let out a yell, then gritted his teeth.

"You take another swing at me and I'll break your arm!" hissed Scott.

"Oh, no, you won't," retaliated Smith. "What would Dad say if you did that?"

Scott rammed the arm higher. "Where you been, Smith?"

Smith winced, sucking air through his teeth. Suddenly his countenance changed. He began to chuckle. "Okay, big brother," he said, "you got me." He chuckled again. "I'll confess if you'll let go of my arm."

Scott eased his brother's arm downward, then let go. "All right. Let's hear it."

Rubbing his arm and shoulder, Smith said, "I've been seein' a woman."

"What woman?"

"Ah, ah, ah!" Smith said, shaking a finger in his brother's face. "I'm not tellin'."

Scott narrowed his eyes. "Is she married?"

Smith grinned impudently. "Sort of."

"Messin' around with a man's wife could get you killed," snapped Scott.

"Not now."

"What do you mean?"

"Her husband's dead now," replied Smith, emphasizing the last word.

Fire flashed in the older Wayne's eyes. "Who you been seein', Smith?"

"Laura Lane," lied Smith. "Have been for a long time. Only it's easier now, since somebody stretched ole Vance's neck."

"Laura Lane?" breathed Scott unbelievingly.

"She's some looker, eh?"

Scott Wayne did not want to believe what his brother was telling him. Had Smith really been carrying on with the homesteader's wife?

However, he would rather it be that than what he had been thinking.

Scott eyed his brother. "You could at least show some respect and let her husband get cold in his grave before you start hangin' around over there."

"Maybe I'll do that," said Smith, wagging his head.

"Now will you get outta here so I can get a little sleep?"

Without a word, Scott opened the door, stepped into the hallway and pulled it shut.

The morning sun was lifting its fiery rim over the eastern horizon when Dan Colt rode away from the Ray Arnold place. He and Ray had slept in the living room on the floor, allowing Laura to occupy one bedroom and Edith the other. Dan wanted to be on the place in case the hangmen decided to show up.

Edith had been sick all night. Laura had stayed up by her side all night. At daybreak, Laura offered to fix breakfast, but Dan and Ray insisted that she go to bed and get some sleep.

Dan held the black to a steady lope. He wanted to examine the saddles of the Box W crew before they scattered.

A golden orange stained the low-hanging clouds as Dan rode through a narrow canyon, topped on both sides with giant rocks. From the early morning shadows just ahead, a large black hawk left the ground and lifted himself skyward. Reaching the level of the rocks, he wheeled and began a wide circle.

Dan watched with admiration as the hawk floated gracefully over the rocky rim. Suddenly, he caught the glint of sunlight on a rifle barrel. A split second after he had left the saddle, two shots filled the morning air. Bullets whined past where he had been sitting and chipped rock on the canyon wall.

Dan was instantly behind a small pile of rocks, guns drawn.

Another shot roared and reverberated through the canyon. The slug hit a nearby rock, then caromed angrily away. Removing his hat, Dan raised his head.

Peering upward to the canyon's opposite rim, he could see the tops of two hats barely visible behind a large rock. He wished for his rifle. The black had trotted forward some twenty yards. There was no way to get the rifle.

Dan could hear some men talking, but could not make out the words. Apparently they were plotting the attack. No doubt they would circle around and try to pin him in a crossfire.

Who were they?

Were they some of the hangmen?

Had Fargo Wayne sent them to stop him from returning to the Box W? Dan did not think so. He doubted that Fargo Wayne was in on the hangings. He had learned to read people's characters. Wayne possessed a certain quality that rang true to Dan Colt.

Another slug chipped a rock and whined away. Whoever his bushwhackers were, they meant to kill him.

Suddenly Dan saw one hat disappear, then a slender shadow darted between two rocks at a slightly lower level. One of them was descending into the canyon along the ridge to his right. The shadow appeared for a second between two more rocks, then was gone again.

Dan could see the route that the man was taking. If he stayed on it, he would appear at another spot about twenty feet lower within a few seconds. Quickly holstering his left-hand gun, he dogged back the hammer of the other one. Steadying the barrel rifle-style with his left hand, he aimed at the obvious spot where the bushwhacker would soon appear.

The Colt .45 roared when the man's body filled the gap. He let out a cry and staggered into full sight. His rifle clattered on the rocks as he fell from view behind a large boulder.

154

The man on top cried, "Lefty . . . Lefty!"

Dan swung the muzzle in the remaining bush-whacker's direction and waited. The hat came into view, then a face. The rifle suddenly barked and the bullet showered Dan with bits of rock. Quickly he returned a shot, causing the man to duck.

Again the bushwhacker called for his friend.

The odds were more even now, but the man with the rifle still had the advantage. He had Dan pinned down. Two more shots were fired from the canyon's rim, when a pitiful cry came from where the other bushwhacker had fallen.

"Manny! Manny . . . help . . . me! Help . . . me . . . please!"

Within seconds Dan saw the second man appear at the place he had first seen the other one. The man was going down the same way his partner had.

Sure enough. He darted between the same two rocks where Dan had spied the first man.

Colt held his cocked revolver on the opening where he had shot the first one. The wounded man let out another cry just as his partner moved into Dan's sight. The Colt .45 spit fire. The bushwhacker buckled and dropped his rifle. He staggered blindly toward the ledge in front of him and peeled off head first. It was a forty-foot drop. He hit the canyon floor with a dead thud and lay motionless.

Dan stood up and walked to the inert form. The man would never ambush anyone again.

Suddenly there was movement above. The first man was on his knees at the ledge. His shirt was red with blood and he was trying to steady a revolver on Dan Colt.

Stiffening his gun arm and dogging back the hammer, Dan aimed straight at him and cried, "Drop it, mister!"

Lefty paid no heed. He fired the weapon. The bullet bit dust near Dan's feet as his own gun roared. Lefty straightened from the impact, pivoted, and fell. He landed at the tip of the ledge, his gun arm dangling over the side. Slowly his fingers relaxed and the revolver fell to the canyon floor.

With no more time to waste, Dan leaped into the saddle and headed for the Box W.

Cowhands were milling about the corral and bunkhouse as the tall man rode up to the house. Dismounting, he ascended the red-brick steps and passed under a fancy Spanish-style arch to the door. Lifting and dropping the heavy knocker twice, he scanned the area around him while he waited.

Momentarily the door rattled and swung open. A broad-shouldered young man appeared, fixing his hazel eyes on Dan's angular face.

"I'm Dan Colt," he said with a friendly tone. "Mr. Wayne is expecting me."

"Oh yes, Mr. Colt. I'm Scott Wayne," said the young man. "Please come in."

Scott led the tall man through the luxuriously furnished house to the kitchen. Dan's spurs set up a metallic echo as he moved across the shiny floor.

Fargo Wayne was at the table, halfway through his breakfast. He stood up as Dan entered the room. "Good morning, Mr. Colt," he said with a weak smile. "I expected you a little earlier."

"I had a couple of unexpected hindrances," the tall man said dryly. "Has anyone left the grounds yet?"

"No," replied Fargo. "I gave orders that everybody stay put till I say different."

"I appreciate that, sir," said Dan.

Fargo's lean law squared. "Colt, I'm just as anxious to find these bloody hangmen as you are. If any of my

156

men are a part of it, I want to know it." The silver-haired man gestured toward an empty place at the table. "Since nobody's goin' anywhere without my say-so, Colt, sit down and have some breakfast."

"I've already had breakfast," said Dan, "but I'll take some coffee."

"Fine. Sit down. I assume you met my son Scott?"

"Yes," said Dan, looking toward Scott, who had returned to his own breakfast.

Fargo poured Dan a cup of coffee and began asking about other ranches he had inspected. Had he found any clues? Were there any prime suspects? What was it he wanted to look at?

Smith Wayne opened his eyes at the sound of spurs jangling in the house. The ranch hands seldom came inside the house and Scott would not strap on his spurs till he was ready to ride. He sat up in the bed and ran his fingers through his dark hair. Muffled voices were coming from the kitchen.

Hastily, the younger Wayne pulled on his pants and opened the bedroom door. Easing his way down the hall toward the kitchen, he stopped when the words came clear. His father was talking to a man with a voice Smith had never heard.

Smith's ears tingled when the stranger said, "I want to look at every black saddle on the place."

His blood turned cold when Fargo said, "There's only three or four of them, Colt. My son Smith has one. I think Bob Elder does. Maybe one or two others."

That was all of the conversation Smith heard. He was in his bedroom putting on his clothes in a hurry.

Within three minutes, he crawled out the window and made his way casually to the barn. None of the cowhands paid him any mind when they saw him gallop away. After all, he was Fargo Wayne's favored son. Smith did not have to obey the mandates issued by the senior Wayne.

Smith swore savagely as the black gelding carried him across the grassy plain toward the canyon. He assumed that would be the spot where Dean and Drake would set up their ambush. Something had gone wrong. Dan Colt was alive and looking for black saddles.

The canyon looked deserted as Smith entered its rocky confines. He approached slowly, eying the lofty crags. Then he saw the lifeless form of Manfred Drake lying on the canyon floor. Smith swore as he dismounted. There was no need to touch Drake's body. He was dead. *Where was Lefty Dean?*

Young Wayne's dark eyes scanned the area. Then he saw the arm hanging over the ledge forty feet above.

As Smith Wayne labored his way up the steep incline toward the place where Lefty lay, he pondered his predicament. He was getting low on men. The Lane woman had killed two of them. Heath Finley might bleed to death. Maze was still weakened from his ordeal with the burning tablecloth. And now Dean and Drake had been killed by Dan Colt. At least he figured Dean was dead. It would be a miracle if he was still alive.

Breathing heavily, Smith reached the ledge. He was surprised to see Lefty's back rising and falling slowly. Kneeling down, he rolled the wounded man over. The bright sunlight stabbed Dean's eyelids, and his face flinched. The rocky ledge was covered with blood. It was evident that Dean was almost gone.

Smith placed his own head so as to cast a shadow over the dying man's face. "Lefty. Can you hear me?"

Dean's eyes fluttered and half opened. They were glazed and bloodshot.

"Lefty," repeated Smith. "Can you hear me?"

Dean's tongue touched his lips again. "Y-yeah. Who . . . who is . . . it?"

"It's Smith. What happened?"

"I . . . I dunno . . . exactly." Lefty swallowed hard. "He killed me, Smith."

"How'd he do it?"

Dean rolled his eyes. "Where's . . . where's M-Man . . . Manny?"

"At the bottom of the canyon," snapped Smith. "How'd it happen?"

Licking his lips, Lefty closed his languid eyes and grunted, "Colt must . . . must have eyes . . . eyes in the back of his . . . head, Sm-Smith. We was . . . just . . . just sightin' in on . . . him He . . . he looked right up . . . right up at us . . . and jumped out . . . out of his s-saddle."

Smith spewed a string of cusswords. "You stupid idiots! How did he shoot you from down in the canyon? You had him covered!"

Dean's voice was barely audible. "I . . . dunno. The man has . . . has special powers. Watch out, Sm-Smith. He . . . he'll get . . . you."

Smith cursed as Lefty Dean died. He should have taken care of Dan Colt himself. Things were going to get sticky. Colt was at the ranch right now. Sooner or later he or Deputy Bill Caley would inspect his black saddle. Anyone would be able to tell that one ornament had been put back on by a different tool than had been used originally.

Abruptly, a thought struck him. Why not rip the other three ornaments off and put them back in the same manner as he had the first one? If all four were fastened in the same way, who could say that they weren't that way in the first place?

159

Smith would have to find a way to get it done before Colt or Caley inspected it. There was no doubt in his mind that he could do it. Certainly Smith Wayne was not going to let a small thing like a saddle ornament keep him from becoming king of the Del Norte valley.

Chapter Fourteen

~~~~~~

Dan Colt finished examining the third black saddle in the Box W barn. "Well, that clears everybody," he said to Fargo Wayne with a smile.

"Everybody but my little brother," put in Scott, who stood by.

Fargo forced a hoarse laugh. "Well now, Scott," he said, shaking his head, "you don't suspect Smith, do you?"

"I have to inspect *every* black saddle in this valley, Mr. Wayne," spoke up Colt. "Since you don't know when or why Smith left, I assume you don't know when he'll be back."

"No," said Fargo, "but if you'll tell me when you're going to swing back this way, I'll have him here."

"I've got several ranches to check out today," said Dan. "I'll just plan to stop here on my way back to the Arnold place."

"Is that where you're staying, with Ray Arnold?" asked Fargo.

"Yessir," answered Colt. "Laura Lane is staying there also."

Scott Wayne's ears perked up.

"Laura was cut up pretty bad when she ran from the hangmen," continued Dan. "She fell off her horse in the dark. A dog attacked her, too. Tore one leg pretty bad. Mrs. Arnold has been taking care of her."

"As you know," said Fargo, "the ranchers and the homesteaders don't mingle much. But I know the Arnolds are good people. That's mighty nice of them . . . taking Mrs. Lane in."

Dan chuckled. "Yeah, it's sort of ironic."

"What's that?"

"Mrs. Arnold brought Laura to her house to take care of her, then last night Mrs. Arnold took sick. Laura ended up tending to her all night."

Scott Wayne's face blanched.

"Well, Mr. Wayne," said Dan to the silver-haired man, "I'll be on my way." Extending his hand, he said, "Much obliged for your cooperation."

Meeting his grip, Fargo said, "Glad to do so. If there's anything else I can do, let me know."

"Sure will," said Colt, swinging aboard his black gelding. "Thanks for the coffee, too."

Fargo smiled and nodded.

Dan swung his gaze to Fargo Wayne's older son. "Glad to have met you, Scott."

"Same here," said Scott Wayne, smiling.

Dan spurred the black, hollering over his shoulder, "I'll be back at sundown!"

Fargo waved his acknowledgment.

Dan reached in his shirt pocket and unfolded the crude map that Bill Caley had drawn. He wanted to check on Anne Braxton. Make sure she was all right. The map indicated that he could stop at two ranches along the way. He would make those stops, then swing by Tod Moore's. Afterward he would move on to the other big one, the Circle L.

Dan had eased the black to a steady trot and had been riding for about fifteen minutes when he heard a distant voice behind him. Twisting in the saddle, he saw a rider coming at a full gallop, waving his hat. Dan reined in and waited. Soon he recognized Scott Wayne.

As Scott pulled his horse to a halt, he said, "Thanks for stopping, Mr. Colt. I'm sorry to hold you up, but I've got to talk to you a minute."

"It's all right, Scott," said Dan with a smile. "What is it?"

"Well, it's about something you said just before you left."

"What's that?"

"Did you say Laura Lane was tending to Mrs. Arnold *all* night?"

"Mmm-hmm. Why?"

"Would there have been a time, even for a few minutes, when Laura was not with her?"

"Nope. Why?"

"Were you there all evening?"

"The entire evening . . . and all night," said Dan evenly.

"Did Laura have any visitors that you know of?" Scott's face was grave.

"Laura had no visitors. I was in the house the entire time. Ray and I slept on the living room floor. Anyone visiting Laura would have to walk over us."

"How about someone crawling through her bedroom window?"

Squinting hard at the younger man, Colt said, "Laura wasn't even *in* her bedroom till dawn. She was with Edith all night long." Firming his jaw, he said, "Now I asked you why."

Scott's face went gray. "Uh . . . one of the men was off the ranch most of last night. I caught him coming in just before dawn. He said that he and Mrs. Lane had been seeing each other for some time . . .

163

and explained his absence last night by saying he had
been with her."

"He's lyin' on two counts," clipped Dan. "Laura
Lane saw no one last night . . . and she's not that
kind of woman. She was very devoted to her husband.
Your man is a liar."

"Guess he's in trouble then," said Scott.

"If you tell me his name, he'll be in *worse* trouble,"
Dan said coldly.

"I . . . uh—I'll handle it, Mr. Colt," said Scott nervously. "See you at sundown. And thanks for the information." He suddenly turned and rode off at a furious pace.

"You're welcome," responded Colt, as he watched
Wayne gallop away.

It was nearly eight o'clock when Dan rode through
the gate on the Moore place. He felt it before he saw
the shattered front door. Something was wrong.

He jumped from the saddle and leaped onto the
porch. He could hear a woman weeping before he
reached the door. "Anne!" he called, pushing the awkwardly hanging door.

Anne Braxton met the tall man as he entered. "Oh,
Mr. Colt!" she exclaimed, wrapping her arms around
him. "I'm so glad you're here!" Releasing him, she
darted to Lila Moore, who sat crying in the straight-
backed chair next to the couch. On the couch was a
shapeless form under a blanket. No one needed to tell
him what had happened.

"Lila, it's Mr. Colt," said Anne, gripping the weeping woman's shoulders.

Dan had met the Moores upon delivering Anne
Braxton to their home the evening before. He spied
the two children sitting soberly in a corner. Lila lifted

her swollen eyes toward the tall man. Her face twisted severely. "They hung him, Mr. Colt!" she sobbed. "They hung my husband!"

Anne stayed with Lila until she calmed down. The new widow sat sniffing and wiping tears, staring at the lifeless form. Speaking softly, Anne said, "Lila, I need to talk to Mr. Colt. We're going to step outside. Okay?"

Lila Moore nodded.

Anne headed for the door. Dan followed.

As they stepped out into the sunlight, Dan noticed the lump and dried blood on Anne's head. Anger welled up inside him. "They hit you, ma'am," he said with tight lips.

"I lost my temper," said Anne, putting fingertips to the wound. "But we've got another one that'll be easy to identify."

"Oh?"

"I got my teeth on an ear, even through his hood. Felt it tear loose from his head. Got a mouthful of blood."

"Remind me to stay on your good side," said Dan, attempting a touch of humor.

Anne Braxton related the events of Tod Moore's hanging in detail. Dan examined the ground under the giant oak tree, but could find no clues as to the identity of the murderers. However, he did notice that the five horses had left a clear trail leading away from the place.

"I'm going to follow the tracks," Dan told Anne. "I think we'd better move you again tonight."

"Funny thing," said the widow Braxton, "one of them asked if I wasn't the Braxton female. In fact, it was the one whose ear I chewed. If they were after me, they had their chance."

"Just the same, I think—"

"Lila really needs me, Dan," she said, touching his arm. "I'm sorry. I mean Mr. Colt."

"Make it Dan, ma'am," he said warmly.

"Okay," said Anne, "but I'm not ma'am. I'm Anne."

"It's a deal, Anne." Colt smiled. Dan liked this woman. She had grit, just like Laura Lane. No wonder the two were such good friends, even though Anne was ten years older.

"I don't think the hangmen will be coming back here," said Anne. "They'll go after another farmer. Like I said, if they wanted to kill me, they'd have done it last night."

"Okay, but we've got to get another door on the house before nightfall," said Dan.

It did not take Maze McLeod long to learn that Anne Braxton was indeed at the Tod Moore place. After returning from hanging Moore, Mel Trent held a wet cloth to Heath Finley's damaged ear and boasted of how he had hit the Braxton woman with his revolver.

"You shoulda killed her," Finley swore hatefully.

"Uh-uh," said Trent. "You know how the boss feels about us killin' females."

At dawn, big Maze got up and dressed. He was going to spy on the Moore place and see if Anne Braxton moved to another farm. She was to die tonight.

Mel Trent was asleep in a chair beside the bunk where Heath Finley lay. Finley rolled his eyes and looked at McLeod as he moved about the room. Maze looked down at Finley and whispered, "How's the ear?"

"Bleeding's stopped," whispered Heath in response. "Pain's better."

"Good," breathed McLeod, heading for the door, hat in hand.

"Where you goin'?" came Finley's hoarse whisper.

"Gotta get away from these four walls for a while," said Maze. "Been cooped up too long. Feeling stronger. Need to stretch my legs. Besides, my horse needs limberin' up. See you later." With that, Maze McLeod stepped out into the sunrise.

Saddling his horse, the big man rode toward the Moore farm. As he moved across the valley, Maze pondered his plan to kill Anne Braxton. He would have to find a way to get away from the hideout tonight without arousing suspicion. Whoever she stayed with would probably have to die, too. That woman could put a rope around his burly neck. She must be disposed of.

Maze McLeod was riding through a dense stand of pine and Aspens when he saw a wagon in the distance, to the right. The vehicle was moving at a good clip and was headed in the direction of Tod Moore's place. Maze had a hunch. He halted his horse at the forest's edge and watched the fish-tailing wagon draw closer. After a few minutes, he recognized Paul Healy at the reins and his wife hanging on for dear life at his side.

The sight troubled Maze McLeod. To him it could mean only one thing. The homesteaders had been frightened by his visit and were rushing to tell Anne Braxton that he was after her. The huge outlaw scolded himself. He should have known this would happen. The Healys left him no choice.

Spurring the powerful animal under him, Maze took off to intercept the speeding wagon. When he was within five hundred yards, Healy saw him coming and snapped the whip over the team's heads, driving them harder. Closing in, McLeod quickly scanned the valley to see if anyone was in sight. There were horses and cattle grazing in the early morning sun, but no other humans around.

Leaning over, he slid the Winchester .44 from its boot and jacked a cartridge in the chamber. He swung parallel with the charging vehicle and shouldered the rifle. The rifle barked and the horse on McLeod's side went down. The other horse stumbled and plunged to the ground. The speeding wagon careened, then lurched cornerwise. As it flipped over, both passengers flew through the air.

Paul Healy was on his feet first, limping toward his wife. Maze urged his mount toward the wagon, working the lever of his rifle. Healy heard the thundering hoofs and looked up from his kneeling position. His eyes widened as he saw Maze taking aim. The Winchester roared and the homesteader crumpled to the grassy earth.

The big man halted the horse and left the saddle. Paul Healy was dead.

Myrtle was stunned and struggling to gain her feet. Her gaze fell on McLeod just as he pulled the trigger. The bullet ripped into her head. She slumped to the ground, jerked twice, and died.

The horse McLeod had shot was dead. The other one was on its side, entangled in harness and gasping for breath. The huge man looked around the valley another time, worked the lever again and said, "You just as well join the rest of 'em, horsie." The shot clattered across the valley floor.

McLeod bounded into the saddle and headed for the Moore farm.

As McLeod lay in the grass on a hillside overlooking the farm, Anne Braxton climbed down from the giant oak tree where she had just cut the rope that held the dead farmer in midair.

Hatred for the woman burned in McLeod's chest. She had thrown the flaming tablecloth on him. The burns would probably leave ugly scars. Not only that, but she could point a finger at him in court and identify him as one of the hangmen. Impulse pressed him to ride down right now and shoot her dead. Maze checked himself. It was after seven o'clock. It would be too easy for someone to come riding in about the time he was shooting Anne Braxton. No, Maze had a better way for her to die.

The woman struggled, pulling Moore's limp body into the house.

Within twenty minutes he saw a man ride into the yard on a black horse. As McLeod watched from the hill, he saw the man come near the house, leap from the saddle, and dash inside. Maze watched with interest until the rider and the Braxton woman came out together. They stood in front of the house and talked. Then they walked toward the tree where the farmer had been hanged. The tall man studied the ground and pointed to tracks that led out of the yard.

Maze McLeod bent low and ran in a zigzag pattern toward the yard. Within half a minute he was in the cover of the trees. He worked his way forward until he could hear what they were saying.

"I think we'd better move you again tonight," said the blond man.

By his low-slung guns, Maze figured this must be the gunhawk that Drake and Dean had talked about, the one who had killed Neal Nix in a stand-up shootout. They had said he was blond.

"Lila really needs me," McLeod heard Anne Braxton say.

Maze watched them chat a little longer, then walk toward the house together. The Braxton woman was convincing the gunslinger that if the hangmen wanted to kill her, they would have done so last night. The blond man said something about replacing the broken door on the house.

A wicked smile twisted Maze McLeod's face. Anne Braxton was not expecting any visitors tonight. She was in for a surprise.

Chapter Fifteen

Dan Colt followed the tracks of Tod Moore's murderers to the Circle L ranch. They led straight into the corral.

Men eyed him suspiciously as he rode past the barn and corral to the large ranch house. It was a single-storey structure of logs, built long and low. A thin thread of smoke lifted from a chimney at the rear of the house, where Colt dismounted. A heavyset Mexican woman was washing clothes on a scrub board.

Approaching the woman, Dan said, "Good morning."

"*Buenos días*," responded the woman.

"Is Mr. Long here?"

Lifting her hands from the soapy water and elbowing a wisp of hair from her eyes, she pointed toward the barn. "*Señor* Long is somewhere aroun' zee barn."

"*Gracias*," responded Colt. He led the black to the corral and wrapped the reins around a pole. Two cowboys were standing just inside the barn door when Dan pulled it open. They both gave him a cold look.

"Gentlemen," he said, forcing a smile, "my name is Dan Colt, and I represent the sheriff's office. Is Mr. Long around?"

"You got here mighty fast," said the shorter of the two.

"Pardon?" said Dan.

"Where's Jeb?" asked the tall one. "You come in Caley's place? You the new deputy?"

"No," said Dan. "I'm not a deputy, but I'm helpin' Bill Caley."

"How come Caley didn't come?" snapped the tall one.

"Wait a minute," said Colt. "Are you tellin' me someone has gone after Caley?"

"Yeah," said the short cowboy. "Jeb Wilkins left for Alamosa at sunup. You didn't come with him?"

"Nope," replied Dan.

"Seems to me, Elrod," said the tall one, "this gent ain't got no business here."

Dan eyed him caustically.

"Now hold on, Rex," said Elrod, "he ain't told us why he's here."

"Pro'bly sneakin' around, spyin' for them scaly sodbusters," said Rex with a sneer. "Lemme see your badge, partner."

Dan felt his blood grow warmer. "I told you I *represent* the sheriff's office." His ice-blue eyes held Rex hard. "I'm not a deputy. Since Palmer and Castin were killed, I offered to help Bill Caley for a while."

"If you're not here because of the stolen horses," asked Elrod, "why *are* you here?"

"I need to see Mr. Long." Dan squinted at the short man. "Did you say you had horses stolen?"

"Yeah," replied Elrod. "Somebody rode in here last night and run off with a passel of 'em. Mr. Long sent Wilkins after Caley. The boss and several of the boys are out right now roundin' up the ones that strayed from the horse thieves."

"Looks like I'll have to wait till your boss returns," said Dan. "Since Caley's comin', that'll even make it better."

Rex had a tobacco plug in his cheek. He turned and spit on the barn floor, then set his eyes on Dan. "Mr. Green asked you a question, partner," he said insolently. "I'd appreciate it if you'd give us an answer."

"Who's Mr. Green?" asked Colt, tight-lipped. "What question?"

"I'm Elrod Green," said the short man, extending his hand. "And he's Rex Dobbs."

Dan shook Green's hand.

"The question, Mr. Colt," pressed Dobbs. "Elrod asked you a question. Now let's have the answer, partner."

Dan Colt's jaw corded. He sized up Rex Dobbs. The man was probably not more than twenty-five. He was about an inch taller than Colt. Probably would weigh around one-ninety. Rawboned and well-tanned. Wore his gun high on his hip, portending that he was not a gunhawk.

Dan fixed his eyes on Rex's. With a ponderous, thick voice, he said, "I said I would discuss my business with your boss. And I'm not your partner."

"You have a smart mouth, Colt," lashed Dobbs. "Maybe somebody needs to smash it for you."

"And you got a burr stuck in your pants, Rex," said Dan with a cold smile.

Dobbs took a quick step forward. Green jumped in front of him.

Looking up at Dan, Green said, "He had a fight a few weeks ago with the ranch champ. Got in a lucky punch and put the champ out. He's been tootin' his whistle ever since, tryin' to get somebody to fight him. Thinks he can lick anybody and everybody."

Dan paused, then spoke to Green. "I'll wait around till Mr. Long gets back. Need to see Caley, too." With that he turned and walked out into the sunlight.

Rex Dobbs was instantly on his heels. "I think you just better ride, mister," he said in a threatening tone.

"Leave him alone, Rex," said Elrod Green, following. "Jeb will be here with Caley soon and the boss will be back. If Mr. Colt wants to talk to them, that's his business."

"Butt out, Elrod," snapped Dobbs, his face red.

Dan stopped and wheeled. Several ranch hands saw Rex's face. They began to gather around. They had learned to ignore his insolent spirit. Maybe this tall, muscular stranger would not. Dobbs needed a good whipping.

"I came here peaceable, Rex," Dan said evenly. "I'm on official business. Now why don't you just go out to the pasture and count cow pies till you cool off?"

A brassy look glinted Dobb's eyes. He rolled the dark mass in his mouth and spit a heavy brown stream across the toes of Dan's boots.

Colt's face crimsoned. "Now you just take your shirt off and wipe that ugly stuff off my boots," he hissed, lips pulled tight over his teeth.

Dobbs flared his nostrils and stuck out his chin. *"Make me."*

These words were just rolling off of Dobbs's lips when Dan's right fist caught him flush on the nose. The arrogant man's head snapped back. His hat took flight. Dan met his jaw on the rebound with a piston-like punch. Dobbs went down like a gut-rotted tree in a high wind. He rolled over in the dirt, shaking his head. Blood was running from his nostrils. He raised up on one knee and ran a sleeve under his nose. When he saw the blood, fire ignited in his eyes.

Dan braced himself as the angered cowboy swore vehemently and charged, head down. Their bodies came together with a *whump* and when they hit the ground, Rex was on top. Colt arched himself and flipped Dobbs head-over-heels. The Circle L hands were cheering the stranger.

Dan pounced on the bleeding man. Rex let out a wild yell and rolled free. He leaped to his feet and came at the blond man, swinging a booted foot. The agile Colt dodged and grasped Dobbs's leg. Giving it a quick twist, he dropped the man and jumped on him again.

This time the powerful Dan Colt threw a hammerlock on his challenger. His hands were like claws of iron, his arms like tempered steel. Dobbs was in severe pain and could not move.

"Now cowboy," breathed Dan heavily, "you've got a choice. You can agree right now to remove your shirt and clean your filth off my boots."

"And if I don't?" asked Dobbs, grimacing.

"I'll dislocate your shoulder and break your arm."

"Go ahead and bust his arm, mister!" shouted one of the hands.

Colt applied more pressure. "Well?"

Rex cried out in pain. Sucking air through his teeth, he said, "I'll . . . I'll clean your boots."

The seven Circle L hands who were gathered around let out a cheer.

Dan released the agonized cowboy and stood up. He was dusting himself off as Dobbs raised to his knees.

"Take off the shirt," commanded Colt, stepping toward him. He pointed to the dust-caked tobacco spittle on his boots. "Clean 'em."

Cowboys snickered as Rex Dobbs, still on his knees, unbuttoned his shirt and pulled the tail from under his pants. His gun was still in its holster. Working the shirt off of his arms, he wadded it up and began rubbing the blond man's boots.

"You can do mine next, tough guy!" shouted one of the hands. Dobbs gave him a hateful stare.

"Mine, too!" hollered another.

Looking up at Dan Colt with eyes of venom, Dobbs said, "Is that good enough?"

"Just touch up the left one a little more on the toe," Dan said evenly. He let Rex rub for nearly a minute. "That oughtta do it. Thank you."

Dobbs stood up and dusted himself off, adjusting his gunbelt. Dan turned his back on him and walked toward his hat. The group of cowboys began to scatter, laughing among themselves.

Suddenly, above the laughter Dan heard behind him the familiar double-click of a hammer being eared back. At the same instant somebody shouted, "Look out!"

Like a well-oiled machine, Colt whirled, both .45s coming out and firing in an invisible blur. The slugs caught Dobbs in the lower chest. He buckled forward, his own gun firing into the dirt, and flopped to his back. Uttering one indistinguishable word, his knees dropped and his eyes closed.

Dan holstered his smoking guns and raised his line of sight from the dead man to two riders who were just dismounting. One was Bill Caley.

"Don't feel bad, Colt," said Elrod Green, who now stood beside him. "It was bound to happen one day. Today was as good as any."

Dan looked at Caley. "I couldn't help it, Bill. He—"

"I saw it, Dan," said the young lawman. "He'd have shot you in the back."

Upon privately asking Colt why he was at the Circle L ranch, Caley learned that Tod Moore had been the latest victim of the hangmen. Dan told him of the tracks of five horses leading from Moore's farm to the east gate of the Circle L corral.

Together the two men crossed the corral, discussing the theft of Jake Long's horses. They were standing at the west gate when a large herd of horses came into view from the direction of the creek to the west. Several mounted cowboys were herding them toward the corral.

Elrod Green and Jeb Wilkins joined them at the gate, gazing at the approaching herd. "Looks like they found 'em, Sheriff," said Wilkins.

"I hope so," said Caley.

Presently the herd arrived and was once again in the corral.

A big man on a blue roan separated himself from the other horsemen and rode toward where Bill Caley and the others stood. Dan knew instantly that he was Jake Long. He was square-shouldered and rawboned. Deep lines in his granite face betrayed his sixty years, but he had a ruggedness about him that would gain instant respect from any man.

Eying Caley as he dismounted, Long said with a deep voice, "Sorry, Bill. We done handed you a false alarm. Every cayuse is accounted for. I don't know what to make of this."

"Could we talk privately, Jake?" asked Caley. "I think I can explain it."

"Sure. Come on to the house," said Long, casting a glance at Dan Colt.

"Oh," said Caley, "this is Dan Colt, Jake. Dan, meet Jake Long."

Jake Long shook Dan's hand with a powerful grip. The trio was making its way toward the house when Jake saw some of the men picking up Rex Dobbs's body. He swore hotly and said, "Who killed Rex?"

"I did, sir," spoke up Dan.

"It was self-defense, Jake," added Caley. "He tried to shoot Dan in the back."

Long swore again. "I knew he'd tackle the wrong man one day." Fixing his gaze on Dan, he said, "You say your name's Colt?"

"Yessir."

"Any relation to Sam? The gunmaker, I mean."

"Not that I know of," said Dan. "But then, I could be. I was orphaned as a small child. Someone else raised me."

The three men passed through the door into the house. Jake led them to the large kitchen where the Mexican woman that Dan had seen earlier was busy making flat bread.

"Have a seat, gentlemen," said the rugged rancher gesturing toward a big table. Turning to the woman, he said, "Lolita, how about some coffee?"

"Sí, señor," she replied. "Un solo momento."

Caley and Colt sat down, and Jake Long dropped his big frame on the chair at the head of the table. Squinting at the blond man, he said, "Colt . . . Colt . . . There used to be a gunslinger—"

"That's me," cut in Dan.

Looking down at the table, Jake shook his head. "Seems like I heard Dan Colt was killed."

"Only a rumor, Mr. Long," said Colt.

"Dan knew my dad, Jake," put in Bill Caley.

"Oh?"

"Yep. Saved his life once, too."

Long nodded, then set his eyes on Caley. "You said you can explain about my horses being turned loose and scattered."

"Since Sheriff Palmer was killed," began Caley, "Dan has offered to help me find his ambushers, who we know are part of this gang of hangmen that are killin' the homesteaders."

Jake Long shook his head and swore. "I hope you

do find 'em. Makin' all us cattlemen look like cutthroats."

"Last night," continued the acting sheriff, "they hanged Tod Moore."

Long's face twisted. "Oh, no."

"Dan found the tracks of five horses leaving Moore's place and coming straight to the Circle L. They went through the east gate of your corral—"

"And out the west gate," said Long, finishing Caley's statement.

Lolita placed coffee mugs on the table and filled them. The rancher smiled and thanked her.

"I guess you're supposed to think the hangmen are Circle L men," said Jake.

"Yeah, but it's too obvious, Jake," said Bill. "Looks to Dan and me like the hangmen used your horses to cover their own tracks."

"Good idea," nodded Long.

"It worked," said Dan flatly.

"Yeah," agreed Caley, "no way to trail them now."

"While we're here, Mr. Long," said Colt, "we need to examine all the black saddles on the Circle L."

Long's brow furrowed.

"Hangmen left a clue at one of the farms," said Bill.

"Sure," said Jake, easing back his chair. "You can start with mine. It's black."

Eight of the seventy-nine saddles on the Circle L ranch were black. A thorough examination convinced Caley and Colt that none of them was ridden by the hangman who lost his silver ornament.

Dan and the acting sheriff agreed to split up and finish checking all the black saddles on the remaining ranches. Dan would ride into town tomorrow morning and they would discuss the results.

The sun was lowering toward the mountain peaks to the west when Dan rode away from the Moore place. Having finished his part of the saddle inspections with no results, he rode to the Moore house and hung another door in place of the damaged one. He offered once again to escort Anne Braxton to another farm, but she insisted on staying with Lila Moore. He headed for the Box W.

Smith Wayne sat on the porch of the hideout, working on his black saddle. Heath Finley lay on his cot inside, moaning over his damaged ear. It was nearly noon. *Where is that stupid McLeod?* Wayne swore under his breath.

Mel Trent had just disappeared into the trees due north to ride to Del Norte and recruit some new men. Smith Wayne's promise of great riches would doubtless entice more money-hungry men to enter his employ.

Smith finished with the last ornament on his saddle just as Maze McLeod came riding in. He threw the big man a hot glare and rasped, "Where you been?"

"Just ridin'," replied Maze with a half smile. "I got tired of bein' cooped up here. Needed to get some fresh air."

"Anybody see you? Those burns on your face are a dead giveaway."

"Nobody saw me," replied McLeod. *At least nobody that's alive to tell it,* he said to himself. Looking around, he said, "Where's the boys? Only Heath's horse is here."

Wayne's face went stiff. "Lefty and Manny are dead."

"Wha—?"

"I sent 'em to bushwhack that Colt dude."

"You mean that blond gunslinger?"

"Yeah. He outsmarted 'em. Killed 'em both."

180

McLeod cursed. "Somebody needs to do somethin' about him."

"You want the job?"

McLeod cursed again. "No, sir! I ain't no gunhawk! If he could take Neal Nix head-on and kill Dean n' Drake when *they* was ambushin' *him* . . . no thanks!"

"I sent Mel up to Del Norte to recruit some more help," said Smith. "He oughtta be back some time to-morrow. You stick here with Heath."

"Okay," Maze lied. Heath would have to be alone long enough for Anne Braxton to die. A wave of relief came over McLeod. It was going to be easier than he had thought to get away tonight undetected. He would just wait until Heath was asleep.

Smith Wayne saddled up and headed for home.

The last fiery rays of the setting sun were burning the mountain tops as Dan Colt rode through the gate of the Box W. The crew was eating supper in the bunkhouse.

Dan slid from the saddle at the house. Fargo Wayne opened the door before he reached it. "Evenin', Colt," he said smiling. "We're about to sit down to supper. Would you like to eat with us before you look at Smith's saddle?"

"Well, I really need to—"

"Aw, c'mon," said Fargo, slapping his shoulder. "You've got to eat supper somewhere. Might as well be here."

The thought of food reminded him of his empty stomach. Dan smiled. He liked this man. "Okay, if you insist."

Scott Wayne was already at the table when Dan and Fargo entered the room. Mabel was placing hot food before him. Scott stood up and smiled. "Hello, Mr. Colt."

"Howdy, Scott," responded Dan.

"Does Smith know supper's ready?" Fargo asked Scott.

"Mabel banged on his door and told him," replied Scott.

"Go ahead and sit down, Colt," said Fargo, gesturing.

Mabel laid a plate and utensils before Dan. "Thank you, ma'am," he said, showing his white, even teeth.

The silver-haired patriarch looked past Dan's head, eyebrows arching. "There you are, son," he said with a fond warmth. "Come in and meet Mr. Dan Colt."

Dan turned his head to see the tall, slender figure of Smith Wayne.

As Dan rose to his feet, the elder Wayne said, "Dan, this is my son, Smith. A real chip off the old block, eh?"

Smith Wayne tried to veil his contempt for the tall, blond intruder, but his icy black eyes betrayed him. Dan read it instantly. Smith's hand was like cold meat in Dan's.

"Mr. Colt," nodded Smith, making the handshake brief.

"Well, gentlemen," said Fargo, "let's eat."

The meal had progressed several moments when Smith set his dark eyes on Dan. With a stoical face, he said, "Understand you're inspectin' saddles."

"Black ones," said Dan around a mouthful of potatoes.

"What for?"

"Official reasons."

"You a law officer?"

"Nope."

"By what authority you pryin' into people's privacy?"

182

Fargo threw his gaze to Scott, then Smith. "Son, you act like you've got somethin' to hide. Don't be rude to Mr. Colt."

"You got somethin' to hide?" chided Scott, purposely rattling his brother.

Smith shot his older brother a dirty look, then made a pleasant one for his father. "I don't have anything to hide, Dad," he said with a tone of innocence. "I just don't like strangers smearin' their gritty paws all over my private property."

"I'll be glad to wear gloves," clipped Dan with heat creeping up his spine.

"What if I refuse?" asked Smith, tilting his head back. "I don't see a badge on your chest."

"Now son," said Fargo, touching Smith's arm, "you're making a mountain out of a molehill. Dan's not going to find anything wrong, so just settle down." Swinging his gaze to Colt, he said, "He's a good boy, Dan. Just a little impetuous. But you'll have to admit he's got a lot of starch. Heh, heh, heh."

I'd call it something else, Dan thought to himself.

"Young feller needs some starch, wouldn't you say, Dan?" continued the elder Wayne. "Reminds me of myself when I was his age."

Scott Wayne's face showed a touch of nausea.

"You can refuse," said Dan in a level tone, "but it would just be Bill Caley out here tomorrow to do the same thing. He *has* a badge."

Smith's countenance did a sudden change. He ejected a belly laugh. "I was just funnin', Colt," he said, slapping a palm on the table. "You want to see my saddle now?"

"We haven't had our apple pie yet, son," said Fargo, smiling. "Let's have the pie fir—"

The smile left Smith's face. "I don't want any pie,

Dad. If Colt is going to paw my saddle, it'll be right now."

Fargo's face slacked. "But son, it will only be—"

"I said it will have to be *right now,* Dad," grated Smith.

"All right, all right," chuckled the silver-haired man with a false smile. "We can eat dessert afterward. Scott, light a lantern, will you? We'll escort Dan to the barn."

As the four men walked toward the barn in the circle of light cast by the lantern, Scott said, "Understand you had a little ruckus over at the Circle L today, Mr. Colt."

"How'd you hear about that?" asked Dan.

"Reggie Owens, one of Long's cowhands, was here this afternoon."

Smith listened with interest.

"What happened?" queried Fargo.

"You've met Rex Dobbs, Dad," said Scott.

"Uh-huh. Don't like him, but I've met him."

"He prodded Dan into a fight. Dan cleaned his plow. After it was over, Dobbs pulled his gun. Was going to shoot Dan in the back. Reggie said Dan heard the hammer being cracked, turned, drew, and fired before Rex could let the hammer down."

"Kill him, Dan?" asked Fargo.

"Yep," replied Dan quietly.

"You must be faster'n a weaver's shuttle," breathed Fargo.

Smith Wayne felt a chill wash over his body. He remembered Lefty Dean's words . . . *The man has special powers. Watch out, Smith. He'll get you.*

The barn door squeaked on its hinges. The familiar smells of hay, old wood, leather, and horse manure met their nostrils as they stepped inside. Smith led them to a stall at the rear where his black gelding

184

stood. A black saddle straddled the gate of an empty stall nearby.

"There it is, Dan," said Smith. "Look all you want."

Scott held the light while Dan examined the four silver ornaments outside and underneath. "Hmmm," he said.

"What's the matter?" asked Smith, knowing very well what Colt was thinking.

"Mighty poor workmanship on these ornaments compared to the rest of the saddle."

"What do you mean?" asked Fargo.

"Look," said the tall man, bending the squared corner upward, exposing the back side of an ornament. "A saddlemaker has a special awl that fastens these with a swirled knot. These have been done by hand. They're crude and irregular."

"So what?" snapped Smith. "What are you lookin' for anyhow?"

"One of the hangmen scraped a tree with his saddle at the Braxton place. Sheriff Palmer found an ornament exactly like these on the ground. That's why Palmer and Castin were ambushed. The hangmen shot them down and took the ornament from Palmer's pocket."

Scott Wayne riveted his eyes to his brother's face. Fargo swore.

"I was with them," added Colt. "I saw the whole thing."

The scene came back to Smith's mind. He remembered seeing only the top of their hats from his lofty position. *Palmer's prisoner had been Dan Colt!* Smith wondered why Colt had been arrested by the sheriff . . . and wished now that they had shot Colt, too.

Holding his face rigid, Smith said, "I'm sorry about the hangin's and the sheriff bein' killed and all that, but I sure didn't have anything to do with it."

185

"Of course you didn't, son," put in Fargo.

Suspicion was evident in Dan's ice-blue eyes. Smith read it.

"Look, mister," Smith said heatedly, "I can't help what some stupid saddlemaker did. This saddle don't prove nothin'!"

Fargo Wayne's brow furrowed. "Dan, you don't think Smith is one of the hangmen."

Colt's jaw squared. "Let's just say he could be a suspect."

The elder Wayne's face flushed with a hint of anger. "Smith's a good boy," he said with conviction. "This is preposterous!"

Dan eyed him coldly. "You told me you couldn't think of any cattleman in this valley who would hang those homesteaders."

Fargo nodded.

"Well, Mr. Wayne, *somebody* in this valley is hangin' 'em."

Chapter Sixteen

At the same moment that Dan Colt rode away from the Box W leaving Smith Wayne with a knot of fear in his stomach, violence was about to break out in the town of Del Norte, twenty miles to the north.

Dave Sundeen left his room at the Sunset Hotel and ambled up the street. He was in the mood for an evening of poker, and his funds were getting low. He hitched up the gunbelt bearing his twin Colt .45s and spoke to an aged man who was lighting the street lamps.

Reaching the corner, Dave paused, eying the two saloons. They stood directly across the street from each other. Numerous horses were tethered to the hitching rails in front of both. He studied the Golden Nugget, then stared across at the Frontier.

Making his decision, he crossed the street toward the Frontier. The tall, blond man elbowed his way through the batwing doors and angled toward the bar. Smoke was thick in the place, ringing a fog around the wagon-wheel chandeliers that hung from the ceiling.

A pasty-faced woman with too much rouge on her cheeks stood near the piano. A fat man banged its keys while the woman sang a sad ballad.

As Dave slipped between two men at the bar, a

bald-headed bartender eyed him and said, "What'll it be?"

"Whiskey," said Sundeen, pushing his hat to the back of his head with a forefinger.

The bartender poured a generous shot and shoved the glass toward him. Dave nodded and laid a coin on the bar. Glass in hand, he turned around and scanned the smoky room. He spied a table with an empty chair. Three rough-looking men were playing poker. He tossed off the glass in two gulps, swishing the second gulp around in his mouth before he swallowed it.

Approaching the table, Sundeen stood for a moment and watched. As cards were slapped down, one man laughed and raked chips from the center of the table. Another looked up at that moment and said, "Howdy, stranger."

Dave smiled. "You boys through, or you gonna play some more?"

"Siddown," said the one who had just raked in the pot. "I just as well go home with some of your money, too."

Dave slacked into the empty chair. Running his ice-blue eyes over their faces, he said, "My name's Sundeen. Dave Sundeen."

The man directly across the table said, "I'm Earl Mound." Pointing to the others, he said, "This is Vince Forbes. This is Arnie Winkler."

Dave nodded and the game began.

About an hour had passed when a portly man of sixty left a nearby table and walked to where Dave Sundeen sat. He stood there looking down at the blond man. Shifting cards in his hands, Dave gave the man a casual look.

"Howdy, Mr. Colt," he said, smiling. "Remember me? I'm Fred Carver."

"No, I don't remember you," said Dave blandly.

"And you don't remember me either. My name's not Colt." Dave was disturbed. He had lost count of the times within the last year that someone had mistaken him for the dead gunfighter, Dan Colt. At least Colt was *supposed* to be dead. Dave had never seen Dan Colt, but he was convinced that the two of them must bear some resemblance. Had to. So many people had thought he was Colt.

Carver laughed as if Sundeen had cracked a joke. "Sure you remember. I was in Alamosa when—"

"You and I have never met," cut in Sundeen. "Now I'm busy, sir, if you don't mind." With that, Dave put his attention to the cards.

Fred Carver gave an insulted grunt, wheeled, and left the saloon. Stiff-legged, he crossed the street to the Golden Nugget. Two drunken cowboys met Carver as he pushed open the batwings. He stepped aside, let them pass, then proceeded inside. Threading his way through the crowded room, he approached a table occupied by four tough-looking men. Each had the mark of a gunslinger.

Setting his gaze on one with a jagged scar across his face, Carver said, "Mr. Bower . . ."

Wade Bower stopped in the middle of something he was saying and lifted his gunmetal-gray eyes to Carver with a petulant stare. He waited for the portly man to speak.

Bower's cold eyes encased in his scarred face sent a chill down Carver's spine. "My . . . my name is Fred Carver, sir."

"So?" snipped Bower.

"Sir," continued the round-faced man, "I'm a drummer by trade . . . and . . . I live here in Del Norte."

"That's exciting," said the gunslinger without expression.

"Business has been a little slow lately—"

"Oh, I'm so sorry," Bower said, blinking his eyes in mockery. His three friends laughed.

Fred Carver wiped sweat from his rotund face. "I overheard you talking at the hotel today at lunch."

"Yeah?"

"I understood you to say that you had ridden all the way from Albuquerque to Alamosa to challenge Neal Nix—"

"Yeah." Bower's cold eyes showed a spark of interest.

"And you were upset because somebody else beat you to him?"

Bower cursed. "Yeah. Stupid kid sheriff wouldn't tell me who it was. Couldn't find out from townfolks. They didn't know his name. Said he was tall and handsome. Blond hair."

"How much would it be worth to you to meet up with him?"

Bower lifted his black flat-crowned hat and scratched his head. "You know where this dude is?"

"I know *where* he is and *who* he is," Carver announced, his round eyes enlarged.

"You mean he's where I can get at him?"

"He's right here in Del Norte."

"Town ain't so big," said the hard-featured gunslinger. "Guess I can find 'im for myself for nothin'."

Disappointment spread over Carver's moon-shaped face.

Wade Bower chuckled and shoved his chair back. Rising to his full height, he said, "However, I might not have found out he was here if you hadn't told me."

Bower's fingers dipped in the pocket of his black leather vest. Gold coins jingled. A broad smile spread over Carver's mouth.

"What's his name?" asked the gunslinger.

"Dan Colt."

Bower's expressionless face stiffened. The jagged scar that ran from the middle of his forehead in a slanted line through his left eyebrow turned white. "Dan Colt is dead and buried."

"He's alive and in a poker game at the Frontier Saloon," said Carver advisedly. "I was in Alamosa two days ago when he bored two .45 caliber holes in Neal Nix's chest. Told me himself he was Dan Colt."

"Tell you what, Carver," said Bower, "you go with me and point him out. If it's Dan Colt and I kill him, you get a fifty-dollar gold nugget."

"It's a deal," said Fred, licking his thick purple lips.

"Let's go," said Bower with a toss of his head.

The other three gunslingers followed, talking among themselves. Wade Bower checked the loads in both his irons as they angled across the well-lighted street. The fat man led the way through the batwings, then side-stepped and stopped. Pointing with his double chin, he said, "That's him over there. Blond one. Has the flat-crowned gray hat with the neck cord."

The painted woman was in the middle of a song. Bower checked the position of his cronies. Two flanked him on the right. One on the left. Fred Carver inched his way to an inconspicuous place at the bar.

Wade Bower took a deep breath and shouted, "Hey, you on the piano! Stop playin'!"

The piano was suddenly silent. The woman was still warbling.

The gunslinger scowled. "Hey, woman! Shut up!"

As the woman gasped and her last word died out in the air, all eyes were turned to Wade Bower, including Dave Sundeen's. Loudly, he said, "My name is Wade Bower. Everybody hear that? *Wade Bower!* Now I understand that the gunhawk who killed Neal Nix in Alamosa a few days ago is in this room right now. I'd like him to stand up and identify himself!"

Heads turned, dozens of eyes roving about. Nobody moved. Bower fixed his gray gaze on Dave Sundeen. "Whatsa matter, blondie," he said bitingly, "you got chicken livers for guts?"

Sundeen looked around as if to find another blond man. Swinging his arctic blue gaze back to Bower, he said, "Were you addressing me, big mouth?" The hair was bristling on the back of Dave's neck.

"You shot Nix, didn't you?" barked the scar-faced gunslinger.

"Nope," Dave said icily.

"You're Dan Colt, ain'tcha?"

"No, I'm not," rasped Sundeen. "But if I see Colt I'll tell him you're lookin' for him. What'd you say your name is, sonny?"

Bower's eyes purpled. "You're yellow, Colt. You know my name. And you know my reputation. Now all these nice people here are wonderin' if you're gonna step into the street and draw against me . . . or find yourself a chicken house to hide in."

Sundeen looked across the table to Earl Mound. "Earl," he said, "I've heard your name around. They say you're pretty fast. Tryin' to work your way up the ladder. Since neither of us is Dan Colt, would you like to move up a rung?"

Mound shook his head. "I'm not in Bower's league yet, Dave."

"You really *are* stinkin' yellow, ain'tcha?" grated Bower. "Askin' someone else to fight your battles. I'm wonderin' now if you didn't shoot Nix in the back!"

The saloon was quiet as a tomb.

Sundeen's temper was near the boiling point. He eyed Wade Bower as he would a pesky fly. "I'm not Dan Colt," he said through his even white teeth. "And I didn't shoot Neal Nix. Now I'm going to give you a chance to walk out of here and be around to see the sun come up in the mornin'."

Bower bared his fangs. "You ain't talkin' your way outta this one, Colt. You gotta be over thirty by now, ain'tcha? Whatsa matter, *gramps* . . . you gittin' old? Maybe you're slowin' some!"

Dave Sundeen's simmering rage was fanned into a blaze.

He stood up and shoved the chair back with his leg. Every eye was glued on his towering figure. Glaring at Bower, he said, "I want you to get one thing straight. When you die out there in the street in a few minutes, it was *Dave Sundeen* that killed you."

Bower waggled his head. "Yeah," he said with an insolent sneer. "I'll remember that."

Sundeen shot Fred Carver a hot look. "You remember it, too, chubby."

Carver swallowed hard, eyes bulging, and watched the crowd follow Sundeen and Bower out the door. They spoke among themselves in low, strained voices.

The street lanterns cast eerie shadows on the dusty, wagon-rutted street as the blond man centered himself and took his stance. Electric current tingled through his body. Dave Sundeen thrived on challenge. As a gunfighter he had had plenty. The west was full of many a young hopeful who yearned to have his name on everybody's lips . . . and a reputation that struck fear to men's hearts.

Wade Bower detached himself from his close-knit group. The other three stood together near a water trough. The cocky gunman moved to the center of the street, flexing his fingers dramatically. Music from the Golden Nugget filled the night air as Bower turned and squared himself with his opponent. He did it with the flair of a showman.

Dangling his hands over his low-slung guns, Bower tilted his head downward and looked at Sundeen out of the tops of his eyes. "Go for your guns!" he bellowed.

"You're the one come looking for me," said Sundeen doggedly. "Draw."

Bower's hands swung downward. Sundeen gave him a second of grace. He did not go for his twin Colts until Wade's fingers had touched the cool grips of his guns. Then Dave's hands moved . . . so fast they seemed invisible. Two guns roared.

Both were Sundeen's.

Bower's revolvers were out of their holsters, spilling from lifeless hands. The .45 slugs exploded his heart. He lived long enough for his expressionless face to register total shock. Wade Bower was dead before his body slammed onto the street.

The piano inside the Golden Nugget Saloon went mute. Silence clung to the night air. Dave Sundeen shifted his gaze among the faces of the crowd as the smoking guns slid into their holsters. "Was it a fair fight?"

Heads nodded. "Sure was," came two voices in unison.

Sundeen took a step toward the side of the street when Bower's three friends bolted toward him, pulling their guns. Instinctively Dave's right hand flashed for his gun. Going into a strange squat stance, he quickly braced the forearm of his gunhand against his thigh. The left palm fanned the hammer three times. Two men went down. The third staggered, bringing his gun to bear.

Dave fanned the hammer twice more. The man's gun fired, the bullet going wild. The impact flattened him on his back.

One of the others rolled over, coming up with his gun. Dave straightened up as his left hand moved in a blur. The .45 boomed. The slug hit the gunman's forehead.

"Fair again?" Dave asked of the crowd.

Eager agreement met his ears. People were now pouring out of the Golden Nugget. Doors were opening along the street.

The broad-shouldered Sundeen eyed the corpses sprawled on the street, then spoke to the crowd. "Tell the marshal he can find me at the Sunset Hotel if he has any questions."

By the time everyone had come out of the Golden Nugget, Sundeen was gone. The crowd milled around the bodies, buzzing like bees.

The last man through the batwings was Smith Wayne's henchman Mel Trent. He eyed the scene for a long moment, then spoke to the bartender, who stood next to him. "Which one is Earl Mound?"

Chapter Seventeen

~~~~~~

Under the black canopy of twinkling stars, Maze McLeod and Heath Finley rode away from the hide-out.

Finley expressed his hatred for Anne Braxton time and again. As he nursed his injured ear, he fumed and wished he had killed the woman when he had had the chance. Maze figured that if he took Heath with him, it would solve his problem of sneaking away from the cabin.

Gambling on Finley's hatred for Anne Braxton being stronger than his loyalty to Smith Wayne, Maze took Finley into his confidence. When Heath learned of Maze's plan to kill the woman who had mangled his ear, he was instantly ready to be in on it. Binding his ear close to his head with a cloth, he saddled up.

Anne Braxton stood on the porch beside Lila Moore and watched the three farmers ride out of the yard and dissolve into the night. They had dug Tod's grave for Lila and would be back at ten o'clock in the morning to help her bury him.

Lila Moore had wondered why Paul Healy did not come with the three. They had explained that in stopping by Healy's place, they had found no one home.

Lila's two daughters stood just inside the door.

Turning toward them, the mother said, "All right, girls. Bedtime. I'll take you to the outhouse first."

Stepping into the kitchen, Lila lifted a burning lantern off the table. Another lantern sat on a shelf.

"I'll turn their beds down," said Anne.

"Thank you," returned Lila. "Come, girls."

"Lila . . ." said Anne as the three stepped out on the porch.

"Yes," said the young widow, pausing.

"Why don't you take the rifle with you?"

"Anne, we're only going a hundred feet from the house."

"I know, honey, but it's just a precaution."

Lila shrugged, crossed the kitchen to the Remington .44 that leaned in a corner. Picking it up, she jacked a cartridge into the chamber. Anne Braxton watched the circle of light and the three figures as they moved toward the outhouse. Leaving the door open for their return, she went to the girls' bedroom.

As Anne turned down the covers, she heard the soft sound of a horse blowing. Thinking it was one of the Moore animals, she paid it no mind. She crossed the room to a chest of drawers and pulled out fresh nightgowns. Hearing footsteps in the kitchen, Anne started down the hallway in that direction. She spoke as she walked, "Okay, girls, your beds are all ready—"

Anne Braxton's heart froze. Before her stood the huge man she had seen the night her husband was hanged. There were ugly patches of discolored skin on his face. Behind him stood a smaller man with his hat tilted to one side, exposing a white cloth bound around his head, covering one ear. Both men pointed revolvers at her.

Maze McLeod's eyes were wild. "Have you said your prayers lately, Mrs. Braxton? You're about to die!"

198

Anne had stopped near the cupboard where the supper dishes had been stacked. In desperation, she grabbed a large bowl and flung it at McLeod's face. Whirling, she darted down the hallway. Maze caught her quickly, sinking his powerful fingers into her shoulders.

Frantically, Anne kicked, bit, and scratched. McLeod's big fist met her jaw savagely. The gallant woman went limp and slumped to the floor. McLeod picked her up.

"I'll get the rope," said Finley fiendishly. "We can hang her from the same tree where we hung Moore."

Grabbing the remaining lantern in the kitchen, Finley led the way across the yard toward the giant oak where Tod Moore had died. Suddenly, a feminine voice pierced the darkness. "Put her down!"

Both men turned to see Lila Moore standing in the light of the lantern she had placed on the ground. The Remington .44 was shouldered in place, aimed straight at them. The two girls stood beside her, faces filled with terror.

Heath Finley's revolver was still in his hand. Without hesitation, he raised it and fired. Lila went down, the rifle falling across her stomach. Both children screamed. Heath fired twice more. The girls both fell instantly.

Anne Braxton was coming around as her wrists were lashed behind her back. Finley slung a rope over the limb. The hangman's noose writhed like a serpent in the light of the lantern.

Anne's eyes cleared just as McLeod hoisted her upward and Finley dropped the noose over her head. Terror filled her eyes. She twisted against McLeod's hands and felt the rope burn her neck.

Heath Finley laughed as he yanked on the rope.

Anne felt herself lifted upward. She choked and gagged as her toes barely touched the ground. Then Maze McLeod lent his weight to the rope and the choking woman was raised toward the dark sky.

Finley anchored the end of the rope to the bottom of the giant oak and said, "Let's get out of here!"

"Get on your horse," said McLeod. "I want to make sure the Moore woman is dead.'"

Maze walked to where Lila Moore and her two daughters lay in the soft dust of the yard. The dead children were huddled together. Lila lay as she had fallen, the rifle across her stomach. Maze stood over Lila's inert form, his face fully exposed by the lantern on the ground. The woman's eyes were open, staring emptily into space. Blood darkened her light-colored dress just below her neck on the right side.

A wicked laugh came from deep in McLeod's throat. Finley approached the circle of light, already in the saddle. He was leading McLeod's horse. "Let's go, Maze."

Anne Braxton dangled limp against the noose as Maze stepped in the stirrup and eased his huge frame into the saddle. Kneeing his mount, he moved ahead of Finley.

Neither man saw the eyes of Lila Moore blink . . . and roll back and forth.

The killers were just moving out of the light cast by the two lanterns when a shot lashed through the night and Heath Finley stiffened in the saddle. McLeod drew his revolver and whipped around. Lila Moore was up on one knee. Maze aimed and fired. Lila flopped to her back and rolled over in the dust.

Finley was doubled over, clinging to the saddle-horn. "Heath, can you ride?" asked the big man.

The wounded man coughed and moaned. "I . . . I think so."

"Let me take the reins," said Maze, looping them over the horse's head. "You hang onto the horn."

They rode about two hundred yards when Finley peeled over the saddle and hit the sod. McLeod stopped and slipped from his saddle. It was too dark to see much, but it was not necessary. Heath was dead.

The big man draped the dead outlaw's body over his saddle and wondered what he was going to tell Smith Wayne. He thought about taking the corpse into the mountains, dumping it over a cliff, and leaving the horse to wander. He could tell Smith that Heath just went for a ride and never came back.

A cold prickling crawled over his skin. Smith would not buy it. Especially when the news hit the valley tomorrow of Anne Braxton's being hanged. And the Moore woman and her girls being killed.

Then it struck the big man. Smith had heard Finley say he wished he had killed the Braxton female. Within minutes Maze McLeod had his story completely constructed. Finley had gone off on his own, and Maze went to look for him. It was going to be all right. He was rid of the woman who could identify him. Smith would never have to know that she had seen his face. Yessir, it was going to work out fine. Maze McLeod would still be in Smith Wayne's good graces. He would still be in on the riches when Smith became the cattle king of Del Norte valley.

Sunrise came with Smith Wayne saddled up and supposedly going to spend the day checking waterholes. He rode away from the Box W corral and headed south. Once out of sight he made a wide circle and rode north toward the hideout.

At the same moment, Dan Colt sat at the kitchen table eating breakfast with Laura Lane and the Arnolds.

"Some more coffee?" asked Edith, looking into Dan's pale blue eyes.

Dan nodded, swallowed his last mouthful of scrambled eggs, and held up his mug. "Mmm-hmm," he said. "Time for one more cup, and I'll be on my way."

"How about me riding as far as Moore's place with you, Dan?" asked Laura. "Then when you go on to town, I'll ride back here."

"Nope." The tall man smiled. "I don't want you anywhere alone."

"Oh, Dan Colt," Laura said, flopping an open hand toward him. "No one's going to hurt me. I'm a woman, remember?"

"Of that fact, ma'am, I need no reminders. But we're takin' no chances."

"I'd ride over and bring you back, Laura," put in Ray Arnold, "but the Homesteaders Association is meetin' again this mornin'. I've got to be there. We should be through by nine. I could take you then."

"That's all right, Ray," said Laura with a smile. "I guess there's no reason to make two trips."

"I'll find out from Lila what time they're buryin' Tod," Dan said to Laura. "If it's possible to get into town, see Caley, and get back here in time, I'll do it. If not, I'll head back here and go to town after the buryin'."

Laura walked the tall man to the door. As his muscular frame filled the doorway, she said, "Dan, thank you again for befriending us."

"My pleasure, little lady," he said, touching his hat brim. "See you later."

Del Norte valley was a long, sweeping panorama of green grass, forests, rolling hills, and rock formations of exquisite beauty. Astride the big black gelding Dan Colt drank in its grandeur in the cheerful light of the early morning sun.

202

As he felt the peacefulness of the land, he wondered how violence could erupt in such surroundings. But erupt it had. He wished that it was over, that he could ride away today in quest of his outlaw twin, knowing that Laura Lane, Anne Braxton, and all the home-steading families were safe. But it could not be, until the brutal hangmen were caught and executed.

The big black carried Colt through the gate of the Moore place and angled toward the house. Dan noticed a flock of sparrows gathered on the ground, hopping around in the inch-high grass. He wondered why they were not in the trees around the house as usual.

At first he thought they were feed sacks that had fallen from a wagon. Then he focused on them clearly. Raking the gelding's sides, he galloped to where Lila Moore and the two little girls lay dead in the yard. The horse was still in motion when his boots hit the ground.

Dan felt sick to his stomach. *Who would*—? He shook his head. It was like a feverish nightmare. The girls were tight-knit in a death heap. Lila lay face down, her fingers buried in the dust like claws. Abruptly his line of sight fell to the soft dirt just above Lila's right hand. The dying woman had swept the palm of her hand over the dirt, smoothing it out. Then in distinct letters she had written a message in the dust.

BIG MAN—BURNS ON FACE

Suddenly Dan thought of Anne. The tree where her body hung was behind him. His attention had been so riveted on the three corpses that he had not seen Anne's body as he rode past it.

203

Leaping to his feet, Colt charged toward the house shouting, "Anne! Anne! Anne, where are you?"

The door stood open. He bounded through it, spurs jangling. He ran through the house, pushing open doors and letting them swing when it was evident the rooms were unoccupied. A cold blade of sadness knifed his heart when he saw the two small beds, covers turned down, nightgowns draped over the sides. Anne Braxton was nowhere in the house. *The filthy hangmen have kidnapped her!* he thought.

Anger was welling up inside Dan Colt with heated fury as he headed back outside. *What kind of scaly inhuman beasts would shoot down a woman and two little gir—*

The angry man caught a sharply etched view of Anne Braxton's lifeless form swaying in the morning breeze.

The shock was like a physical blow to Dan Colt . . . a powerful, paralyzing blow. Suddenly his brain was a swirling mass of buzzing noise and confusion. Fire, like a boiling maelstrom of white-hot lava, coursed through his body. For a long, numb moment, he did not move. He just stood there staring with enlarged, disbelieving eyes.

Within seconds Dan was at the tree, eyes fixed on the knotted cords that held Anne's slender wrists behind her back. The face was bloated, purple. They had let her die a slow, tortuous death of strangulation.

His breath was hot with wrath and came in short gasps. Dan felt something like a hot iron run across his forehead and seep burningly into his brain. A wild yell escaped his lips. He had not felt fury like this since the day he had found his own wife brutally murdered.

Suddenly Colt's attention was drawn to a lone rider

coming at full gallop from the gate. It was Sheriff Bill Caley.

Caley's horse plowed dirt as the young lawman pulled rein. Leaping to the ground, he darted his gaze in three directions. First at Anne Braxton's swaying corpse, then at the three bodies on the ground near the house . . . then at Dan Colt's florid face.

"The hangmen," Colt said, teeth bared.

Caley walked to where the rope was tied to the tree. "You get ahold of her, Dan," he said. "I'll let her down."

Dan tenderly laid Anne's body on the ground and released the noose from her neck. Furiously, he slung the rope against the giant oak. It popped like a whip. "I'm gonna find 'em, Bill!" he bellowed. "Those dirty rats are gonna pay!"

"They sure are, Dan," agreed Caley. "They sure are."

"Come over here," said Colt, walking toward Lila Moore's body. "I want you to see somethin'."

The man with the star on his vest followed and stopped beside Dan. Pointing at the message in the dust, Dan said, "Must've been the man Anne threw the tablecloth on."

"Tablecloth?"

"The night they hanged her husband and burned her house down, Anne threw a burning tablecloth on a huge man who came after her. She said the cloth had to have burned his face and head even though he was wearing a hood."

Bill Caley ran his gaze over the soft ground. "Aren't there supposed to be seven or eight hangmen, Dan?"

"We're not sure just how many there are," said Colt. "They may not all go to every hangin'. Laura killed two, but we've no way of knowin' how many are left."

"How many would you say were here last night?" asked Caley, pointing to the hoofprints in the dirt.

Dan studied the prints in the immediate area, then followed them to where the grass began. Walking back, he said, "There were only two, Bill."

Caley rubbed his chin. "This is the first time there've been less than five. Do you suppose it was because they knew all that was here were two women and the children?"

"Probably."

"But why kill *them*?"

"I was going to say to throw a real scare into the homesteaders," replied Dan. "But it may be something else."

"Oh?"

"Before Anne threw the burning tablecloth over the big man's head, she had seen him without his hood. He knew it. I wonder if she didn't have to die because he figured she could identify him." Dan rubbed the back of his neck. "But then . . . why didn't he kill her when they came in here and killed Tod?"

"That's a puzzler," agreed Bill.

"Well, at least we know that the big brute with the burns on his face was one of the two here last night," said Dan. "Tell you one thing," he said, turning his eyes on Caley. "If I find him before you do, he won't need hangin'!"

Bill Caley pulled at his ear. "I hope you find him before I do," he said. "That's unofficial, of course."

"I haven't thought to ask you," said Dan. "What're you doin' out here this mornin'? I was supposed to meet you in town."

"Oh!" said Caley, shaking his head. "A drifter came into town at dawn this mornin'. Said he'd found the bodies of a man and woman in the valley at sunset last night. Their wagon was overturned. Both horses dead. Man and his wife had been shot."

"Who was it?"

"Paul and Myrtle Healy."

Dan swung his fist in the air angrily. "Bill, these bloody killers have got to be stopped before they wipe out every farmer in the valley!"

"The Association is meeting this morning at Hank Carpenter's place," said Caley. "I was heading over there to inform them of the Healy murders." He looked again at the bodies on the ground. "Now I've got to tell them about this."

"What do you think they'll do?" asked the tall man.

"I don't know," said Bill, wiping a hand over his face. "But it could launch a full-scale war. The homesteaders may decide to start killin' all the ranchers in the valley."

"We've got to find the hangmen before that happens."

"You get anything checkin' saddles?" asked the acting sheriff. "I didn't turn up a thing."

"Maybe so, maybe no," replied Colt.

Caley's eyebrows arched. "Tell me."

"Smith Wayne has a black saddle with four ornaments like the one Sheriff Palmer found."

"So do a dozen others."

"But all four of Smith's had been removed and put back on. He tried to tell me it came with them just like they are, but it's an expensive saddle. Top-grade workmanship. Except for the way the ornaments are fastened on."

Caley nodded. "So there's a skunk in the woodpile?"

"I smell one," said Dan. "You hold the farmers off till I can flush him out."

Chapter Eighteen

~~~~~~

Smith Wayne dismounted at the hidden cabin and
eyed Heath Finley's bloody saddle laying on a corner
of the porch. Abruptly big Maze filled the doorway.

"Mornin', boss," said McLeod with sober face.

"How'd all that blood get on Heath's saddle?" demanded Smith.

Clearing his throat, Maze said, "He got shot last
night. He's dead."

Wayne's eyes widened. "Dead?"

"Siddown, boss," said McLeod. "I'll explain it."

Smith cast a gaze toward the north. He wondered if
Trent had been successful in hiring some more men.
He sat down on the porch step, slipped a thin cheroot
from his shirt pocket and lighted it. As the smoke
curled upward, he said, "All right, let's hear it."

"Well, boss," began the huge man, "Heath got to
carryin' on yesterday about that Braxton woman
chewin' his ear. I mean, boss, he was full of vengeance.
Next thing I knew, he's saddlin' up his horse
right after dark. I asked him where he was goin'. He
had a mean look in his eye. Said he was goin' after
Anne Braxton."

Smith blew smoke and listened.

"I know how you dislike killin' wimmin, boss, so I
tried to talk him out of it. Purty soon I could see he
was gonna go kill that woman no matter what I said. I

was gonna grab him and manhandle him, but he threw a gun on me."

The boss tossed another glance northward, then looked back at the big man.

"So he got on his horse and took off," continued Maze. "I stewed around here for a while, then decided maybe I'd better go stop him somehow. Well, I guess I waited a little too long. Apparently he had rode up when Mrs. Moore and her kids and Anne Braxton were out in the yard carryin' lanterns. He shot the Moore woman and the two kids. Then he grabbed Mrs. Braxton and tied her hands and strung her up to the same tree where you hung Moore."

Smith Wayne swore, shaking his head.

"Well," proceeded McLeod, "the Moore woman had been carryin' a rifle. I rode in just as Heath had finished hanging Mrs. Braxton. There was nothin' I could do then, so I told him let's get out of here. But Mrs. Moore wasn't dead. As Heath mounted up, she shot him in the back. There was no choice then, boss. She'd have fired again if I hadn't shot her."

Smith stood up, dropped the cheroot in the dust and stepped on it. "I guess you did what you had to," he said dryly. Eying the rugged north horizon again, he said, "There's somethin' I have to do, too."

"What's that?"

"I gotta get rid of this blond dude, Dan Colt. He's breathin' down my neck and I know he suspects me."

"Whatcha gonna do, boss? Try another ambush?"

"I'm not sure yet," replied Wayne. "But I'm gonna figure out somethin'."

Dan Colt rode back to the Arnold farm and broke the news of Anne Braxton's death to Laura Lane. He then told her of Lila Moore's dying message scratched in the dirt. He stayed with her until Ray Arnold returned from the Homesteaders Association meeting. Bill Caley came with him.

"What's the farmers' frame of mind?" Dan asked Caley.

"They're scared and angry," replied the young lawman. "Talkin' vigilante."

Dan shook his head. "Lot of innocent people will die if they go that route."

"That's what I told them," said Caley. "They agreed to give us a couple more days. If we haven't produced the hangmen by then, they're goin' on a killin' spree of their own."

Ray Arnold spoke up. "Can you blame us, Dan?"

"I don't blame you for bein' angry," replied the tall man, "and I want to put a stop to these killings as much as you do. But declaring war on all the cattlemen is not the answer." Colt's blue eyes narrowed. "I've got a hunch the hangmen are outsiders."

"Really?" asked Arnold.

"Why would outsiders want to drive us from the valley?" asked Laura Lane, eyes red from weeping.

"Let me add to my statement," said Dan. "Outsiders plus *one* cattleman."

"But which ranch owner would it be?" asked Edith Arnold.

"I don't think it's a ranch owner, ma'am," responded Colt. "I think it's a *potential* ranch owner. A man who figures to one day rule the roost in this valley. He would have more roost to rule if the farmers were out of the way."

Bill Caley looked knowingly at Dan. "I've had some thoughts along the same line," he said evenly.

"Who?" asked Laura.

Dan's face was grim. "Smith Wayne."

Ray Arnold's bushy eyebrows arched. "Smith

Wayne is an egotistical bird," he said, "and spoiled rotten. But why do you suspect him?"

Dan explained about Smith's attitude when they met and about the "doctored" saddle. He went on to remind them that the Box W was the biggest spread in the valley. The heirs of Fargo Wayne would be rich. Especially with no homesteaders to use up grazing land.

"But you don't suspect Scott, Dan?" asked Laura.

"Not in the least."

"If Smith's guilty," said Arnold, "he's goin' to a lot of trouble to own only half of the empire."

"I got a feelin' he plans on ownin' *all* of it," said Colt flatly.

Laura's eyes widened. "You mean—"

"A man who'd hang innocent people . . . especially innocent *women* . . . would murder his own brother," breathed the tall man.

"So what do you suggest, Dan?" asked Bill Caley.

"The way to get a skunk out of the woodpile is to rattle the wood," said Dan. "I think we need to put some pressure on Smith." Looking at the lawman, he said, "Bill . . . after the burials, let's you and me ride over to the Box W and ask Smith some more questions."

"Let's do it," agreed Caley.

Smith Wayne sent Maze McLeod deep into the woods to bury Heath Finley. He paced back and forth in front of the cabin, glancing periodically toward the north.

It was nearly eleven o'clock when five riders appeared on the northern hills, silhouetted against the azure sky. Trent had done a good job. Four new men! Smith waited, grinning.

The five horsemen drew up to the cabin and dismounted.

"Howdy, boss," said Trent with a wide smile. "Gotcha some new recruits."

As the riders approached the slender man with the pencil-line mustache, Trent said, "Boys, meet your new boss . . . Smith Wayne." Gesturing toward the four rough-looking gunmen, he said to Wayne, "Earl Mound . . . Vince Forbes . . . Arnie Winkler. These three been ridin' together. I met them in Del Norte."

Smith shook hands with each one.

Gesturing to the fourth one, Trent said, "This here is Zack Robins. We picked him up along the trail. Looked tough and hungry. Deal sounded good to him. So he came along."

Wayne shook hands with Robins, then eyed Earl Mound. "Seems I've heard your name somewheres, Mound. Didn't you brace . . . uh . . . what's his handle . . . uh . . ."

"You thinkin' of Darrel Ramsey?" asked Mound.

"Yeah!" said Smith. "Over in Trinidad?"

"Mmm-hmm," hummed Mound, a smug look etched on his face.

"He was pretty well known," said Smith. "You must be plenty fast."

"I'm learnin'," said Mound in a casual manner.

"He outdrew Spanky Gonzales, too," put in Arnie Winkler. "Shot the Mex dead center in the heart."

Smith Wayne had not heard of Spanky Gonzales, but he nodded and said, "Well, let's get down to business. I assume Mel has given you boys the big picture."

The four hardcases nodded.

"And he gave you some advance money?" queried Smith, swinging his dark eyes toward Trent.

213

"Yessir," replied Mound. "This appears to be the kind of situation we been lookin' for."

"Me, too," put in Zack Robins.

"Good," smiled Wayne. "Mel told you about the hangin's, of course."

All four nodded.

"You're not queasy about hangin' farmers?"

"Nope," said Mound, answering for himself and his two partners.

Wayne looked squarely at Zack Robins. "I'd hang the governor of this here territory of Colorado for this kind of money," said Robins.

The sound of hoofs came from the deep shadows of the trees to the south. Presently Maze McLeod appeared astride his horse and leading Heath Finley's.

"What's goin' on, boss?" asked Mel Trent.

"Maze was just buryin' Heath," said Smith tonelessly.

Wayne filled Trent in on Heath Finley's death . . . according to McLeod's story. Afterward, he gathered the gang together in a half-circle by the porch and said, "Our biggest problem at the moment is a gunslinger that's hangin' around sidin' with the farmers. He's got to be eliminated."

"What's his name?" asked Earl Mound.

"Dan Colt," said Wayne with a hateful sneer.

"*Dan Colt?*" echoed Mound. Instantly he remembered that the fat drummer in Del Norte had thought Dave Sundeen was Colt.

"Dan Colt's dead," put in Robins.

"No, he ain't," spoke up Vince Forbes. "We heard over in Walsenburg that Colt is alive and well. He done some fancy shootin' over in Albuquerque like no dead man can do. You can bet your spurs. Dan Colt is alive and faster'n ever."

"He's helpin' the homesteaders, you say?" Arnie Winkler asked the boss.

"Yep. He's gotta die."

"Let's ambush him," said Mound.

"Tried that," said Smith. "The dude's got eyes in the back of his head. Killed the ambushers I sent to get him." He shook his head. "I haven't figured out what to do yet."

"Colt wouldn't back out of a quickdraw fight," said Earl Mound.

Smith Wayne's eyes lit up. "You willin' to face him?"

Mound's face blanched. Thrusting palms up, he said hastily, "N-no sir! I'm not in his league! I'm still workin' my way up the ladder."

"Be great if we could find some fast hawk who'd challenge him and leave Colt layin' dead in the dust," said Maze McLeod.

"Wait a minute!" exclaimed Earl Mound, snapping his fingers. "I've got just the man!"

"Who?" asked Wayne.

"A gunslingin' dude like you've never seen before in your life! Me and Vince and Arnie saw him last night," Mound said excitedly. Looking at Wayne, he asked, "You ever hear of Wade Bower?"

"Yeah," said Smith. "S'posed to be pretty good."

"This gunslingin' dude killed Bower with ease. Then Bower's three pals went after him like vultures after dead meat. He fanned his two guns faster'n you could blink. Left 'em all dead in the street."

"You think he'd do it?" asked Wayne. "Challenge Colt, I mean?"

"We can try," replied Mound. "How much you willin' to pay?"

Smith thought for a moment. Whatever the cost, it would be worth it to be rid of Colt. "Tell you what,

215

Earl. Are you willin' to ride back to Del Norte and talk to him?"

"Sure, boss."

"Tell him that your boss sent you. He's got this gun-slinger that needs eliminatin'. Tell him he'll get ten thousand dollars. I'll meet him at the Yellow Rose Saloon in Alamosa at nine o'clock tomorrow mornin'. At that time I'll give him half of it. He'll collect the other half when he does his job."

"Shall I tell him he'll be facin' Dan Colt?" queried Mound.

Smith rubbed his chin. "Uh . . . no. Tell him he will get the details when we meet at the Yellow Rose."

"I'm sure the sound of ten thousand dollars will put him in the Yellow Rose at nine in the morning," Mound said, smiling.

"What's this dude's name?" asked Wayne.

"Dave Sundeen."

"Seems like that name has run through my ears a time or two," said Smith. "Has a familiar ring to it."

"He's greased lightnin'," said Mound.

"You tell Sundeen that your boss's name is Mr. Smith. Tell him to sit at a table. I'll find him. Now what does he look like?"

"Real tall," said Earl. "Well-built. 'Bout thirty. Blond. You can't miss him."

Smith Wayne laughed. "Really?"

"Yessir," answered Mound, blinking. "What's so funny?"

Wayne spit in the dirt. "You could just as easily have been describing Dan Colt."

Earl laughed. "You're kidding!"

"No," chuckled Smith. "I'm serious."

"Funny thing," said Mound, looking at Forbes and Winkler. "At the saloon last night we were playin' poker with Sundeen and this sweaty little fat man comes up to him and calls him Dan Colt."

"I guess they must have some resemblance, huh?" Smith said and laughed. Getting serious again, he said, "Mel, I want you and Maze to ride into Alamosa tonight. Grab that kid sheriff. He sleeps at the jail. Wake him up about an hour before dawn. Head this way with him. Get him far enough away from town and send him to be with the angels. Understand?"

"Yes." Trent nodded.

"Then hightail it back here by sunup so I'll know it's done. Colt will be at the Arnold place tonight, I'm sure. He's had Maze's description. Maze can't go. So Mel, you will go to Colt in the mornin' and tell him that Bill Caley sent you. He's got some new evidence on the hangmen and will be waiting at the Yellow Rose. Be sure you time it so that Colt will arrive in Alamosa about nine thirty."

"Okay, boss," nodded Trent. "But what if he ain't at Arnold's place?"

"Wherever that Lane widow is, he'll be near," grinned Wayne coldly. "Especially since Finley hanged the Braxton woman. You get him to the Yellow Rose on time, hear me?"

"I'll do it, boss," said Trent, squaring his bristly jaw.

Smith Wayne laughed heartily. "Tomorrow will be interesting. I'm going to bring Dan Colt and Dave Sundeen together. Face to face. Gun to gun!"

Chapter Nineteen

Dave Sundeen lay on the bed in his hotel room, wondering if he could get through the coming evening without a gunfight. Killing four men last night had interrupted his poker game. His cash reserves were getting progressively lower. He did not want to pull a robbery. Things were going smoothly right now with the law. A holdup would mean riding hard again.

The setting sun cast slanted orange rays through the window. A light breeze toyed with the curtains. Footsteps sounded in the hallway, then a knock at his door.

The tall man swung his boots over the edge of the bed and stood up. Slipping one of the Colts from the holsters that hung on the bedpost, he moved toward the door. "Who is it?" he called.

"Earl Mound, Dave," came a muffled voice. "We played poker together last night."

The lock rattled as Sundeen turned the key. He pulled open the door. "Come in, Earl," he said. "Sit down."

As Dave closed the door, Mound took a seat on the only chair. Sundeen sat on the bed, holding the .45.

"You're not going to shoot me, are you?" asked Earl, smiling.

"Oh," said Dave, suddenly realizing the gun was still in his hand. "Not at the moment." He reached over and dropped the gun into the holster. Setting his candid blue eyes on the young gunfighter, he said, "I suppose you want me to teach you how to fan a gun."

"Uh . . . no," Mound said with a smile. "At least not today."

"Usually when the young hopefuls see me use it, they want to enroll in the Sundeen School of Gunfanning right away."

"No, that's not it," said Mound.

"If you need to borrow some money," said Dave, palms upward, "I can't do anything for you. I'm a little financially embarrassed myself right now."

"On the contrary," said Earl. "I've come to offer you ten thousand dollars."

Sundeen eyed him suspiciously. "You *what*?"

"Well, not me, actually . . . but I work for a man named Smith."

Dave chuckled. "Smith? Now what's the punchline?"

"It's no joke, Dave. My boss has a problem, and I told him about you. He needs a man who can handle guns like you do."

Sundeen's ears perked up. "Now you're rakin' the yard near my tree. Go ahead."

"There's a fancy gunslick who's standin' in the way of my boss makin' a whole lot of money. He has authorized me to offer you ten thousand dollars to ride to Alamosa and challenge this dude."

"That's all there is to it?"

"Yep. He'll pay you five thousand earnest money and the other five thousand right after you kill the man."

"I *did* hear you right," said Dave. "You did say *challenge* him."

"Yessir."

"Good. I don't murder people."

"After what I saw last night, I know you can take this dude," said Mound with confidence.

"What's his name?"

"The boss said he'd tell you that when he gives you the earnest money. You are to be at the Yellow Rose Saloon in Alamosa at nine o'clock in the mornin'. The boss will meet you there. He's already got the wheels rollin' to lure this gunslick to the Yellow Rose about nine thirty."

"You mean before you return with the message of what takes place here?"

"Yep."

"Now just what happens if I don't take the job?" Dave asked, then pursed his lips.

"The boss was sure you would," grinned Earl.

Dave ran his fingers through his heavy blond mustache. "This dude must be a top gun."

Earl's brow furrowed. "Why do you say that?"

"If you felt he was in *your* class, *you* would be going after the ten thousand. Right?"

Mound's face flushed. "Yeah, guess so," he said, dipping his chin. "You takin' the job?"

"Yeah. I'll be at the Yellow Rose at nine o'clock sharp. How will I know this Smith?"

"You just take a seat at one of the tables," said Mound, grinning. "He'll find you."

The sun had dropped behind the mountains and dusk was lingering as Dan Colt and Bill Caley rode through the impressive Spanish-style gate of the Box W.

Smoke threaded skyward from the chimney of the bunkhouse and that of the big stuccoed house. Scott Wayne came out of the barn and stood talking to a cowhand. His eyes eventually fell on the two riders approaching. He quickly finished his conversation and walked toward the riders.

"Evenin', Mr. Colt . . . Sheriff," he said pleasantly. The riders drew rein.

"Howdy, Scott," said Caley.

"Good evenin', Scott," Colt said with a smile.

"You gentlemen seem to like it here," mused Scott.

"A few questions to ask your brother," said Caley.

Dan saw something flash into Scott Wayne's eyes. He could not think of a word for it, but something strange was there.

"He just rode in," said Scott advisedly. "He's at the barn."

"Thanks," said Caley.

As both riders nudged their horses toward the barn, Scott followed. Smith came out of the barn just as Colt and Caley were dismounting. Anger touched his dark eyes. His face hardened and his mouth drew into a grim line.

"Need to talk to you, Smith," said Caley.

Temper flared in Smith Wayne. Face flushed, he said, "What is this, Caley? You think I hung those poor homesteaders? Is that it?"

"I didn't say that," spoke Bill Caley softly. "But can you account for your whereabouts at the time Russ Morton and Ed Cleaver were murdered?"

Smith cursed. "No, and neither can you. That was a couple of months ago. Who can remember where they were at a particular time on a particular night that long ago?"

"All right," sighed Caley, tilting his hat to the back of his head. "How about within the last few days? Where were you Monday night when Vance Lane was murdered?"

Smith Wayne forced a veneer of calm. Inside, he churned like a whirlpool. "Uh . . . let's see. Uh . . ."

"That's the night of the storm," put in Dan Colt.

Dan saw a glint of hatred in Smith's eyes, then it quickly disappeared.

"Uh . . . I was in my room from early evening on," said Smith, speeding up the last few words.

Looking at Scott, Caley said, "Can you verify that?"

"I can verify that Smith *went* to his room immediately after that," replied Scott. "But I cannot say that he *stayed* there."

"Well, I can!" came the voice of Fargo Wayne. Moving hastily into the group, the elder Wayne scanned the faces of Dan Colt and Bill Caley. "What is the problem, gentlemen?"

"No problem, Mr. Wayne," answered Dan. "The sheriff, here, was just doing some routine questioning."

Smith hawked and spat. "Routine, nothin'! You're doggin' me for some reason!"

Eying Fargo narrowly, Billy Caley said, "Was Smith home all night Wednesday night, Fargo?"

Fargo's face formed a blank look.

"That's the night Tod Moore was hanged," put in Dan Colt.

"He sure was!" snapped the silver-haired man. "He was here all night!"

Scott threw a glance at Smith. The latter glared at his brother for a brief moment, then looked away.

"You're positive of that, Fargo?" asked Caley.

"I know when my boys come and go," said Fargo emphatically.

"Okay," said Caley. "Thanks for the information." Turning toward the tall man, he said, "Let's go, Dan."

As the two men mounted, Caley looked at the elder Wayne.

"Don't mean to rile you, Fargo. But I must leave no stone unturned."

"You haven't riled me, Bill," said Wayne with a weak smile. "It's just rubbin' my nerves sore . . . all this hangin' business."

"I guess you heard about last night's hangin'," said Dan with a raw edge to his voice.

"No," said Fargo.

"This time they hung a *woman*." Colt's jaw corded.

Fargo Wayne's mouth fell open. "Who?"

"Anne Braxton," said Dan, his eyes steady and cold in the gathering dusk. "They also shot Lila Moore and her two little girls."

"Dead?" asked Fargo.

"We buried them this mornin'."

Fargo swore. "This has got to stop!" he said with conviction.

"That's what we're workin' on," said Bill Caley. "See you later."

Smith Wayne's hard eyes followed them as they rode away.

Out of hearing distance, Bill Caley said, "I think we shook the woodpile, Dan."

"I hope the skunk surfaces before the homesteaders start the war," said Colt.

"Wish I knew where the hangmen were going to strike next, Dan," Caley said.

"Me, too," said the tall man. "I'd love to be there waitin' for 'em."

"You think the Arnolds would mind if I stayed at their place tonight?" asked the acting sheriff. "I want to look around the Moore yard some more in the mornin'."

"There's room for another yokel on the floor," chuckled Colt.

As the two riders faded into the gloom, Smith Wayne turned toward the house and said, "I'm hungry. Let's eat."

224

Conversation was at a minimun during the meal. It disturbed Scott Wayne that his father had told Caley and Colt that Smith was on the place all night Wednesday. Monday, too, for that matter. Fargo, in blind devotion to his spit and image, was taking Smith's side when he knew very well Smith could leave the place without his knowledge.

Scott could not say if his brother had left the house Monday night. But he had caught him red-handed Wednesday night. If Scott's suspicions were true, Smith had a gang of cutthroats stashed in a hideout somewhere. It was, no doubt, the gang that did the killing at the Moore farm last night. Smith had been in his room and Scott had stayed awake to watch.

Smith broke the silence as the meal was finished. "Dad," he said in that nauseating tone that made Scott sick, "I need to talk with you in the den if we could."

"Of course, son," Fargo said, smiling.

The elder son watched them walk from the dining room and disappear down the hall. When they were out of earshot, he moved down another hall toward the bedrooms.

In the den, Smith said, "Dad, I appreciate your vouching for me this evenin'."

"You're my son," said Fargo. "I can't let all these groundless suspicions throw a load on your shoulders." His smile faded away. "If I thought you were in on these brutal killings, I—"

"Oh, Dad!" Smith said, laughing. He put his arms around Fargo. "You know your little boy wouldn't be a part of an awful thing like that!"

The silver-haired father hugged his son and laughed with him. "What did you want to see me about?" he asked tenderly.

"Well . . . uh . . . Dad . . . I *was* gone till late

Wednesday night. I was in town . . . uh . . . playin'
a little poker . . . and—"

"How much?" asked Fargo, moving behind his desk
to the safe.

"Well," chuckled Smith, "I signed an IOU for ten
thousand."

Without blinking, the senior Wayne ran the combination and pulled open the heavy door. Presently, he
extended a neatly banded pack of hundred-dollar bills
to his favored offspring. Smiling, he said, "Good thing
both of you boys don't play poker. I'd have to hock
the herds to keep you out of trouble!"

Fargo would have preferred that Smith stay away
from the gambling establishments, but at least the boy
never drank. For this he was thankful.

Smith hugged his father and pecked his cheek.
"Thank you, Dad," he cooed sweetly.

Feeling smug and satisfied, Smith Wayne left his father in the den and moved through the house to his
room. He hummed a happy tune as he stepped into
the dark room and closed the door. Fumbling momentarily at the dresser, he struck a match and touched
the flame to the lantern wick. He gasped at the sight
of Scott, who was seated in the corner.

"Scott!" Smith bellowed in a hoarse whisper. "One
of these times I—"

"If you break that man's heart," said Scott heatedly,
"I'm gonna wring your puny neck!"

"Now, look—"

"You got him lyin' for you now," butted in the angry brother. "You corrupt everything you touch."

"Get outta my room!"

"You lied to me, Smith," hissed Scott.

"What're you talkin' about?"

"You weren't with Laura Lane Wednesday night."

"I was too! I—"

"Dan Colt is stayin' at the Arnold's. Mrs. Arnold was sick all night long. Laura never left her side."

Smith swore, face blazing. "You butt out, big brother! Do you hear me? Butt out of my business!"

"I didn't tell Colt the real reason why I asked if Laura had any visitors. You want me to?"

Suddenly Smith Wayne's features softened. "Look, Scott," he said placatingly, "please don't think hard of me. I was ashamed to tell you the truth."

"And that is?"

"I was in town gambling Wednesday night. Got in pretty deep."

"How much did Dad just fork over?" Scott asked with disgust.

Smith reached inside his double-breasted shirt and produced the pack of bills. "Ten thousand."

Scott walked to the door, pulled it open, and said, "If you break his heart, you have my solemn promise. I'll beat you to a pulp!"

Chapter Twenty

~~~~~~

The sun's rays coming through the east window awakened Ray Arnold and Dan Colt. Lifting his head and blinking, Dan looked toward the spot on the floor where Bill Caley had slept. He was gone.

Dan rolled out of the bedroll and put on his pants. His eye caught a piece of paper on the table. A pencil stub lay on top of it. Lifting the paper, he read the message.

Dan—

Took off at first light. Wanted to get an early start. Am going to the Moore farm, then back to town.

Hope our skunk comes out of the woodpile today. Why don't you ride over to the Box W and talk to Scott Wayne alone. I think he knows more than he is telling us.

See you later.

Bill

At breakfast, Laura Lane sipped coffee and read Caley's note. "You really think Smith is one of the hangmen, Dan?" she asked, setting her large brown eyes on his angular face.

"I do," Dan replied around a mouthful of biscuit. Swallowing and washing it down with coffee, he added, "I think he's more than just one of them. I think he's the leader."

"He'd be in a good position to do a thing like that," put in Arnold. "I understand he gives account to nobody where he goes, or when. It's common knowledge the old man gives him all the money he needs."

"But if Smith has a gang stashed somewhere in this valley, it seems to me it would take a lot of money to keep them around," said Edith. "Would Fargo shell out that kind of money to Smith?"

"Don't know," said Dan. "But mark my word. Smith is the leader of the hangmen."

Laura's face twisted. "I hope you and Bill nail him soon."

"I'll ride over to the Box W in a couple of hours. I'd like to get there when Smith is gone. I agree with Bill. I think Scott knows more than he's tellin'."

As Smith Wayne rode eastward from the ranch house at sunup, a pair of suspicious eyes watched him through a bedroom window. The younger brother announced he would be gone all day. He would ride into Alamosa and pay his gambling debt, then check the water holes along the east ridge.

Once out of sight of the ranch buildings, he cut north and beelined for the hideout.

On his heels, unseen and undetected . . . was Scott Wayne.

Arriving at the hidden cabin, Smith greeted Mound, Forbes, Robins, and Winkler, who sat lazily on the porch in the morning sun. He swung his gaze toward the rope corral at the edge of the trees. Trent and McLeod's horses were missing.

With furrowed brow, he said, "Those two aren't back yet?"

"We ain't seen hide nor hair of 'em, boss." said Earl Mound.

Wayne swore. "They should've had Caley dead and been back here by now." Pulling the gold watch given to him by his father from his vest pocket, he noted the time. *Seven twenty.* He would have to ride away from the hideout within the next twenty minutes in order to meet the blond gunslinger by nine o'clock. Dan Colt would have to receive the bogus message by eight o'clock, or he would not be at the Yellow Rose in time to face Dave Sundeen.

Scott hid among the trees and watched his brother pace nervously back and forth in front of the cabin. His suspicions were confirmed. Though he could only pick up a few of the words, there was no question that Smith was the leader of the hard-featured men who sat on the porch.

Abruptly from the forest to the east, two more riders appeared. Smith met them with fury. Scott moved in closer, leaving his horse back in the dense thicket. He peered around a tree near the rope corral.

"Whattya mean he wasn't there all night?" Scott heard Smith say.

"I can't have that stupid Caley buttin' in on the shootout!"

"But boss," said the biggest man, "we can't help—"

"Don't give me any lip, Maze!" raged Smith. "You were supposed to kill that kid sheriff! You bungled it! Now I'm gonna have to worry about him showin' up!"

Scott Wayne could not believe his ears. He knew his brother was greedy and aspiring . . . but Smith was talking about *murder.* Then it all came clear as Smith continued his railing at the huge man . . .

"It's just like when I left you here to watch my old man's cattle that day, Maze. When the buyers came, you'd let 'em stray! Or the night we hung Roy Braxton. You let that little pint-sized woman nearly burn—"

"Boss!" cut in Mel Trent. He had heard one of the horses at the rope corral nicker. Scott Wayne pulled his head back when the nicker came, but not in time to escape Trent's eye. Mel's gun was out. "We got company."

Smith whirled in the midst of his raving as Trent ran toward the tree where Scott hid. The others followed. Scott knew he could not take on that many men, nor outrun their bullets. Casually he stepped around the tree, gun in holster.

"Gitcher hands up!" barked Trent.

As Scott slowly lifted his hands skyward, Smith's eyes focused on his face. His jaw slacked.

"We got a spy, boss!" bellowed Maze McLeod, glad for the sudden interruption in his scathing.

"It's my stupid brother," snarled Smith.

Scott stepped up and faced Smith. "So *you've* been stealing the Box W cattle. And you've been murdering the homesteaders." There was cold loathing in Scott's eyes. "You gonna kill me, too, little brother? Better think twice before you do. You've never taken time to read Dad's will. If either of us dies before he does, it's set up that the dead brother's children receive their father's inheritance. Dad has been expecting us to get married and raise families. If the dead brother has no children, then his inheritance goes to the children of the surviving brother. Dad has made provision for the grandchildren he hopes to have."

Smith stood motionless, digesting what he had just heard.

"So either way," said Scott, stepping close, "you only get forty percent. Killing me won't gain you a thing . . . except a rope around your neck." Scott's breath was hot.

The big man had taken Scott's gun and each man in the group had holstered his own. The elder brother's eyes were like red-hot coals.

Without taking his defiant gaze from Scott's face, Smith spoke from the side of his mouth. "Mel, get on your horse and run your errand. Colt must be at the Yellow Rose by nine thirty."

"You better get goin' yourself, boss," warned Trent. "Or you won't be there at nine to meet Sundeen."

"I'm leavin' in about one minute," said Smith, still glaring into Scott's eyes. "You git!"

Mel Trent mounted and galloped away.

"I told you what I'd do if you broke Dad's heart," rasped Scott. His fist flashed and caught Smith on the cheekbone.

As Smith went down, Scott piled on him like an angry dog, fists flailing. The five outlaws pulled guns, but found them useless. There was no way to fire without a chance of hitting Smith.

The brothers rolled, kicked, and punched wildly. From inside of Smith's shirt, hundred-dollar bills came flying and scattering in the breeze. Men began chasing them and gathering them up.

It was evident that Smith was getting the worst of the fight. His gun slipped from the holster into the dirt. Soon his arms lost their strength. Scott stood up and hoisted him to his feet. A savage blow sent him reeling, rolling in the dust.

As the elder brother went after him again, Earl Mound shouted, "Hold it right there, cowboy!"

Scott checked himself and turned to face Mound's dark-eyed muzzle. "This is family business, Buster," lashed Scott. "You butt out!"

"You touch him again, I'll bore you," rasped Mound.

233

Smith struggled to his feet, aided by big Maze McLeod, and holstered his dusty gun. He was sleeving blood from his face when Scott gave him a disgusted look and turned away. As Scott walked toward the trees, Smith whipped out his gun and fired.

The slug hit Scott in the left shoulder. He staggered and turned around, eyes wild. Smith aimed carefully and fired again. The slug entered his chest. Scott Wayne flopped to his back, eyes glazing and empty.

Smith studied his dead brother for a long moment. Holstering the gun, he said, "Maze, can you do something right for a change?"

"Sure, boss," breathed McLeod eagerly.

"My brother's horse will be back there in the trees somewhere. Put his stinkin' corpse on him and lead him down to those two haystacks about a half mile from the house."

"Yeah?"

"Turn him loose. From there, he'll carry the corpse to the house."

"Okay, boss."

"Maze . . ."

"Yeah?"

"Take one of the hangmen's hoods and plant it on him. Let 'em think some sodbuster shot him. It'll puzzle old Fargo, but it'll do the old goat good to think Scott was one of the hangmen."

"Okay, boss," said big Maze, smiling.

"Now don't botch it, Maze," clipped Smith tightly.

"I won't, boss," said the huge man. "I won't."

Zack Robins placed the crumpled hundred-dollar bills in Smith's hand. He jammed them in his shirt and strode to his horse.

"You want we should wait here, boss?" asked Earl Mound.

234

"Yeah," answered young Wayne, without turning around. Once in the saddle, he set his dark, evil eyes on the clustered group. "If this Sundeen-Colt shootout works, we're about ready to take over the whole valley. As soon as I can talk my old man into changin' the will, I'll kill him. We'll drive the rest of the sodbusters out and get filthy rich."

Smith pulled his hat tight. "I want you boys right here in case anything goes wrong in the shootout. Sit tight. I'll be back shortly." With that he raked the black gelding's sides and darted eastward.

Worry tugged at Smith Wayne's mind. He would have to push his horse hard. Even then, he might not reach Alamosa before Dan Colt did. Colt did not have as far to ride. Sundeen would not even know it was Colt he was supposed to kill.

"No," said Ray Arnold to the stranger. "Dan isn't here. He rode off to the Box W ranch about twenty-five or thirty minutes ago."

"I'm new in these parts, Mr. Arnold," said Mel Trent. "Which way is the Box W?"

Pointing due east, Arnold said, "Take a straight line that way. You can't miss it. Big iron and stone gate. Spanish-style. Box W on top."

"Thanks," said Trent, stepping off the porch.

Calling after him, Arnold said, "Is there a message I should give Dan if somehow you miss him and he comes back here?"

"Uh . . . yeah . . ." replied Trent. "Sheriff Caley sent me to tell Colt that he has some new evidence on the hangmen. He's got business to tend to in town. He was workin' hard at it when I left. Said to tell Colt to meet him at the Yellow Rose at nine thirty. I guess a little later would be all right."

Ray Arnold nodded and turned toward the women, who stood directly behind him.

As he galloped eastward, Mel Trent assured himself that even if Dan Colt was late, Smith would detain Sundeen till Colt showed up. With ten thousand dollars in the offing, Sundeen would no doubt be glad to hang around for a while.

Laura Lane eyed Ray Arnold quizzically. "Did I hear him correctly?" she asked.

"What's that?"

"Did he say that Bill was in town when he left?"

"Yep."

"Impossible," said Laura, eying the clock on the wall.

Arnold's eyes widened.

"She's right," put in Edith.

Laura stepped to the table and palmed Caley's note. "Bill says he left at first light. There's no way he could do that, ride to Moore's place, look around . . . and have been in Alamosa when that man left town."

"Somethin's wrong," said Arnold, shaking his head.

"It's some kind of a trap!" Laura said hastily and darted out the door. "I've got to beat that man to the Box W! I've got to warn Dan!"

Ray Arnold was on her heels. "Laura, you can't go off alone!" he exclaimed.

"Which is your fastest horse, Ray?" she asked, opening the corral gate.

"The red roan, honey, but you'll never have time to saddle him and—"

"Not going to saddle him," she said, clipping each word. "I learned to ride bareback last Monday night."

Ray Arnold wrung his hands as Laura sidled smoothly up to the roan. The horse lifted his head and laid back his ears. "Take it easy, boy," she said softly.

With one hand she lifted her skirt to her knees. In a single bound she was on his back. The other horses gave her a wide berth as she steered the roan out the gate.

Ray was shouting her name as she galloped away. He hurriedly went for a saddle.

Laura's long, dark hair fluttered in the wind as the big horse carried her like a feather across the valley. Dan would be somewhere near the buildings. Laura veered the horse slightly south. She would approach the Box W from a southerly angle. She must get to Dan before the rider did.

The black gelding's sides were heaving rapidly as Smith Wayne rode into Alamosa. Halting the tired animal at the hitching rail in front of the Yellow Rose Saloon, he dismounted stiffly and wrapped the reins around the rail. Three other horses stood near. He yanked the gold watch from his vest pocket. *Nine twenty-five.*

Inside the saloon, the bartender looked up at the tall blond man with the ice-blue eyes. "I don't know what Mr. Smith it might have been, stranger," he said apologetically, "and I don't know an Earl Mound."

Disgustedly, Dave Sundeen eyed the big roman-numeraled clock on the wall and walked back to the table where he had been seated for the last half hour. Maybe something came up. Maybe this Mr. Smith had been delayed.

A dark thought seeped into his brain. *Or could it be this was some kind of hoax?* Ten thousand dollars sounded like a lot of money to take out one dude. Dave would wait till ten o'clock. If Mr. Smith did not show up by then, he would charge it off as a ruse and ride out.

Smith Wayne eased up to the batwings and looked inside. His eyes roamed the room. Two dirty cowboys sat at a table near the bar. When his gaze lined on the face of the only other occupant, a cold, hard ball of ice formed instantly in Smith's stomach. *Dan Colt!*

Smith jerked his head back.

Something had gone awry. Somehow Mel had reached Colt in time. In fact, if Colt had been sitting there very long, he was *early*. Where was Sundeen? His mind went in a whirl. Maybe they had already shot it out. If so, Sundeen was dead.

Spotting a man across the street, he dashed toward him. "Hey, Steve!"

The man stopped. "Howdy, Smith."

"Steve, have you been in town all mornin'?"

"Sure have," the man smiled. "Why?"

"Has there been a gunfight this mornin'?"

"Nope. Sure ain't. All's quiet."

Leaving the man to wonder, he ran back to the Yellow Rose and peered in again. The tall, blond man had a heavy look of impatience on his face. Smith eyed the bartender, who was looking casually toward the door. He caught the bartender's attention with a wave of his hand. Quickly he placed a vertical index finger over his lips, then beckoned with the other hand.

The bartender slipped around the end of the bar and pushed through the batwings. Smith whispered, "Al, how long's the big blond dude been here?"

The barman's eyes widened. A settled look formed on his face as of a man who had just solved a perplexing mystery. "Since before nine o'clock."

Smith could not believe his ears. How was it possible? There was no way that Colt could have done it. Not as late as Mel Trent left the cabin. Fargo Wayne's treacherous son was hopelessly confused.

Then came the words that turned his brain into a total fog of bafflement.

"He's been waitin' for you, Smith. Seems quite perturbed."

Slowly the bartender's words collected in the fog. *If Colt is waiting for me, he knows the plan. He'll gun me down like a rabid dog! What in the world could have happened? Where's Dave Sundeen?*

"Don't tell him I'm here, Al," gasped Smith. "I'll explain later." With that, he vaulted into the saddle and galloped away.

Seventeen minutes later, Dave Sundeen left the Yellow Rose and mounted his horse. Mumbling under his breath, he rode out of town.

Chapter Twenty-One

Dan Colt was told by the Box W's cook that Scott Wayne was gone. He had ridden out not long after Smith had headed for town. Thanking the cook for the information, he decided to ride on into town and see if Bill had turned up anything concrete at the Moore place.

He was just leaving the gate of the Box W when a rider came galloping toward him from the west, waving wildly. He drew rein and waited. The horse skidded to a stop.

"You're Dan Colt, aren't you?" asked Mel Trent.

"Yep," replied the man on the black.

"Sheriff Caley sent me. He needs to see you right away. I mean *pronto*. He has some new information for you about the hangings. He'll be at the Yellow Rose Saloon." Trent removed his hat and sleeved sweat from his brow. "My horse is winded. You go ahead. I'll follow after he cools off."

He did not look like the type of man Bill Caley would ask to do *anything*, but Dan figured Bill must have grabbed the first messenger he could get. Apparently the acting sheriff had sent him from somewhere in the valley, then headed for town.

"Right," said Colt. Spurring the black, he bounded across the open range, then disappeared in the forest to the east.

* * *

Laura Lane rode out of the trees slightly south of the Box W buildings and pulled hard on the horse's mane. The roan stopped immediately. North of the buildings at the big gate was the strange rider talking to Dan Colt.

It had taken Laura longer to reach the Box W than she had hoped. Suddenly Colt spurred his horse and galloped eastward. There was nothing to do now but ride hard for Dan. Goading the roan and slapping his rump, she put him into a full lope. "Dan!" she screamed. "Dan!"

Colt did not hear Laura calling him. But Mel Trent did. Dan was already out of sight when Trent aimed his horse in a direct line to intercept the red roan.

Laura saw him coming. A feeling of helplessness washed over her.

Seeing that the woman was barebacked without even a bridle, Mel Trent deliberately steered his mount directly into the roan's face. Both horses shied. Trent held tight to his saddle, staying aboard. Laura lost her hold and landed in a heap on the ground.

Trent slipped from the saddle as Laura gained her feet, unhurt.

"Now, Mrs. Lane," the hard-faced man said evenly, "you're going with me. Conscious or unconscious. Choice is yours." The look in his eye told Laura he meant business.

Her face was deathly pale, her eyes wide with fear. "All right," she said. "I won't give you any trouble."

Placing the tiny woman in his saddle, the outlaw sat behind her and headed north for the hideout.

Laura questioned Trent along the way. "What's going to happen to Dan Colt?"

"He's gonna die," the outlaw laughed wickedly.

"Ambush?" queried Laura.

"Nope. Fast-draw shootout."

"You mean with one man?"

"Yeah, lady," chuckled Trent. "One cool, lightning-fast dude who'll leave your Danny boy in a pool of his own blood." He laughed hoarsely. "You shoulda kissed him good-bye, honey."

Laura's back stiffened. "There isn't a man alive who can outdraw Dan Colt."

Trent spit out of the side of his mouth. "This one can."

"You mean Smith Wayne hired a gunfighter to come to Alamosa and kill Dan?"

Laughing again, he said, "Yes ma'am, he shore did! He—" Mel Trent swallowed hard. "How'd you know about Smith?"

"I didn't," rasped Laura. "I was only guessing. But I know it now."

"Lotta good it'll do you," Trent said coldly.

Laura said no more to the outlaw. His last words gripped her heart like a cold hand.

When they reached the hideout, Maze McLeod had just returned from sending Scott's corpse back to the Box W. Earl Mound and his two friends, plus Zack Robins, sat around the porch. All five outlaws stood to their feet as Trent pulled his horse to a halt.

"Wowee!" exclaimed Zack Dobins, eyes bulging. "I don't know where you got that one, but rush right back and git me one jist like her!"

Laura flashed a look of pure disgust. Trent pushed himself over the horse's rump and landed flat-footed. Stepping to the animal's left side, he raised both hands. "Lemme help you down."

"I'll get off by myself," Laura retorted crisply.

243

"How did this happen, Mel?" asked Maze McLeod, recognizing Laura.

Her brown eyes fell on McLeod's burn-splotched face . . . and took in his size. As Trent gave his explanation, Laura thought of Lila Moore's dying message in the dust. This vile monster was the fiend who had hanged Anne Braxton and murdered the Moore children and their mother. A burning paroxysm of hatred welled up in Laura Lane. She scanned the faces of the motley group. These men, at least some of them, had murdered Vance. These men and *Smith Wayne*.

Laura was looking for a man with a chewed ear, when Smith Wayne bolted out of the forest, his black gelding shiny with sweat. Wayne dismounted, not bothering to tether the animal. His dark eyes were riveted on Laura.

Swearing profusely, Smith said in anger, "Who brought her here?"

"I did, boss," spoke up Mel Trent.

"What for?" lashed Wayne.

"Well—"

Before Trent could say another word, Smith said, "Never mind! We'll talk about it later. We got more important matters right now!"

It dawned on Mel that Smith was back too soon to have stayed in Alamosa for the shootout. Before he could phrase his question, the irate boss answered it.

"Sundeen never showed up!" hissed Wayne with fury. "And I don't know how he did it, but Colt got to the Yellow Rose before nine o'clock!"

While those words were slowly oozing into Mel Trent's brain, Laura pushed back enough fear to say, "Smith, did I hear you say Sundeen?"

Wayne eyed her coldly without answering.

"Dave Sundeen?" continued Laura.

"So what?" lashed Smith.

"You hired Dave Sundeen to kill Dan Colt in a shootout?"

If things had not been so serious, Laura Lane would have laughed. Instantly she understood Smith's confusion. He had taken Dave Sundeen for Dan Colt. There was no way Dan could have made it from the Box W to Alamosa before nine o'clock. It had to have been nearly that time when he left.

Mel Trent spoke. "Boss, Dan Colt was not at the Yellow Rose before no nine o'clock."

Smith Wayne was already beyond the edge of reason. Panic gripped him. His plan for Dan Colt to be shot to death by Dave Sundeen had gone askew. Colt was still alive and stood as a threatening barrier between Smith and his dream of riches. Fury ran like liquid fire in his veins. Ignoring Trent's statement, he turned on Earl Mound.

"Earl!" bellowed Wayne, eyes bulging. "Your hotshot gunfighter yellow-bellied out!"

Mound hunched his shoulders, extending palms upward. "He told me he'd be there. I don't und—"

Mel Trent cut in doggedly. "Boss, I tell you Dan Colt was not at the Yellow Rose anywhere near nine o'clock."

Smith's eyes flashed with fiery rage. Anger burned with feverish heat within him. It greased his face with sweat. His teeth protruded like fangs. "Trent, you callin' me a liar?" he breathed. "I saw Dan Colt sittin' at a table in the saloon. Al Bunker even told me Colt had been askin' for me!"

Retaliating fury surfaced in Mel Trent. Pointing an accusing finger at young Wayne, he roared, "You're callin' *me* a liar! I said Colt could not have been at that saloon before nine o'clock. I found him at the Box

W and gave him the message you told me to. It was nearly nine o'clock then!"

Wayne's lips were blue. "I'm lyin', then. Is that what you're sayin'?"

Trent met Wayne's hot glare eye to eye. Nodding his head vigorously, he charged with venom, "Unless Colt's horse has got wings, *you are a liar!*"

Blind passion dropped Smith Wayne's hand to his gun. Whipping it from the holster, he shot Trent in the stomach. The man jackknifed and fell to the ground.

Forgetting her own precarious position, Laura Lane broke from her place and stood in front of the wild-eyed man with the smoking gun. "Smith, you fool!" she shrieked. "Dan Colt has an identical twin brother! He goes by the name of Dave Sundeen!"

Laura's words came over Smith Wayne like an arctic wind. His jaw sagged. He looked down at Mel Trent, who had rolled to his back, hands covering his bloody wound. Trent had heard what Laura said. Eyes glazed, Trent gasped, "Sm . . . Smith . . ."

His countenance totally altered from the anger only seconds before, Smith knelt beside the dying outlaw. "Mel," he said with quivering voice. "I . . . I'm sorry. Please forgive me, Mel. I . . . I didn't know nothin' about no twin. Please, Mel . . ."

Trent gritted his teeth. "I'll get you in hell." His eyes rolled back. His body went limp.

Smith stood up. Fixing his black eyes on Laura Lane, he said, "Why didn't you jump in and tell me about this twin business before I shot my friend?"

"I tried. You were too angry to listen to me," said Laura heavily.

A cold smile parted Wayne's lips. "I guess you're right." Swinging his gaze to the lifeless form at his feet, he mumbled to himself, "Twins. Colt and Sundeen . . . twins. Who'da thought it? Twins. Sundeen really did show up. Twins. For the love of—"

"Boss," interrupted Earl Mound.

Smith raised his head slowly, his gaze finding the young gunfighter's face. He waited for Mound to continue.

"I've got an idea," said Mound, pointing to Laura Lane. "I take it she and Colt are friends."

"Yeah," put in Maze, "mighty good friends. Like sweeties, mebbe."

Laura's face flushed. "That's not true!" she snapped. "He's just a kind and good man who saved my life when you would have killed me!"

"I watched you from the trees a couple days ago," said Maze with a fiendish smile. "Looked like sportin' stuff to me."

Wordlessly the angry woman glared at the huge monster.

"So what's your idea?" Wayne asked Earl Mound.

"You still want to force Colt into a shootout?"

"Yeah, but who—?"

"Me."

"You?"

"Yep."

"Be suicide."

Earl Mound was anxious to move up the ladder in the world of gunfighters. If he were to outdraw and kill the famous Dan Colt, he would be feared and honored from California to the wide Missouri. Narrowing his eyes, he said, "Not with his sweetie-pie's life at stake."

Laura's face blanched, fingertips finding her gaping mouth.

A look of triumph crawled over Smith Wayne's face. "You mean—"

"I mean we send him the message that we have his girlie," clipped Mound. "He's to face me head-on in the middle of Main Street in Alamosa. He's already there by now."

"Go on," said Smith, liking what he had heard so far.

"We tell Colt that he draws slow and goes down in the dirt . . . or she dies. If he don't draw slow, he murders his girl friend."

Smith rubbed his pencil-line mustache. "What if he chooses to do that? Draw fast, I mean."

"Then it's my gamble, isn't it?"

"Mmm-hmm," said Smith, smiling.

Mound grinned. "For that ten thousand in your shirt, I'll take the gamble."

The smile drained from Wayne's face.

"You were willin' to pay ten thousand to Sundeen for a dead Dan Colt," Earl said defensively. "Why ain't it worth the same if I kill him?"

Smith's hollow smile returned. "Okay. With one difference."

"What's that?"

"Sundeen was goin' to get half before killin' Colt . . . half after. You'll get it all at the same time."

Mound eyed Smith warily.

"*After*," said Smith.

Reluctantly Earl Mound agreed. Forbes, Winkler, and Robins would go along behind him. Smith Wayne would ride with them. At the edge of town, he would drop back and watch the shootout from a distance. Maze McLeod would keep Laura at the hideout.

"Now we've got to convince Colt that we have his girlie," said Mound.

"What you got in mind?" asked Wayne.

Turning to Laura, Mound said, "Were you wearin'

248

that dress when your boyfriend left the house this mornin'?"

Laura's lips pulled tight. "Dan Colt is not my boyfriend." She lanced Mound with a cold stare. "Yes. I was wearing this dress when he left Mr. and Mrs. Arnold and myself this morning."

The dress Laura wore was cotton print with wrist-length sleeves. Before she could dodge, Mound sank his fingers into the sleeve of her left arm where it joined the shoulder and ripped it loose. Laura screamed and pulled away. Smith seized her and held her until Mound could pull the sleeve from her arm.

Turning to Vince Forbes, the gunslinger handed him the torn sleeve. "Vince, you, Arnie, and Zack will go ahead of me when we get to town and show this to Colt. It'll be plenty enough to convince him we've got her. Tell him we ain't playin' games. It's him or her."

Forbes nodded. Laura swallowed hard.

"If he agrees," continued Earl Mound, "tell him to walk out in the middle of the street."

"And if he don't agree?" queried Vince Forbes.

Setting his vicious glare on Laura, Mound said, "Then the beautiful lady has a beautiful funeral."

A chill traveled down Laura's spine.

Smith Wayne did not like the thought of Laura being murdered, but his doubts had to be put aside. At all costs, the barricades that stood in his way must be removed. "We'd better hurry," he said to the others. "We want to catch Colt while he's still in town." Turning to McLeod, he said, "Maze, I'll take your horse. Mine needs a rest."

"Okay, boss," said the huge man. "You want I should tie the lady up?"

"It would be a good idea," said Wayne. "She's pretty tough, you know. Remember Jim? She put a hatchet in his face. Took Dobie's gun away from him and shot him in the gut."

With that, Smith leaped in the saddle of McLeod's horse and the five men thundered eastward.

As the wind cut his face, Smith Wayne laughed to himself. There was no question in his mind what Dan Colt would do. He would place a higher value on Laura Lane's life than his own. Earl Mound certainly felt sure of it.

An evil grin formed on Wayne's imperious mouth. Before sundown today, the blond gunslinger with the pale blue eyes would be dead.

Chapter Twenty-Two

Dan Colt arrived in Alamosa a few minutes after ten o'clock. He was about to dismount at the Yellow Rose Saloon when he looked up the street and saw Bill Caley's horse tethered in front of the jail. He figured his young friend had grown tired of waiting at the saloon and decided to go to the office.

Guiding the big black to where Caley's mount stood, he lowered himself to the ground and crossed the board sidewalk to the door. Pushing it open, Dan saw the acting sheriff examining a cigarette butt that he had laid on a large piece of paper.

Looking up pleasantly, Bill said, "Oh, good mornin', Dan. Take a look at this cigarette butt I found at the Moore place."

Colt leaned over the desk and eyed the object of attention. "So it's a machine-made cigarette," he said casually. "Does that tell you something?"

Without looking up, Caley said, "Not too many men in these parts buy ready-made smokes, Dan."

The tall man straightened up. He eyed the youthful lawman curiously. "You mean this is the evidence you were so all-fired anxious for me to see?"

"Huh?" asked Bill, studying the butt.

"This is what you sent that mean-lookin' dude after me for?"

Caley's gaze came immediately upward. "Mean-lookin' dude? What mean-lookin' dude?"

Dan reflected on his friend's question a moment. Leaning over and leveling his eyes with Caley's, he said, "You didn't send a rider to find me this mornin' with the hot news that you had new evidence on the hangmen and I was to burn horseflesh to get here?"

Caley slowly shook his head. "No, sir."

Colt hammered a fist on the desk top and spun around. "Somebody's pullin' somethin', Bill," he said, turning back again. "We must be gettin' too close to the board our skunk is hidin' under."

"Where'd this guy approach you?" asked Caley.

"I was just pullin' away from the Box W. He came ridin' from the west, so I figured you had sent him from somewhere around Moore's place."

"Don't make sense, Dan," said the young lawman, scratching his head.

"I know," agreed Colt. "He had to have been one of Smith Wayne's hired hangmen."

"We gotta nail that sidewinder," said Caley. "Did you get anything from Scott?"

"No," replied the tall man. "He wasn't there. The cook at the Box W said Smith had left for town at sunup and Scott had ridden out not long afterward." Adjusting his gunbelt, Colt asked, "Have you seen Smith in town this mornin'?"

"Nope," answered Caley.

Fingering his heavy blond mustache, Dan said half to himself, "If the gang wanted me to head for town, they wanted me here for a reason . . . or they wanted me out of the valley." A cold feeling moved next to his spine. "Bill, you don't suppose they would go after Laura?"

"I doubt it, Dan," reflected Caley. "They've had other chances to get her if that's what they wanted."

"Yeah, but—" Dan was starting to say that since the brutal hangmen had hanged Anne Braxton, they might do the same to Laura Lane. His words were interrupted by the sound of heavy boots on the boardwalk.

The office door came open. It was Fargo Wayne and two cowboys Dan recognized from the Box W. Wayne's face was drawn. His eyes sagged.

"Howdy, Fargo," said Bill Caley, rising to his feet.

Fargo Wayne spoke solemnly in a grave monotone. "Somethin' outside I've got to show you, Sheriff."

Caley followed the silver-haired man out into the harsh sunlight. Dan Colt followed. Fargo led them to a bay mare that was on a lead rope, tied to his own horse. Draped over the saddle on her back was the lifeless form of Scott Wayne.

Bill Caley breathed an oath. Dan repeated it.

"He was shot twice," said Fargo with gravel in his voice. "Once in the back. Once in the chest. The horse came walkin' in by herself. I haven't touched a thing. Wanted you to see it just as it was."

Dan Colt and Bill Caley knew that Fargo Wayne had the manpower to declare war on the homesteaders and literally wipe them out. They eyed each other with apprehension.

Cautiously, Colt said, "Who do you think did it, Mr. Wayne?"

"Homesteaders," came the steady reply.

"You going to retaliate?" asked the acting sheriff nervously.

"Nope." Wayne's manner was that of a broken, defeated man. Gesturing toward the left saddlebag, he said, "Take a look."

Dangling outside the tightly buckled saddlebag was a black hood. Round holes were cut in for the eyes and a narrow slit for the mouth. Dan lifted the hood upward. It was attached inside the bag.

"How can I retaliate?" asked Fargo. "Scott was one of the hangmen. Someone among the homesteaders found it out. I can't blame them. I'm so ashamed. I can't face people anymore." The silver-haired cattleman shook his head sorrowfully. "Just wanted to let the law know the truth."

Dan Colt unbuckled the strap and looked inside the bag. "I don't think what you're believin' is the truth, Mr. Wayne," he said emphatically.

"Huh?" said Fargo, looking at Colt with dim eyes.

"This hood is tied securely in the bag to the strap that runs through it. The flap was buckled down tight. There's no way it could be hanging on the outside unless somebody *put* it there, *then* buckled the strap. Why would it be knotted to the strap inside and dangling outside unless Scott's killer wanted the hood to be very obvious?"

Fargo Wayne's eyes revealed that Dan's words were registering and making sense.

"Scott was not one of the hangmen, Mr. Wayne," said Dan with conviction. "I'll lay you a bet that it was the hangmen who killed him. He had probably discovered them and got himself shot for the effort."

The owner of the Box W nodded vigorously. "You're right, Colt! You're right!" Stepping to Scott's inert form, he broke into tears. Patting his dead son's head, he said, "Forgive me, Scott. Please forgive your foolish old dad. I should have known you wouldn't be one of those cold-blooded murderers. You were a good boy. Just like Smith . . . you were a good boy."

Colt's eyes met Caley's. They both were thinking the same thing. *How was Fargo Wayne going to take it when he found out the truth about his favored son?*

Bill Caley stepped to Fargo, touching his shoulder.

"Why don't you take Scott home now, Fargo?" Looking at the two Box W men, he said, "You fellas help him into the saddle, will you? Take him home."

As the three men prepared to ride, Dan Colt said, "Mr. Wayne, Bill and I are about to crack this hangmen thing open. I promise you. We'll bring in Scott's killers."

Wayne nodded soberly. The dismal train moved slowly up the street. Scott Wayne's two hands hung downward, swaying with the movement of the bay mare.

"Now what?" said Caley, eying Colt's rugged face.

"I'm headin' for Arnold's place," replied Dan. "I want to make sure Laura's all right. Then I'm going back to the Box W. I'm gonna force Smith's hand. Wouldn't surprise me if it was him who killed Scott."

"I'm ridin' with you, Dan," said Bill. "This thing's got to bust open. We'd better be together when the skunk comes out of the woodpile."

"Okay," agreed Colt. "Let's go."

Stepping out into the driving sunlight, the two men ducked under the rail. Dan caught sight of the three horsemen just as one of them barked, "Dan Colt!"

Bill Caley whirled at the sound and set his eyes on the squalid trio. Dan walked from between the horses and faced them.

"Wanta talk to you, Colt," Vince Forbes said gruffly, dismounting.

Dan squinted as the other two left their saddles and led their horses, along with Vince's, to the rail. "Do I know you?" asked Dan heavily.

"Ain't necessary," said Forbes, stepping close. "We got a little proposition for yuh."

Bill Caley's eyes followed the other two hardcases while Dan fixed his own ice-blue eyes on Vince's stubbled face.

"Proposition?"

"Yeah. You got a big decision to make."

"I've already made one," Dan said with cool precision.

"Yeah?"

"I don't like you."

Forbes guffawed, exposing crooked yellow teeth. "Yer gonna like me less when I show you this." Reaching in his shirt, he whipped out Laura's tattered sleeve. "Recognize this, lover boy?"

Dan's jaw tightened. Anger welled up in him. "Where is she?" he asked, a jagged edge in his voice.

"Never mind that," retorted Forbes. "We have her. This is our proof."

"What do you want?" Colt spit each word.

"You ever hear of Earl Mound?" Vince's eyes were wide.

"Yeah," clipped Dan. "Two-bit gunslick."

"Well, he's makin' you an offer," rasped Forbes.

The other two were standing beside him now. Bill Caley stood at Dan's flank. Dan remained silent, eyes boring Vince Forbes.

"Yer life for hers," came Forbes's cold words.

Colt heard Bill Caley grab his gun. Turning quickly, he said, "Put it away, Bill."

"But, Dan!" argued Caley. "You can't let them do this!"

"They've got Laura," Dan said, tight-lipped.

"If we don't show up at the hideout by sundown," Forbes put in quickly, "she dies!" The outlaw squared his shoulders. "I mean all of us. Includin' Earl Mound."

Dan Colt's scalp tightened. "You mean Mound is goin' to square off with me . . . and I'm supposed to be slow on the draw."

Zack Robins spoke up. "Hey, Vince, he ain't as all-fired stupid as you said he was. Mr. Dan Colt figered that proposition out all by his lonesome!"

Dan glared at him.

Bill Caley touched the tall man's arm. "Dan, you can't—"

"I haven't got any choice," said Dan without looking at Caley.

"But, Dan," argued Caley, "we don't even know she's still alive. They may have killed her already! And even if she's alive, how do we know they'll really let her loose if you go through with this?"

Vince Forbes laughed fiendishly. "You don't, kid. But I tell you what. You have Mr. Earl Mound's solemn promise. If you don't breathe a word about this setup, she'll go free. Now yer gonna have to make that promise . . . or else."

"Promise him, Bill," breathed Dan.

Reluctantly, Bill Caley made the promise.

Laura Lane watched Smith Wayne and his malicious devils ride into the forest and disappear. Cold chills danced on her spine. A ball of fire settled in her stomach. Dan Colt was about to be crowded into the tightest corner he had ever faced.

She looked up at the huge ugly man who had helped hang her husband and was identified by the dying Lila Moore as the beast who had hanged Anne Braxton. Laura's insides were burning, seething, alive with hate.

"Okay, lady," said Maze McLeod in his deep voice, "inside the cabin. I'll tie you up in there."

Laura stiffened. "You mean a great big brute like you has to tie up a little woman? You afraid of me?"

Without answering, McLeod walked to the end of the porch and picked up a length of lariat rope. Laura's eyes darted about. Smith's black gelding was standing forty feet away, untethered. The rope corral among the trees was twice as far. The three horses within the rope were unsaddled and unbridled.

Laura figured she could outrun the big man. If the black did not shy when she ran toward him, she could be aboard and out of reach before Maze could catch her. It would take him at least three minutes to saddle one of the horses.

Then she remembered that the black had just had a long run. The horses in the corral were fresh. Three minutes was not enough time; Maze would catch up if she jumped on the tired horse. Laura's mind was whirling. The huge man would have to be delayed longer. She must think of something. She must get to town before Dan—

"Inside!" barked Maze, shoving the woman toward the door.

Laura spied a six-foot length of logging chain hanging from a large spike in the wall, just outside the door. The spike was about seven feet from the porch floor. The chain hung loosely along the edge of the doorway. On the porch floor within a foot of the chain was an ax handle without the head.

Another shove put her through the door. Roughly, McLeod forced her onto a straight-backed chair and jerked her arms around its back. Laura winced as the rope burned her wrists.

Cinching it tight, the huge man said, "There. That'll hold you till the boss gets back and decides what to do with you." He turned and walked outside, leaving the door open.

Laura was facing opposite from the door, toward the back of the cabin. There was a window offering a view of the trees to the rear. Her mind went to Dan Colt, who was about to face a horrible decision.

Then she thought of the chain hanging outside the door . . . the heavy ax handle . . .

Her eyes suddenly focused on a small structure nestled in the trees behind the cabin. *It was worth a try.*

Raising her voice, she said, "Maze!"

Nothing.

"Maze!"

Still nothing.

This time she hollered as loud as she could. *"Maze?"*

Heavy footsteps thumped behind her. "Yeah?"

"I . . . I need to . . . uh . . . uh . . . visit the little house out back."

McLeod swore and untied the rope. Dropping it on the floor, he said, "All right, I'll walk you out there."

Five minutes later, Laura emerged from the outhouse. Maze McLeod fell in behind her as she followed the path back to the cabin. As she stepped onto the porch, her heart was slamming her ribs. She must time it just right. The big man would have to be exactly three feet behind her when she reached the door.

He was lagging a little. Laura paused, head slightly turned. As the monster moved closer, she gripped the chain midway in its length and whirled it at him with all her strength. The heavy chain swirled around and around his neck, gaining momentum. The tail end whipped at his mouth, breaking two teeth.

As the surprised man howled and reached for her, she grasped the ax handle and backed up. Maze hit the length of the chain and the spike held. He gagged and stumbled off balance. Wide-eyed, he saw the heavy ax handle coming in a full arc. Laura was swinging it savagely, teeth gritted. The big man was helpless to avoid it.

The handle met his skull with a vociferous crack.

Maze's knees buckled. His full weight fell against the chain. He gagged and choked, clawing at the log wall for support. Gaining his feet, he reached up and slipped the top link in the chain over the head of the spike. Laura arched the heavy handle and swung again. It met McLeod's temple with a meaty sodden sound. The huge man toppled to the porch floor and lay still.

The determined woman bounded off the porch and made for the black. The beautiful animal stood absolutely still as Laura sprang into the saddle. She allowed herself a quick glimpse of Maze McLeod. He was stirring, but still on the floor. Shouting in the horse's ears like a wild Indian, Laura put him to an immediate gallop.

Chapter Twenty-Three

~~~~~~

"Now, Mister Blue Eyes," said Vince Forbes, facing Colt. "Earl Mound is watchin' from where you can't see him. If you accept the proposition, you are to step out right now into the middle of the street and face west. Me and the boys will take about five minutes to get all these Alamosa citizens gathered around. Earl wants a nice big audience. He wants them to spread abroad how they watched him outdraw and gun down the famous Dan Colt!"

Bill Caley ejected a woeful moan as Dan walked woodenly to the center of the street.

While the three henchmen ran up and down the street announcing the pending gunfight, Dan faced the stark reality of the moment. He was trapped. There was nothing he could do but stand there, draw slow . . . and take Earl Mound's hot lead.

He figured these were some of Smith Wayne's men, since they knew about Laura. *Ironic,* he thought. *Every gunfighter dreads the day when he must meet that inevitable faceless man who will outdraw him. But I have to die in a way I never dreamed. Taken out by a two-bit gunslick who couldn't shoot his way out of a bubble bath.*

Looking down at the pallid-faced acting sheriff, he said, "Bill, you've got to get Smith Wayne."

Caley could not speak for the hot lump in his

throat. Coughing it loose, he said, "Dan, there's got to be an answer. I can't just stand here and watch you be gunned down in cold blood!"

"Laura's life is at stake, Bill," said the tall man evenly. "There is no choice. Just you bring in Smith. He's responsible for all this. I know it as well as I know the sun sets in the west."

"I'll get him if it's the last thing I do," said Bill Caley through clenched teeth.

When ten minutes had passed, most of the town lined the street, eyes roving the west end.

Abruptly, the dastardly trio appeared at the far end of the street. The westerly sun was at their backs. They walked shoulder-to-shoulder toward the tall man with the sky-blue eyes. Presently a rider swung from between two buildings and followed. Earl Mound was making a spectacle of the occasion.

Forbes, Winkler, and Robins veered to the side as they drew within ten feet of Dan Colt. Bill Caley still flanked his blond-headed friend, breathing heavily.

With a circus-style flair, Mound dismounted forty feet from Colt and led his horse to the rail. Wrapping the reins around it with a flourish, he walked to the center of the street.

Mound raised his voice to the curious crowd. "Ladeez and gennulmen! In case some of you don't know . . . my name is Earl Mound! Did you hear correctly? Earl Mound! *Earl Mound!* The famous gunfighter! That tall man down there is none other than the great Dan Colt! Dan Colt! You've all heard the name."

Mound strutted in a small circle. "Now Mr. Colt has been top hog in the trough for too long! I, Earl Mound, have issued the top hog a challenge. Fastdraw duel! Just wanted you to get the names and facts straight so you can tell it abroad. You saw Earl Mound kill the great Dan Colt!"

262

With that, the cocky Mound turned to face the towering Colt, a mocking, triumphant grin on his lips. His back was toward Smith Wayne.

Leaning against a faded frame building, Smith Wayne watched the scene, intent on seeing Dan Colt die on the sun-bleached street of Alamosa. He was about a hundred yards behind Mound and could only hear a few words of his speech.

Dan eyed Mound with a malevolent glare and went into his stance. Every eye was on the two gunfighters.

"Move, Bill," Dan said from the side of his mouth.

Caley stepped toward the crowd silently and reluctantly.

Over Earl Mound's shoulder, Dan saw a slight movement down the street.

Suddenly Wayne's own horse thundered past him, lathered and foaming. Laura Lane was in the saddle. Thirty yards from where the startled Smith stood, the weary horse spied a water trough and turned toward it. As he buried his foamy muzzle in the water, Laura fixed her eyes on the two men in the center of the street and slid from the saddle. Waving her arms wildly, she caught Dan's attention.

Colt focused on Laura in the cotton print dress with one arm bared just as Earl Mound's hand swooped toward his gun. Mound never saw Laura.

Colt palmed the twin .45s with the speed of a rattler's tongue. Both of Colt's guns roared. Dan purposely shot low. He wanted Earl Mound to live long enough to know what hit him. One bullet tore through Mound's big belt buckle. The other hit just beside it.

Mound dropped his unfired gun with the impact and fell to his back. His eyes bulged with shock. He cried out as splinters of pain spiraled up from his wounds. A slogging sickness clawed at his stomach.

Dan stepped up and kicked Mound's gun across the street, then holstered both of his own. Laura was coming toward him on the run.

Suddenly Bill Caley shouted, "Dan! Look out!"

A gun boomed from the side of the street. People were scattering. Women were screaming. From the corner of his eye Colt saw Caley go down. Vince Forbes turned his smoking muzzle toward Dan. The tall man's invisible hands drew and fired. The bullets hit Vince in the chest with terrific force. His gun discharged as he was flung to his back on the boardwalk, the slug going wild. Forbes lay dead, sightlessly staring upward.

At the same instant Dan's guns were spitting death at Forbes, Arnie Winkler and Zack Robins were drawing theirs. Winkler was standing in the dirt, just off the boardwalk. Robins was on the wooden sidewalk, midway between the edge and the white wall of a clothing shop.

Dan's guns roared again. The slug from the lefthand gun ripped through Winkler's heart. He died before he hit the rough wooden slats. The slug from the righthand gun hit Robins in the windpipe at the base of his throat. He let out a gurgling cry as his back slammed the white wall. He was still on his feet and still could shoot.

Robins raised his gun. Dan fired again. The desperate man grunted with the impact and raised the gun again. Instantly Dan dropped his lefthand Colt and fanned the remaining one. The .45 boomed three times in rapid succession, tearing three smoking holes in Zack Robins's chest.

Quickly Dan retrieved the other gun, ready to give him more. Trying to kill Robins was like trying to kill a mad grizzly, Dan thought. The outlaw's gun slipped from his fingers. He was still standing, back against the wall, blood spurting from the wound in his windpipe. His eyes were glassy as he slid slowly down the wall and slumped to the boardwalk. Two bullets had gone clear through him. They were planted deep in the wood. A shiny crimson trail followed his body down the wall.

Dan hurried to Bill Caley, who was sitting up in the middle of the street. Blood soaked his shirt at his left shoulder.

"Is it bad?" asked Dan.

"Just nicked me a little," said Bill, forcing a weak smile.

Doc Cummings detached himself from the crowd, knelt beside him and examined the wound. "First one's still alive," the physician said to Dan. "But not for long."

Standing up, the tall man walked to where Earl Mound lay dying. Laura Lane had been pulled into the crowd and was being held tight by two women. Dan looked at her and smiled, then dropped his gaze to the dying man.

Mound's eyes were glazed. His face had the waxen pallor of death. He tried to focus on Dan's face. "Colt . . ." he gasped.

"If you can talk, Mound," said Dan firmly, "why don't you do a decent thing before you die? Tell me who's behind this."

Mound nodded slowly.

Turning toward Bill Caley, Dan lifted his voice. "Bill, can you make it over here?"

The doctor helped Caley to his feet. Two men stepped in and half-carried the wounded lawman to where Dan stood. Caley eyed the dying man.

"Mound, the sheriff is here to witness your statement," said Colt. "Can you hear me?"

"Yes."

"Who hired you?"

"Sm . . . Smith Wayne."

Caley looked at Dan and smiled.

"Mound," said Dan, "is Smith Wayne the leader of the hangmen?"

"Yes."

"Who shot Scott Wayne?"

Earl Mound licked his lips. "Smith . . . Smith did. Sc . . . Scott found hideout. Smith . . . shot him."

"Where's Smith now?" asked Bill Caley.

"West . . . end of . . . street."

Caley looked in that direction. "Some of you men run down that way," he said, pointing with his good arm. "Smith Wayne has just been named as the leader of the gang of hangmen. He might still be down there among those buildings!"

Several men pulled their guns and ran toward the west end of town.

Mound was working his jaw.

"What is it?" asked Colt.

"Smith . . . Smith . . . is going . . . going to kill his father . . . as . . . as soon as . . . he can get . . . the old man . . . to change the . . . will."

Dan eyed Bill Caley. Caley shook his head.

Earl Mound coughed painfully and said, "Colt . . ."

"Yes," answered Dan.

"I . . . I did . . . I didn't think you'd do it. Maze . . . Maze will kill her now."

Dan raised his head and beckoned for Laura Lane. As she drew near his side, Dan put his arm around her shoulder. Moving Laura to give the dying gunslick a view of her face, Dan said, "Mound, can you hear me?"

"Y-yes."

"Take a look."

Earl focused as much as possible. "Is that . . . her?"

"It's me," said Laura. "I got away from Maze. I rode in just in time for Dan to see me before you drew on him."

A slow, painful grin slanted across Earl Mound's mouth. "You . . . must . . . be . . . quite a . . . woman." His eyes closed. He was dead.

"Who's Maze?" Dan asked Laura, leading her away.

"He's the man Lila Moore wrote about before she died. The big one with the burns on his face."

Dan's rugged features hardened. "He's the one who hanged Anne."

"Yes."

"He was holding you?"

"Yes."

"How'd you get away?"

"It's a long story."

"Where is he?"

"I left him at Smith's hideout. It's at the north end of the valley. I can take you there, but we'd better gather up a posse. He's a huge monster."

Dan's eyes flashed fire. "I want him all to myself."

"You've got him!" came Maze McLeod's heavy voice.

The crowd was breaking up. The doctor had taken Bill Caley to his office. The men searching for Smith Wayne were running from building to building. No one had noticed big Maze ride into town. He had left his horse and was standing in the street, big as a mountain. Dried blood was caked on his face. His eyes were wild.

"First, I'm gonna kill you, cowboy!" McLeod bellowed. "Then I'm gonna kill her!"

Dan eyed the monster with fury. "You've killed your last woman," he said, lips pulled tight over his teeth.

Pushing Laura toward the boardwalk without taking his eyes from McLeod, Dan said, "Get away from here, Laura."

The dainty woman backed away, trembling.

Slowly Maze moved his hands to the buckle of his gunbelt and released it. Throwing the gun aside, he said, "I ain't drawin' against yuh. I'm gonna do this with my bare hands."

Laura gasped from the boardwalk. People were noticing the two men.

"Nothin' I'd like better," said Colt with a crooked grin. Unbuckling his own gunbelt, he threw the guns aside. "I want my hands on you, woman killer!" The picture of Lila Moore clawing the dirt in death and her two daughters crumpled on the ground flashed into Dan's mind. Slowly it faded to the clearly etched form of Anne Braxton hanging by her neck, swaying in the breeze.

The veins in Dan Colt's neck stuck out like swollen rope. His frosty-blue eyes chilled McLeod for an instant with a poisonous look.

McLeod scowled and moved his huge shoulders. His slitted eyes were evil. "Come and get me, cowboy!"

Chapter Twenty-Four

~~~~~~

Dan Colt charged the hulking giant, fists ready.

Maze tried to dodge the first punch, but Dan was too fast and accurate. The punch struck the hollow of the jaw and McLeod's head snapped back. On the rebound, Colt popped him with a stiff left jab, then followed quickly with a second smashing right to the jaw. The big man staggered, then closed in. A massive fist glanced off of Colt's head, but he felt its effect.

Dan pounded Maze's nose, then caught a blow on his own temple. He felt his feet leave the ground. The lowering sun was in Dan's eyes as he rolled over in the dust. Suddenly a monstrous shadow came over him like some gigantic bird.

Adeptly Dan rolled in time to escape the nearly three hundred pounds of angry man. Maze hit the wagon-rutted street with a heavy thump.

Colt waited for him to rise to his feet and charged again. He drove four punches in succession to the big man's face. McLeod staggered, but came back strong.

"I'm gonna kill you, little man!" bawled the monster.

The gathering audience stood spellbound. Laura was biting her lower lip, eyes fixed on the two men.

Dan ducked a whistling fist and popped Maze's thick lips. They both split and spurted blood. Another slammed his nose. In a rage, McLeod swung wildly as

Dan was coming in again. Dan connected, but so did Maze. The ponderous fist chopped Colt's jaw. He felt as if he was falling through a black, endless hole. Bright lights whirled and flashed in Dan's head as the hard earth jumped up and slammed him violently.

Again, the blond man moved in time to avoid the diving giant. While Maze rolled, Dan rose to his feet. They were fighting near the large doorway of the livery stable. Sucking air, Dan caught the odor of horses, leather, hay, and manure.

McLeod came like a charging bull elephant. Dan's back was to the wall of the stable. Maze swung a ferocious blow. Colt ducked. The huge fist banged against the solid wood. Maze howled and grabbed the fist with the other hand. Blood oozed from the knuckles. His big face was now wet with blood from his nose and lips.

Dan steadied himself until the town stopped reeling before his eyes. He shook his head. He caught a glimpse of Laura's white face as the flashing bright lights stopped whirling.

McLeod was coming again. Dan backed up against the wall. The big bloody fist was aimed at his face. Adeptly, Dan sidestepped and Maze's wounded fist cracked against the wall again. He let out a painful yell. Snarling viciously, he threw his weight against the blond man, who was still a bit unsteady.

Suddenly Dan felt himself wrapped in a vise. His feet were off the ground. McLeod apparently had broken his right hand and could no longer use it as a fist. He had Dan Colt in a deadly bear hug, gripping him under the arms.

Colt felt the breath leave his lungs. His ribs were popping. Maze was behind him, breathing in one ear. Dan's fury grew. Like a prairie fire in a high wind, it grew. Gritting his teeth, he threw both hands back and planted a thumb in each eye. Maze tried to shake the hot irons loose from his eyes. Dan had a firm grip.

Screaming wildly, the huge monster threw Colt ten feet through the air. Dan hit the ground rolling, gasping for breath. McLeod was holding his hands to his eyes, staggering around the yawning doorway of the livery. Dan saw a rope dangling from a rafter and thought again of Anne Braxton's lifeless body hanging from the tree in Tod Moore's yard. Thunderous, burning fury raged within him, possessing him until everything blurred in his vision except big Maze McLeod.

Colt went after him like a hungry wolf. McLeod was rubbing his bloodshot eyes, trying to clear the haze that filmed them. Dan planted his feet and sent a raw-boned fist pistonlike to the monster's jaw. Maze staggered, blinking. One, two, three more hissing punches dumped the big woman-killer on the ground. He was lying halfway through the door of the stable.

"Come on!" yelled Colt, sucking air. "I'm not through with you yet. You're still breathin'!"

McLeod rolled to his knees, shaking his ponderous head. Leaning against the wall inside was a new single-tree for harnessing horses. Maze gained his feet. He purposely stumbled toward it. Seizing the single-tree with both hands, he came into the orange sunlight, swinging it violently. Dan ducked as it cut air over his head.

The big man moved in again, wielding the single-tree. The metal rings in the ends made a metallic ringing sound. Dan spun around, placing his back to the livery doorway. Maze chopped at his head. Again, the lithe man ducked. The single-tree slammed the door-jamb with a deafening bang, showering splinters in every direction.

As McLeod righted himself, Dan sent another blow to his nose. Wildly, the giant charged. Their bodies thumped with the impact and they went down, McLeod on top of Colt.

Maze jammed the single-tree downward horizontally at Dan's throat. The blue-eyed man met it with both hands, pressing against the giant's weight and strength. The wooden instrument quivered between them. McLeod grunted, forcing it downward. Colt glared at him with defiant rage, meeting strength for strength.

The spellbound crowd stood in awe. Laura Lane prayed.

In a desperate effort to force the single-tree against Dan's throat, Maze moved himself forward to add weight. Colt's keen senses, born of many hand-to-hand battles, told him the big man had moved too far forward. He was over-balanced.

Suddenly Colt flung his knees upward, catching McLeod on the rump. The top-heavy giant peeled over head first. Whirling around, Dan wrung the single-tree from the surprised man's grasp. Now the lethal piece of wood and metal was in the other combatant's hands.

Both men came to their feet. Maze attacked, attempting to overpower Dan with his weight and brute force. The single-tree rattled and hissed. McLeod's head split open with the impact. He staggered and dropped to one knee. Dan thought of the helpless little Moore girls, shot down in cold blood . . . their mother cut down in the same way. He remembered Anne Braxton's bloated face. She died at the hands of this vicious brute with no mercy, choking to death.

Maze McLeod's head and face were a bloody mass. His foggy eyes were fixed on Colt with raw fury coursing through his veins. Then like a wild, wounded beast, McLeod sprang at Colt. Dan planted his feet and put every ounce of his muscled body into the swinging single-tree. The impact against Maze's big head clattered and echoed amongst the clapboard buildings. People gasped.

The huge man went down like a rotted fence post. He lay absolutely still. Maze McLeod did not get up this time.

Dan dropped the bloody piece of wagon equipment and staggered to a water trough beside the livery barn. Easing down to his knees, he buried his blond head in the water. As he lifted it out, he could hear the excited crowd cheering. Laura Lane was quickly beside him.

"Dan, are you all right?" she gasped.

"Will be with one more dip," he said, submerging his head again. He held it there a long moment, then came up spitting water.

Laura took his hand and helped him stand. Her eyes were swimming with tears. "Dan," she said softly, "what can I say? You rode into this troubled valley a complete stranger and saved my life. You stayed to help and you got ambushed. And now today, you stood out there in that street and looked death in the face to save me again. You wouldn't have killed Earl Mound if I hadn't shown up, would you?"

The tall man's dripping face flushed.

"You would have taken his bullet to spare my life." Laura palmed tears from her cheeks. "Dan, how could you do that?"

Towering over her, Colt looked down and smiled. "There was a beautiful lady I knew once," he said. "She buried a hatchet in a man's face, took a gun from another one and shot him with it. When she was asked how she did it, she said, *I guess you just do what you have to do.* Well, I couldn't let them kill you. To quote the beautiful lady . . . I guess you just do what you have to do."

Doc Cummings left the inert form of Maze McLeod in the street and approached Dan and Laura. "He's dead, Colt," said the physician dryly. Cummings shook his head. "You're a real tornado when you get riled, aren't you? Whew! You must've spotted him a hundred pounds, nearly!"

"Well, Doc," said Dan, "I guess you just do what you have to do."

Laura smiled up at him.

As the physician walked away, the crowd began to disperse. A man stepped up to Dan. "Smith Wayne musta took off, Mr. Colt. He's not in town now. I told the sheriff."

Dan thanked him and said to Laura, "Let's see how Bill is." He walked to where his guns lay in the street and buckled them on. As he tied the thongs around his sinewy thighs, Laura picked up his gray Stetson and dusted it off.

Entering the doctor's office, Dan and Laura found Caley sitting in a soft chair, his arm in a sling.

Arching his eyebrows, the youthful lawman said, "I'm sure glad you're on my side, Señor Colt. I watched you destroy that monster. Whew!"

"I guess you just do what you have to do," chuckled Dan, throwing a look at Laura.

Colt swung his gaze to Caley. "We've got enough on Smith to arrest him, Bill. You're in no shape to ride to the Box W. I want you to deputize me and swear out a warrant for his arrest. I'll go get him."

Caley agreed. Within fifteen minutes, Dan Colt had taken the oath and Caley had pinned a badge on him. The warrant form was quickly filled in and signed.

Laura rode Smith Wayne's black gelding as Dan escorted her to her temporary home at the Arnold farm.

It was dark before they arrived. Leaving the twinkling lights of the farmer's house behind, the tall man rode toward the Box W. Smith Wayne's black gelding followed on a lead rope.

Clouds were forming an ominous curtain over the stars as Dan rode through the Spanish-style gate. The wind was picking up. The smell of rain was in the air.

A sentinel stepped out of the deep shadows as Dan halted the two animals in front of the big house. He held a rifle. "That you, Mr. Colt?" he asked, using the faint light from the windows to see Dan's face.

"Yep, it's me," replied Colt. "Smith home?"

"Yessir. That's his hoss, there, ain't it?"

"It's his."

"Smith'll be mighty glad to see him. Came home this evenin' on a borrowed nag. Said his'n had been stole. Where'd you find him?"

"Alamosa," said Dan, mounting the red-brick steps.

The knocker clattered as the wind gusted across the front of the house.

Presently the door opened, flooding the porch with a rectangular shaft of yellow light. Fargo Wayne's haggard face appeared. His shoulders drooped. His eyes were dull.

"Hello, Colt," he droned. "What brings you out here tonight?"

Gesturing behind him, Dan said, "For one thing, I have Smith's horse."

Fargo's face brightened a little. "Good. Is he all right?"

"He's fine."

"You find the thief?"

"Yep."

"Good."

"There's another reason I'm here, Mr. Wayne," said Dan evenly.

"Oh?"

"I need to see Smith."

Reluctance formed on Fargo's tired face. "He's with Scott's body, Colt. Smith is mourning his brother. Couldn't it wait till tomorrow?"

"No, sir. I must see him now." Dan emphasized the last word.

Looking past Colt to the shadow of the sentinel, Wayne said, "Charlie, put Smith's horse in the barn."

Speaking over his shoulder, Dan said, "Never mind, Charlie. Smith's going to need him shortly."

Fargo Wayne's face twisted. "Colt, what is this?"

"I'd rather you heard it when I address Smith," said the tall man.

"Go into the den," said the stoop-shouldered rancher. "I'll bring him in there."

Dan was standing as Fargo entered, Smith trailing. The latter flashed Colt a savage look of murderous hatred. Fargo rounded his desk and sat down in the chair behind it. "Sit down, Colt," he said, pointing to a chair.

"I'd rather stand, sir," replied Dan, sober-faced.

"I understand you want to see me, Colt," said Smith insolently. Moving to stand in front of his father's desk, he said, "Can't a man mourn the death of his brother in peace? What do you want?"

Dan pulled back his vest, exposing the shiny badge for both men to see. Sliding the folded warrant from his shirt pocket, he said, "As deputy sheriff of this county I have a warrant for your arrest."

Fargo's eyes widened, face blanched.

Smith sneered. "What's the charge?"

"Plural, Smith," said Colt levelly. "Charges."

"Well, spit 'em out! I'm not guilty, I'll tell you that right now!"

"You are under arrest for the murders of Russell Morton, Edward Cleaver, Sheriff Bradley Palmer, Deputy Ron Castin, Vance Lane, Roy Braxton, Anne Braxton, John Jack, Jonah Jack, Tod Moore, Lila Moore, Stephanie Moore, Lucy Moore, Paul Healy, Myrtle Healy—"

"Shut up! Shut up! Shut up!" screamed Smith Wayne. "How can you think I would be party to those poor people dying? I didn't even know some of them were dead."

"This is preposterous!" bellowed Fargo, jumping to his feet.

"Please sit down, Mr. Wayne," said Dan gently. "There's one more name on this list."

Smith was seething. "I'm not listening to another word!" he hissed.

"Apparently you didn't understand me, Smith," lashed Colt. "You are in a present state of arrest. Now you button your mouth."

Smith's eyes were hot, burning with hate.

"The last name on this list," said Dan, taking a deep breath, "is *Scott Wayne.*"

Fargo was on his feet again. Smith stood numb. "Sit down, Mr. Wayne," said Dan. "The sheriff and I heard testimony today from a man your youngest son hired to kill me. He saw Smith shoot Scott to death."

Fargo's mouth hung open. Slowly he sagged into the chair.

"Dad!" yelled Smith. "Don't listen to him! He's lyin'!" Smith glared at Colt. "How could he testify? You killed—" Smith's eyes bulged.

"You were in town hiding and watching today, weren't you, Smith?" rasped Dan. Looking at Fargo, he said, "Not only was Smith party to all the hangings, Mr. Wayne. He was the leader of the pack."

"Dad! It's not so!" screamed Smith. "Somebody's framin' me!" Fixing his dark eyes on Dan Colt, he blurted, "This blue-eyed wonder is a criminal, himself, Dad! Sheriff Palmer had him shackled, takin' him to jail!"

Dan let those words echo in the high-ceilinged room.

"How'd you know that, Smith?" asked Colt, bolting him with his ice-blue stare.

Young Wayne turned gray.

"Only the hangmen who ambushed Palmer and Castin knew that," said Dan coldly. "The hangmen who murdered them in order to get back a silver ornament from a black saddle. An ornament that the chief hangman left at the scene of one of the crimes!"

Smith was unarmed. He glanced toward the door.

"Don't try it," warned Dan. "I'll cut you down before you get halfway."

Fargo angled his languid eyes toward Smith, who stood near the left corner of his desk. "You murdered your own brother?"

Smith stood frozen to the spot, guilt etched deep in his face.

"You murdered all those people?"

"Not all of 'em!" Smith's face was a twisted, distorted mask of horror.

Fargo's voice was ragged. "You stole my cattle, too, didn't you? You're the one that's been smuggling whiskey to my men, aren't you? All that money I gave you—"

"D-Dad," stammered Smith, "the whiskey was so we could keep good men around. The money . . . the stolen cattle . . . well, it was just so I could hire enough m-men to r-run the sodbusters out of th-the valley. I did it all for us, Dad. All for us!"

"You killed Scott for *us?*" Fargo's features had turned to granite.

"Let's go, Smith," said Colt. "We'll lock you up. You'll have a trial."

Smith's face contorted with fear. He looked pleadingly at his father. "Dad, I'm your son! Your own likeness. I'm just like you, Dad! You can't let them take me! You can't let me stand trial! You can't let me hang!"

Fargo Wayne's face was old, gaunt, tired. But there was a light of determination in his eyes. From beneath the desk, he lifted a long-barreled .45 revolver. The hammer was eared back. The muzzle was aimed loosely in Dan Colt's direction. Dan tensed.

"You won't stand trial, Smith," Fargo said evenly, his eyes on Colt.

Smith wiped a nervous hand over his face and smiled.

"You won't hang either," said Fargo through his teeth.

"Shoot him, Dad! Shoot him!" screamed Smith.

Slowly Fargo swerved the black muzzle, lining it on Smith's chest. The youthful hangman's eyes bulged with terror. His mouth gaped.

The revolver roared, belching fire. Smith grunted as the impact slammed him against the wall. Clutching his chest, he staggered toward an overstuffed sofa, reeled in place, and sprawled across the arm of the sofa. His head and arms hung down. Smith Wayne looked like a broken doll. He was dead.

The pallid-faced father stood up, the gun still in his hand. The room was heavy with the bitter smell of burnt gunpowder. The old man walked unsteadily through the pall of blue smoke. He passed Dan Colt as if totally unaware of his presence. Dan watched him move through the doorway. For half a minute the sound of his shuffling feet in the hallway was audible to Dan's ears. Then a door opened and closed. For a moment, all was still.

Then a clattering shot echoed and reverberated through the massive house.

Chapter Twenty-Five

Lightning chewed angrily at the black sky as Dan Colt rode past the house on the Arnold farm. He saw the light of a single lantern burning in the kitchen. Thunder rumbled as he dismounted and led the gelding inside the barn.

The tall man relieved the big black of the saddle and bridle. Then he forked him a generous supply of hay.

Crossing the yard, Dan eyed the yellow shaft of light and the small drops of rain beginning to fall. Laura Lane's shadow moved across the window toward the door. As the porch squeaked under his weight, the metal bolt rattled and the door swung open.

Laura had washed her hair. Soft and shiny by the lantern light, it hung in fluffy waves, curling on her shoulders. She wore a full-length robe and slippers. A warm smile greeted Dan as he stepped inside.

"What are you doing up this hour, young lady?" Dan asked softly. "I was planning to sleep in the barn, but I saw the lantern burning."

"I couldn't sleep," replied Laura. "I got to thinking about Vance. Had myself a good cry."

"The Lord gave you tears so you could let out some of the hurt," said the blue-eyed man. "Don't be afraid to let them fall."

"You're earlier than I expected," mused Laura, looking at the clock on the wall. "It's barely eleven o'clock. Didn't you take Smith to jail?"

"No," said Colt, removing his hat and slacking onto a chair. "You haven't got some coffee, have you?"

Ray Arnold could be heard snoring from where he slept on the floor.

"I think there's some coals left in the stove," said the beautiful young lady. "I'll stir them and throw in some wood. Heat you some coffee in a jiffy." While she did so, she said, "You didn't answer my question."

"No . . . uh . . . I didn't take Smith to jail. He's dead."

Laura stopped what she was doing and set her brown gaze on Colt. "Dead?"

"Mmm-hmm."

"You kill him?" Laura turned back to the stove.

"Nope. Fargo killed him."

She whirled, eyes wide. "Fargo?"

"I cornered Smith in front of his father. He broke down and admitted the whole thing. Smugglin' liquor on the ranch. Stealin' Box W cattle. Runnin' the gang of hangmen. Murderin' Scott."

A look of sadness pinched Laura's comely face. "That poor dear man. It must have crushed him."

"He pulled a gun from his desk," said Dan. "At first I thought he was going to shoot me. Smith did, too. He egged him on. Yelled for him to shoot me. Then Fargo turned the gun on Smith. Shot him dead."

"Do you have to arrest him?"

"Nope."

"No?"

"Fargo aged forty years tonight, Laura. He shuffled like an old man down the hall to his room, still carryin' the gun. Closed the door, put the muzzle in his mouth, and pulled the trigger."

Laura shook her head in disbelief.

"I sent a couple men into town to give the story and my badge to Bill," said Dan.

Neither person spoke until Laura poured two cups of coffee and sat down at the table, facing Dan.

"You hungry?" she asked. "I can get you some—"

"I could eat a grizzly bear, claws and all," cut in Colt. "But I'm more tired than I am hungry. I'll just drink this and hit the sack."

Silence prevailed again for several moments.

Rising and refilling Dan's cup, Laura replaced the coffeepot on the stove. Sitting down again, she said, "Well, now that the hangmen are all dead, this valley can know real peace once more."

"Yep," said the weary man. "And I can head north and work at pickin' up my brother's trail again."

A sly smile found Laura's lips. "That won't be difficult."

"Well," said Dan, clearing his throat, "I won't say I'm the best tracker in the world. I do all right. But it's had a week to cool."

"Huh-uh," said Laura. "It's had about fourteen hours."

"What are you talkin' about?" he asked, leaning forward.

"That scuzzy-looking rider that found you at the Box W this morning?"

"How'd you know about that?" asked Dan, eyebrows arched.

"He came by here. Asked about you. Said he had a message from Caley. Said Caley had sent him from town. After he rode away, it hit me. That was impossible. I climbed on Ray's roan and rode to warn you that something smelled foul. Just as I cleared the trees, you were heading east. The scuzzy dude dumped me off the roan and took me to the hideout."

"So that's how it happened," nodded Dan. "But what's that got to do with my brother?"

"At the hideout, the gang talked openly in front of me," said the lady with the big brown eyes. "Smith Wayne had hired a gunslinger by proxy to challenge you to a gunfight at the Yellow Rose Saloon. Isn't that where you were told to meet Caley?"

"Yeah."

"Smith rode in ahead to pay this gunslinger that Earl Mound had lined up."

A light glinted in Dan Colt's blue eyes. "Wait a minute! Are you tellin' me that gunslinger was—"

"*Dave Sundeen,*" said Laura. Almost laughing, she said, "Smith looked in the saloon and saw Dave. He thought it was you and got spooked!"

Dan broke into a laugh, slapping his leg. Ray Arnold rolled over, mumbling. Dan stifled his laugh.

"So you see, Mr. Dan Colt," said lovely Laura, "Dave won't be far up the trail."

Laura made her way to Edith's room, bidding Dan good night.

The tired man blew out the lantern and slid into his bedroll. He had a passing thought about what might have happened if he and Dave had met this morning. Then sleep hit him like a freight train.

Morning came with a dark sky and a heavy wind-driven rain. Having belted down a healthy breakfast, the tall man shouldered into his slicker and made his way to the barn. He emerged shortly, leading his faithful horse to the porch.

Once again in the kitchen, Dan shook hands with Ray Arnold and was embraced in motherly fashion by Edith. They both expressed profound thanks for what he had done.

Laura fought the hot lump in her throat and walked him to the door. Tears touched the corners of her eyes as she looked up at his angular face. "Mortal language has no words for my gratitude, Dan," she said.

Dan opened the door. The roar of the rain filled the room. The wind drove it against the house. Tenderly, he pulled Laura to him and held her tight for a long moment. Tears ran freely down her cheeks.

Releasing her, he said, "Good-bye, Laura," and stepped out into the rain.

Laura watched him swing into the saddle. He set his smoky blue eyes on her, touched his hat brim and headed toward the gate.

He was almost to the gate when he heard a voice behind him in the rain. "Dan! Dan!"

Tightening the rein, he swung around in the saddle. Laura was running toward him, splashing through muddy puddles. Reaching the horse's side, she beckoned him out of the saddle, curling her forefinger repeatedly. Dan swung to the ground and faced the tiny woman. Rain pelted her beautiful face.

Reaching a hand behind his muscular neck, she pulled his face down and pressed her lips to his. The kiss was short, but warm. Smiling and blinking against the rain, she said, "I guess you just do what you have to do!"

The tall man grinned. Wordlessly, he mounted and rode through the gate. The big black veered northward.

Dan rode a hundred yards, stopped and looked

back. He could see her standing where he had left her. Laura looked smaller than ever, a forlorn, shadowy figure. She waved.

Laura's tears mingled with the raindrops as Dan Colt waved back.

Then he turned and rode into the slanting rain.